YOU FORGOT MY FACE

Cover Design | Editing | Book Design and Typesetting
Enchanted Ink Publishing

The text type was set in Garamond Premier Pro

ISBN: 979-8-9909987-0-4 (E-book)
ISBN: 979-8-9909987-1-1 (Paperback)

Thank you for my best friend and soul sister who knows these

characters almost as well as I do. Thank you for volleying

ideas back and forth. Thank you for your honest criticism.

Thank you for your constant support.

TRIGGER WARNINGS

Domestic violence

Psychological abuse

Murder

Character's fascination with death

YOU FORGOT MY FACE

LUELLA SHANAE

PROLOGUE

RED. RED ALL OVER THE FLOORS. RED smeared across the walls. The air was rancid with fear, with death. No amount of perfume could hide the stench of the room, foul enough to turn the strongest of stomachs. Cinnamon and frankincense polluted the corridors. Corruption such as this had to remain hidden; it had to stay buried.

The paranoia of discovery, of relapse, led to restless nights. Restless nights meant exhausted days, the pattern unhealthy for any soul to endure. The cause for his madness may have stemmed from the lack of sleep. It may be blamed on his inheritance. Little blame existed. No shame. Difficult to concentrate, difficult to redeem himself in the eyes of God.

If the echoes of his past rang true, his existence was not dependent on God. Only for the reminder of shame, of indignity. Rare as it was for him to believe the words spewed from the pulpit, the appearance had to be maintained. If any appreciation existed from the conflict and the rage that he remembered of his upbringing, it was the mask. A face seen only in public, expressions and words spoken only to strangers and acquaintances. The truth . . .

The truth existed only in their home. The truth buried deep beneath layers of anger, beneath the grime of wrongs. No escape. No power. It changed in a matter of minutes, his entire world. The change happened before. The loss of a life and then the aftermath. The aftershocks continued to ripple through the present and into the future.

Balance. Everything had balance. Everything had a cause and an effect; a voice possessed an echo. A figure forever entangled with a shadow. Darkness and light. Joy and sadness. Life and death. Everything had balance.

So why did he not seem to feel balanced? Why did he yearn for more, for depravity? No clear answer appeared. The question repeated itself over and over in his mind. No answer. The silence heavy, the truth veiled behind a curtain of fog. Unreachable. Only a handful of memories evaded him. The truth was one.

Who defined what is true? Who declared what is false? A power struggle continued despite an unfamiliar freedom gained. A struggle remained between his old self and this new self. The change proved too sudden, too drastic. Again and again, the echo of the past reminded him of his faults, of his weaknesses. It had to change. He had to change. But the face seen by the world, this face would remain as it always had been. Since life required more. Society demanded more.

Life styled in the right light, with the right accents. Everything expected to be a certain way. Heaven forbid any subtle changes; for then, flames consumed and destroyed it all.

June 1790

I attended another of Madame Immortelle's parties. This one, she had the corpse of a young woman. Freshly deceased. The woman's cheeks were still tinted pink.

It exhilarated me to look upon the corpse. My heart pounded, and my hands felt warm. Warm and powerful.

I dared to touch the woman's face. She felt cold. So, so cold. Did the warmth of my hand burn her? No. For she was dead. The dead cannot feel. Or can they?

Someone showed up without a mask on. The prideful and boasting son of the duke of Barrington, Edward. Fool that he is.

I showed him my face and offered to take him under my wing. He rejected me. The fool.

-M.L.G.

CHAPTER ONE
Bring Me Your Heart

THE WORLD WAS NOT GOING TO BE THE SAME. Not after Henri, Lord Geoffrey, had seen the beautiful young woman. Her curves were accentuated in a resplendent gown of rose pink. Henri could not recollect a name for her as he stared across the ballroom to examine the auburn tresses and the bright blue eyes. The woman had a rosebud mouth, now parted with laughter, the sound of bells and angels. Henri was smitten.

Henri took time to observe the young woman. She took turns around the room, speaking with a few individuals and smiling at groups of people. The beauty cast a smile in his direction, and his heartbeat quickened similar to the gallop of a first love in the summertime between childhood and manhood. It was an unfamiliar sensation to him. Unfamiliar and pleasing.

Henri was not one to forget what gave him the thrill of feeling, because feeling anything meant he was alive. It meant he was here. The demons of the past remained at bay so long as he could roam beneath the stars. And oh! How the stars shone so bright on this night, the hours of darkness a meager contrast to the day.

A thousand candles illuminated the guests as they socialized and danced in the ballroom—a display of wealth every individual in the great room took for granted. The windows were opened wide to allow the guests to feel the warm breeze from the gardens.

An hour passed as Henri stalked the auburn beauty throughout the ballroom. His pursuit was subtle, so there were no whispers or murmurs to follow him.

The first murmurs came when Henri planted himself to the right of the young beauty while she spoke with Lady Rockwell and another young woman. Henri made the proper introductions and gestures of acknowledgement to Lady Rockwell. Then his full attention turned to the unnamed beauty.

The different shades of blue in the woman's eyes seemed to swirl in merriment as, at last, she looked up at him, her cheeks flushed and her complexion flawless.

"I am Henri, Lord Geoffrey, and you are . . .?" Henri bowed at the end of the sentence, his voice fading into silence as he put the power of the conversation into the beautiful woman's hands.

"Oh, a pleasure to make your acquaintance, Lord Geoffrey. I am Annabelle Stanley, Dowager Countess of Hemming."

"The pleasure is all mine. May we take a stroll about the room, Lady Stanley?" Henri reached out his left arm in an offering to escort her, presuming Annabelle would not deny him.

"Be warned, Lady Stanley, for Lord Geoffrey does not possess a single purity in his intentions toward a single woman," Lady Rockwell interjected, a frown directed at Henri.

"Believe me," Henri murmured, "you are going to mean everything to me."

Lady Rockwell huffed in dismissal of the flirtation she was witnessing. Her fingers curled tight around the slim wrist of her niece, Justine, and they were off. Justine gave a glance and then two over her shoulder in admiration of the ease with which Lady Stanley was speaking with Lord Geoffrey. The pair were lovely together.

"Everything, you say?" Annabelle quipped. Her thick lashes lowered to her cheeks as she flashed Henri a dazzling smile. She placed her hand nimbly over his forearm as she acquiesced to the stroll with the bold lord.

"Yes, my lady, everything."

The duo took a leisured stroll on the perimeter of the ballroom, each fixated on their conversation. As the minutes ticked on and turned into an hour, a ripple of whispers followed in the couple's wake. It was a curiosity that Lord Geoffrey was so taken with the Lady Stanley.

THE WARMTH OF SUMMER NIGHTS BECAME CRISP and cool. As the seasons changed, so did Annabelle's behavior toward Henri. She went from cool shards of glass to the beaming warmth of sunshine, ebbing and flowing. As their relationship became public interest, more gentlemen began to court Annabelle. Quiet and discreet at first, and then the sons of nobility began to criticize Lord Henri.

One such youth was the firstborn son and heir of a duke. His confidence bordered arrogance in a brittle way, as his temper flared often. Henri referred to the boy as Edward, an intentional slight as the youth was Edward the Fifth of a great family.

"Edward, you must restrain yourself . . ." Annabelle simpered as her hand rested on the young man's elbow. An innocent touch but for the spark of lust in her eyes. Edward leaned down to whisper in her ear, causing Annabelle to tilt her head back with a bubbling laugh.

The two were strolling through the gardens of a lavish manor home on the outskirts of London. Another social event at which Henri was proud to adorn his arm with Annabelle, and she had proved a willing trophy. Henri had stepped away from Annabelle to engage in a discussion, something about business and trade. Edward had taken the opportunity to approach and escort Annabelle into the gardens.

Edward possessed a temper and lacked the craft of court. His intentions were written on his face, with his wide eyes and grinning mouth. It was no secret Edward was in pursuit of disentangling Lady Stanley from Henri.

"My love, Mother said young ladies are always the blossom of spring. You are the beauty in the heavens. When I pray, I see your face smiling down on me," Edward was saying, his hand over his heart in a poetic gesture.

"That is blasphemy, my lord. You must seek the confessional," Annabelle chastised him even as a giggle passed through her parted lips, her eyes dancing with humor.

"I will confess nothing because your love is worth it all." The boy continued for another few minutes in a monologue of passion, of love, of eternal worship for the woman beside him.

Henri approached the two with fists clenched at his sides. He took in deep breaths—a failed attempt to calm himself. Neither Edward nor Annabelle saw Henri advance toward them. Not until Henri shoved Edward roughly away from Annabelle's side. The young man's feet tripped over the uneven cobblestone of the garden's path, and he landed on his back. Scarlet flushed his cheeks, down his neck, and Edward scrambled to his feet.

"Why do you keep toying with fire, boy? Lady Stanley is my companion this evening and every evening hereafter. Do you not understand this?" Henri asked in a monotone.

"Annabelle seemed to gain tremendous enjoyment from my company. You abandoned her the moment you stepped through the entry," Edward goaded Henri, a sneer on his young face.

"Henri, he meant nothing by it," Annabelle began to explain, then fell silent, cut off by a death glare from her lover. Her mouth snapped shut, and she lowered her gaze.

"You should be tracking your younger brother's whereabouts, not Annabelle's. I hear that Michel has a taste for the obscene. Did I not see him the other week at Madame Immortelle's? Yes, I did! He had a peculiar look of infatuation when the corpse of a girl came out . . ." Edward was talking to himself, although his gaze fixated on Henri. Further details spilled out as he stood with his shoulders squared and his jaw jutted out. Defiant and shallow.

"Be quiet, before I cut out your tongue!" Henri seethed, advancing a step toward Edward. "You incriminate yourself by speaking such filth. Everyone knows that Madame Immortelle is a debauched madwoman."

"A madwoman who is too familiar with your brother, my lord," Edward threw back.

"You are an imbecile. Be. Quiet."

"Let me have another hour with Lady Stanley, and I will not speak about that lewd evening." Edward smirked, arms crossing over his chest. So proud, so ignorant.

"Annabelle, you seem parched from being outdoors for too long. Come along so that we may return to polite company and refreshments." Henri ignored the youth, explicit in turning his back to Edward and pivoting Annabelle with him.

With a possessive hand placed on the small of his lover's back in the line of sight of young Edward, Henri gave a dismissive wave over his shoulder and drawled a farewell: "Until we speak again, Edward. Take care."

"Henri, he may be foolhardy and young, but he has power. Please be warier of him. What is this about your brother, about Michel? Madame Immortelle is a notorious miscreant," Annabelle whispered into her lover's ear as they walked back into the crowded room.

"Nothing. It is nothing but slander. Edward is trying to undermine me and take you for himself. There is nothing to his words. They are fickle."

"But Henri, there are other whispers—"

"Hold your tongue, woman!" Henri hissed.

Annabelle snapped her mouth shut, though anger flashed across her face as she stared up at him. Resentment brewed beneath the surface at the dismissive tone Henri had used with her. She was more than a charm he could use at his whim; she did not accept disrespect. Not without another cost. What was the cost to be this time? Annabelle could not name the price since they had reentered the townhome—to a wave of smiles and curious eyes.

This meant she held her peace while keeping an eye on her companion. Was he the great love the poets often spoke of? No, Annabelle knew Henri did not have a heart. She questioned if the man had a soul. He seldom showed any signs of guilt or self-doubt. The man was crude and efficient. He knew what to say and when to say it, and he also knew when to stay quiet. This knowledge she had gained from the last few months of observing her new paramour.

Glimpses had been caught—scratches on the surface of the mirror he held up for the world. The inner layer of Henri Geoffrey proved frightening. The harder Annabelle looked, the more fear she felt. But her curiosity grew alongside the fear. She wanted to know more. No, she *needed* to know more. Henri Geoffrey as a courtier was perfectly flawed; what was he beneath the surface, behind the mask?

Her thoughts remained in a state of curiosity as the evening continued. She nodded and smiled as conversations took place around her. She replied in single words, her inner peace shattered into survival mode. Out of the corner of her eye, she saw Edward. He kept a short distance, but his stare was focused on Henri's back. Annabelle caught his gaze once, and she gave a subtle shake of her head and mouthed *"No"* to Edward.

Edward ignored her warning. The young man stalked over to where she and Henri stood. Annabelle was too slow to put her hand on her lover's arm, her voice too quiet to draw his attention. *No, no.* Henri turned away from her, his arm warm beneath her touch. *No, no, no.*

"I challenge you," Edward spat out, his right hand lifting higher and higher until it swung forward. A flash of white and the sound of a slap followed. "I challenge you to a duel. You are sheltering a monster beneath your house. Michel needs to be sent to an asylum, where you all belong."

Annabelle gasped. No other sound followed. Those crowded around the trio had gone quiet, stilled with shock.

Henri stood as solid as a statue. The muscles of his forearm beneath her fingertips were tense, as if his entire body had frozen. How many seconds passed after Edward had spoken the challenge aloud?

"You are a foolish child, Edward. I accept your challenge, but let it be known that I accept your challenge only for the sake of Lady Stanley." Henri spoke the words louder than he needed to while he bent down to retrieve the white glove.

"So be it," Edward agreed and then strode away, not bothering to look at Annabelle nor at any of the other guests around them.

The silence surrounded them for another heartbeat, then whispers broke loose and freely flowed as Henri and Annabelle suddenly found themselves isolated, with a clear distance between the other guests and themselves. Oh, the prince had forbidden duels in the last few months. Henri knew this, right? Why accept the duel at all?

Annabelle inhaled an unsteady breath. Her hand felt frozen in place, hovering where his arm had once been. Why hadn't Henri listened to her caution? The evening had soured.

"Henri, send a note to the estate of Edward's father, a note that declines the duel because it is outlawed. Anything but moving forward with it . . ." Her throat was dry, and her words sounded weak, her voice shaky.

"The bastard needs to be taught a lesson, Annabelle. No one speaks about my brother the way he did." Henri's voice was calm, his demeanor cold. "This duel is a calculated move; the risk does not outweigh the justice it will bring."

"He is just a boy, Henri!"

"You need to return to my townhome, and there you will remain. One of Edward's servants is bound to update me about where the duel will take place. I command you, Annabelle, to stay at my home. Do you hear me?" Henri looked down at his mistress, not bothering to smile or offer reassurance.

"Please . . ." Annabelle whimpered.

"Be quiet. The matter is settled. I will call the carriage for you."

July 1790

Henri is getting annoyed at my debts. He thinks they are for gambling and whoring.

Henri thinks that I am a nuisance, a parasite.

I am so much more. Madame Immortelle tells me so. She is compliant to my requests when I frequent her establishment.

She does not ridicule my fantasies.

She does not shy away from my . . . darkness.

But, she does cost a fortune. Discretion and bodies are not common.

-M.L.G.

September 1790

Annabelle Stanley. This is the first time I have written her name. Henri is besotted with the woman. I do not blame him. She is everything beautiful and everything sharp.

-M.L.G.

CHAPTER TWO

WHAT HAVE YOU DONE?

SCREAMING. ALL AROUND HIM WAS SCREAM-
ing. The ringing in his ears overwhelmed him; the
blood pouring into the earth startled him; and
the screaming, all the screaming, threatened to
undo him.

The young man was face down on the ground twenty
paces ahead of Henri. It took only a few precious seconds
before the unconscious man was surrounded by a crowd.
One woman wept; two men knelt beside his still form. One
was pointing a finger at Henri and cursing him. The other, a
doctor, confirmed the passing of the young man. Henri did
not feel any remorse as he steadily lowered the pistol to his
side. The stench of gunpowder was putrid and calming, a
welcome distraction from the noises around him.

The world felt as if it had come to a standstill. Where was
he? Henri tightened his fingers around the pistol in his right
hand, flexing and relaxing, flexing and relaxing. A search to

become grounded once more. It did not settle the spinning in his head, nor did it quiet the buzzing of the crowd.

A duel. The young man had been a fool to challenge Henri Geoffrey to a duel. It was hot-blooded and fueled by jealousy, the challenge. It was Henri who stood and stared down at the bleeding young duke. The other man had spat insults at him mere minutes before.

Inhale, exhale. Breathe in deep. The air burned his lungs as the residual smoke of his pistol wafted through the air. *Inhale, exhale.* Henri had killed before.

"What have you done?" The woman continued to scream, her wrinkled face contorted with grief and with rage. "WHAT HAVE YOU DONE?"

The woman's screams and question repeated, over and over again, as continuous as the ticking of the pendulum clock.

Time began to move forward again—*ticktock, ticktock*—with the thrumming of his heart. Calm. Henri had remained calm throughout the duel, but now he needed a release. He needed to commit violence with his hands. It was not enough to kill from a distance.

The vision of the crowd and the bloodied corpse on the ground became blurred and then hidden as he blinked once, twice. Then Henri was staring into blue eyes, crystallized and cold.

"Henri?" A gentle whisper as cool fingers curled around his forearm and the pistol was removed from his fingers, inch by inch. Until Henri's hand curled into a fist. "We need to leave before the King's Guard comes, Henri. Do you hear me? Henri?"

"Annabelle, why did you come? You were supposed to stay at the house," Henri said back, a burning in his throat when he registered Annabelle Stanley, his paramour, had disobeyed his command.

"Who are you to tell me where I am to stay?"

"The one who killed for you."

"A pity he wasted his youth. Henri, we need to leave." Annabelle was cold, merciless in the way she spoke about the dead young man, when mere hours before, she had been giggling and cooing over his love letters. Begged for his life, even.

Henri remained impassive. The screams and the curses of before had subsided into a white noise like the sound of the ocean crashing along rocks. Inconsequential yet powerful.

Annabelle stared up at her lover with questions rolling through her mind, questions and calculations as she observed that Henri was detached. He held no guilt over the duke's young son. Was he not aware this duel might end his successful life at court? It did not matter if the prince favored him; it could all change so flippantly if the tides of society shifted. Why was he not reacting to her words of caution to leave? Why was he not aware of the growing crowd and the unrest?

Annabelle made a deliberate change in her demeanor. The slender woman went from gentle and cautious, transforming into a hurricane of wrath, of emotion, of turmoil. Annabelle's lovely features became contorted and twisted as she slammed her fists into Henri's chest. Again and again, harder and harder, as she opened her mouth and began to scream at him.

"Why did you kill him, Henri? He was just a boy! A lovesick boy!" Her voice broke as it rippled through Henri's mind. Annabelle's blue eyes were filling with tears, glistening and warping. "What have you done? WHAT HAVE YOU DONE?"

The mantra of the mourning mother became an echo from Annabelle's mouth. This was the key that broke Henri's resolve, and his gaze snapped between Annabelle's grief-stricken face to that of the crowd. The scene his lover had created was bringing more and more gazes in their direction, the dead body soon forgotten.

"You do not understand. It was necessary. I could not simply fire a warning shot to scare the boy. I prefer to live." Henri had leaned in close to whisper in Annabelle's ear, his lips gently caressing her earlobe.

"You are a beast! Heartless and cruel!" she screeched.

"So bet it, Annabelle. The fool threatened me about Michel and about my brother's secrets. There could be nothing but his death."

"What have you done?" She began to pant, shoulders trembling and her chest heaving. Annabelle was fully aware of the dozens of stares watching her. Aware and undaunted. "You need to leave. The boy's mother witnessed the duel, the duchess herself." These last words were murmured beneath her breath so only Henri could hear.

His gaze remained distant even as realization dawned bright and loud in his mind. Henri did not bother a second glance at the crowd of nobles. Slowly, he reached up to curl a hand around Annabelle's tear-streaked cheek. "Do not toy with my affections again. When you are mine, there is absolutely no one else." His words were laced with malice. There could be no mistake. This was a warning.

Henri withdrew his hand from her cheek and reached down to curl his fingers once more around his pistol. The barrel had cooled just as his thirst for violence had cooled. Enough damage had been dealt.

It was simple to ignore the crowd and the young man who remained face down on the ground. It was child's play to take the first step away from the sight of the duel, to take the second step away from the crowd. The third and fourth steps proved effortless as Henri walked away from it all. Chaos had begun to sprout within the crowd, with murmurings and finger-pointing. Blame was going to be placed at his doorstep, and Henri was no fool when he mulled over the social consequences this scandal was bound to cause.

The challenge had come as a surprise, a rare moment of shock when Henri had turned to the sound of his name on a stranger's lips. Then the sting of a slap across his cheek and the white glove falling at his feet. Henri had been strategic in the seconds following the initiation of the challenge. Henri stared down the smooth-faced boy in front of him. A circle of echoes had sounded around the two.

Henri had accepted the challenge. He had bent down to pick up the white glove and held it firmly between his curled fists.

None of the facts were relevant in the minutes the exchange took place. It was an impairment on the Geoffrey name, but the scandal could not be avoided. Either Henri accepted the duel, or he rejected it but became the target of ridicule.

The ground squelched beneath his feet as he walked faster and faster away from the scene of the duel. The noises of the crowd had grown tenfold since his departure, and Henri assumed this occurred because the palace guard had made their appearance.

"Let them brood over the breaking of the law. Let them learn that I am not to be regarded as passive." Henri was muttering to himself, with each step more deliberate than the last.

Less than a half an hour had passed when Henri slowed down to stand at the edge of a dense line of trees, the fields sprawled out at his back. A figure stepped out from the shadows of the trees with both hands raised in a gesture of peace. As the other person moved into the light of the newly risen sun, Henri made a dismissive *tsk* noise between his teeth.

"You are the second person to disobey me today."

"Oh? I had thought to be the first. Did Annabelle not play by the rules?" The words were said through a sinister curvature of the younger man's lips. "Shall I speak with her, brother?"

"I do not want you anywhere near Annabelle. I've already told you this once. Michel, my patience is gone, and the day has just started. Do not try me," Henri warned as he stopped directly in front of his younger brother.

The two stared at one another as the air around them grew heavy with tension and unsaid words. Henri felt a second surge of ferocity boil through his veins. And he did not fight this. A second and then two passed before his fist collided with his younger brother's jaw. There was a crunching noise; it reverberated through his head as he withdrew his hand and took a single step closer to Michel.

"You need to be more discreet, Michel. A duke's son threatened to reveal your demons. I ended his life this morning. Do not be so imprudent with our family name. Do you understand?" Henri asked in a voice intertwined with rage and murderous intent.

Michel had curled both hands around his throbbing jawline, the familiar metallic taste sliding down the back of his throat as he swallowed. "The duke's boy was at one of the parties—" Michel began to explain until there was a resounding slap on his other cheek. It smarted, and Michel glared at his brother.

"Be more discreet," Henri snapped. "You and I are going to take a trip to the countryside. We are going to let society quiet down about this duel and the threats this man-child had made. You will not contact Annabelle in this time. Do you understand?"

Although there was murder in his eyes, Michel nodded in agreement with his brother, surrendering when there was nothing else he could do, nothing else he could say. Nothing other than, "I understand, Lord Geoffrey."

"Let everyone think I killed for Annabelle. Let them assume I am that overcome with lust for her. Your discretion is key to this façade. If you come this close to exposure again, it will be your heart my bullet enters next. Do you understand?" Henri spoke each word clipped and short, his gaze unblinking as he stared into his brother's eyes.

November 1790

Annabelle Stanley.
Annabelle. Annabelle. Annabelle.
I love you.
Do you see me when you kiss Henri?
Do you feel my hands in your hair when he dances with you?
Annabelle, Henri wants me to stay away from you.
Henri wants to control me, to control us.
But I will not let him.

-M.L.G.

CHAPTER THREE
You Forgot My Face

Henri had been rather withdrawn from society over the last few weeks, or was it months? It was said he was grieving the loss of his paramour, Annabelle, the Countess of Hemming, as he was previously seen at public events with her at his side—too close beside him to merely be an acquaintance and far too many appearances of them together to pass off as a social coincidence. There was servants' gossip that whispered the lady was often seen entering and exiting the Geoffrey estate, Henri's London home, during the oddest of hours. Thus, it was concluded by those members of high society that Henri had become committed to this lady, this unknown siren who'd entered their midst as a mist in the early dawn. Subtly, quietly, and ever so transient. Yet, where had their relationship gone awry? No one dared to broach the subject with the young man now appearing before them, calm, collected, and dashingly attired. He did not appear to be grieving, not in the least.

The few gathered around Henri spoke of nonsensical subjects to avoid any unpleasantness. Despite this, they were unable to hold his attention, but he let them think he was preoccupied. Engaged and charming one moment, and then suddenly, he let his mind go. Physically, he still stood there with a smile and a reserved expression, but his gaze was vacant. Distant and empty.

Another quieter person had also been observing the changes in Lord Geoffrey—a young woman who stood, still and poised, as a wallflower in such a splendid social setting. Her eyes were light, sparkling with curiosity and innocence as she looked between Lord Geoffrey and Lady Annabelle Stanley. The two of them made quite the beautiful couple! Justine Ayling sighed to herself as she also noticed the young lord by Lady Stanley. Such a love story she had watched unfold between Lord Geoffrey and Annabelle, and she watched it transform into a love triangle as the second young lord began to court Annabelle.

Henri heard her unmistakable voice. He felt the ghost of Annabelle's breath against his cheek as he stood rooted with his eyes closed. Her voice echoed through his mind. *What have you done?* she had screamed. *What have you done?* she had yelled and beat her fists against his chest, berating him about the duel, when the lovesick duke's son had died at the end of Henri's pistol.

Her low voice with its sultry tones—he envisioned the pout of her rosebud lips as she spoke with some lord's second son. He knew she was merely stalling, biding her time on the poor youth, who gazed upon her with adoration.

There was a roaring in his ears. The roaring resembled the crashing of waves against jagged exposed rocks. Exposed as if they were made vulnerable. Henri was vulnerable, but he kept tight rein of his composure. A thread held his self-control in place.

"Really, Michel, you are too much," Annabelle was saying, her slender figure turned away from Henri and toward the youth. "I am yours to command, sweeting, but for your brother . . ."

The roaring in his ears increased tenfold. All he saw was her touch against his brother's cheek, her sapphire eyes, and the smirk upon her lips as she caught Henri's stare. The room around them darkened. The sounds became muffled. He felt a pulsing throbbing ache in the back of his skull as he strode forward.

"Annabelle, I didn't know you would be here. And with my little brother. Michel, you should head home. The hour is late." Henri spoke as calmly and as quietly as he could.

The youth, Michel, blanched when looking up at his elder brother, with his mouth agape and trying to form words, but only silence ensued. Always, always silence. There were the screams and the silence, the resounding silence. The room had gone red, so very red.

Annabelle spun around to face Henri with an entrancing smile. Her eyes remained cold and remote. "Oh, Henri! I had hoped to see you tonight! The dancing has been oh-so dull without you as a partner—for me or any other lucky girl," she murmured.

"Go home, Michel," Henri said. There was no emotion in those three words, simply a command. One to be obeyed. Henri did not want to handle another of his brother's social mishaps this evening, not when he had his own to avoid. Annabelle was supposed to have left, disappeared into obscurity, and gone abroad. The rumors of their illicit affair had become too infamous to ignore the picture society was painting with insinuation. Annabelle was to be his wife, they had whispered. Then their public appearances had ended abruptly, and their circle had been left wanting answers.

Why, on this evening, was the lady seen with Michel? Was she not almost engaged to the Lord Henri? Why was she now so tantalizingly close to young Michel? Curious eyes watched the trio hungrily, their curiosity not yet sated.

Henri turned toward Annabelle, smiling. "Darling, why not come to my London townhome tomorrow morning? We shall discuss our future then, as I am forever yours."

Annabelle tossed her head in acknowledgement of Henri's proposition. "Until the morning, then." Her voice was loud enough to carry to those near to them, much to Henri's annoyance. It seemed a survival tactic of hers to let as many be aware of her plans as possible, or was it merely a ploy to crawl beneath Henri's skin? Either way, Henri gave a curt bow to Annabelle as an acknowledgement of her words.

Annabelle gave an odd smile to her once lover and ignored those around them as she brushed her fingertips along Henri's cheek. He was too much in control of himself to openly react to her touch, but she knew it would bother him. And there was the intent. The smile disappeared rather quickly as she turned away from him and made her way through the crowd. She nodded here and there as others offered to welcome her to their circle, but she kept going toward the exit. Her plan had come to a completion with the invitation to the Geoffrey London house.

Thus, Annabelle was last seen approaching the town-home of her former and her current sweetheart. Why aim for brothers? Jealousy would swear them both to her and simply tear them apart. They were heirs to a great, great fortune and were eligible bachelors at the time. Her blue gaze flickered down to assess the periwinkle gown she had chosen to wear beneath a heavy cape with its lavender trim at the neckline. She had a simple silk cord tied about her throat with a giant pearl at its center. She knocked once, twice.

Annabelle was startled to witness Henri opening the front door for her. He was handsome in the soft light of dawn. There was something peculiar about the twinkle in his eyes, or had she imagined the flash of emotion?

"Good morning, sweeting. I have refreshments set for us in the parlor—you know, the one with the blue-and-gold walls. Please, enter the parlor while I tend to another matter."

"Of course, of course."

Annabelle turned away from Henri and began to walk toward the blue-and-gold parlor. She sauntered away with a confident step, which had her skirts rustling across her legs, her hips swaying. Then she was alone in a rather elegant room. Its furnishings were rich yet simple.

"Exquisite," she murmured.

Deftly, her chilled fingers unclasped her winter cape, and she carelessly tossed it over the back of an armchair. She appraised the room with a single sweeping glance before she settled herself upon an ivory couch, her feet tucked beneath the length of her gown. She turned her head at an angle, her gaze was faraway, almost wistful. Her back was to the open door. She did not hear the gentle step of Henri as he stood in the doorway, his silhouette sleek and predatory.

He was entranced for a moment by the memory of their last encounter in the gold-and-blue parlor. There had been white roses. There had been splatters across the floor and much of the furniture. Fractured memories. Flashes of red, all the red. *Forgive me, forgive me . . .* He lifted his hand and pulled it across the front of her white swanlike neck.

Look at me with your beautiful eyes, smile at me with your lying lips, and tell me you hate me . . . He stared at her profile with its flawless complexion, its serene expression. *Look at me!* He began to pace. At his footfall, she turned to face him. Her gaze was vacant, void of feeling as a vase was hurled at her. There was a shattering, a fracturing. Red rose petals fluttered down to the floor.

Henri continued to pace back and forth within the front parlor. He was the epitome of tension from his furrowed brow to his taut shoulders as he prowled through the gold-and-blue room. The floor was littered with the fragments of a shattered vase, ruined dreams, and dying roses. Henri had just been overcome by a violent outburst, and he'd thrown the vase of roses at the wall just inches from his guest. A warning. A mistake. Annabelle had looked at him as if he were a stranger, a nuisance.

"You should have left," was all he could say through his clenched teeth.

"You should not have left. It hurt to watch you walk away from me, not even turning back when I screamed for you. It humiliated me."

"You humiliated yourself."

"I loved you with all my heart. Then I heard those vile rumors about you and the actress!" She spat out the accusation. Her gaze was downcast, her eyelashes curling against her cheeks.

Henri prowled toward her with a raised hand. There was a stinging against his palm and a welt forming upon her cheek. He had an uncivilized savage streak, and Annabelle knew just how to provoke him.

The light of the setting sun outlined her silhouette; she was curvy and had a cascade of auburn curls tumbling down her back. Her face was turned away from him, always away from him. She scorned him. *Do you even love me, my sweet Annabelle?*

"Look at me, you lecherous woman. I know why you have made Michel fall in love with you. I would not wed you, so you sought my younger brother—a child." His words were clipped, and his voice rose from a menacing whisper to an icy threat.

Those lips were pouting as she stared off into the gardens of the Geoffrey townhome, idly watching the snow fall over the cobblestone path. She shrugged at the accusation being laid at her feet by Henri with a simple lift of slender shoulders. She scorned him with her silence, her indifference.

"Annabelle . . . my love, my sweetheart, you are too worldly for Michel." He was whispering now, for he was standing just behind her. Close enough to breathe in the faint aroma of orange blossoms, but he forbade himself from touching her velvety skin. *I love you. I loved you.* Henri was furious at her calm against his previous temper. She knew him too well, and her knowledge was the issue. Annabelle knew him to his corrupt guiltless soul.

When had the glass appeared in his grasp, cutting his fingers as he held it too tight? The blood trickled down, down, down. The red roses were dying, gone.

Henri only heard silence. The roses at his feet had become withered and ruined. How much time had passed? He was lost. Where . . .? He saw her then. Annabelle was still seated upon the ivory couch; her posture was odd. Her complexion had become sallow. Her gaze was empty. Her eyes had become a clouded unfocused blue. The bodice of her gown was a crusted messy display of crimson where it had once been a soft, soft purple.

"Annabelle. Annabelle! ANNABELLE!"

She did not hear his voice crack and break. She did not feel the stale air of the room. She did not see the dead roses. She did not see the sun as it finally set. She had not even heard him when he first spoke to her. Henri stared down at her as the whirlwind of emotions sifted through his mind: confusion to anger, anger to dismay, dismay ebbing into emptiness. It was when the emptiness of comprehension settled within him that he realized . . . he finally realized his mistake. Annabelle had not laughed at his banter; Annabelle had not reacted to his outrage.

Had she been breathing, had she been alive, when he first walked into the blue-and-gold parlor to speak with her? Had their conversation truly taken place? Henri could not catch his breath. He inhaled and exhaled, repeatedly. Again, and again. The emptiness remained. Her body did not move, did not alter in any way. He closed the distance between them and inspected her.

The corpse was days, but not possibly a week old. Henri could not tell. The scent of orange blossoms lingered in the air when he moved closer to her. Her signature perfume. His chest constricted; he did not dare touch her. The memory of her warmth beneath him, of her laughing eyes could not be corrupted. Not by her death. It was complete. Utterly complete.

December 1790

It's still my birthday, even though it's nearly midnight . . .

I turned twenty-three today. I was hurt when Annabelle did not care. If you love someone, you're supposed to remember their birthday. My father did not love me. He never remembered. ~~My stepmother, Alice, loved me. She always remembered.~~

Annabelle loved me. She promised.

Henri invited Annabelle over to our house. Why? He didn't answer me. He never does. Annabelle ignored my notes, and . . . well, she can never ignore me again.

-M.L.G.

CHAPTER FOUR
How Could You Forget Murder?

HENRI WHISPERED INTO THE DYING LIGHT. "What have I done?"

There was a rustling from the other side of the closed doors. Someone approached. Whoever stood beyond the door hesitated. They seemed to take in the deathly silence—the same silence he was suffocating in. Henri had to force air into his lungs as he waited for the knock. No one ever dared to barge in to his presence, only Annabelle . . . but she was gone. She was dead, and her corpse lingered within his parlor, as if she had envisioned dying with the sunset.

"Henri . . . Henri, we must speak. It has been days since you left this room. The servants are whispering, and there are rumors floating through the London streets. Rumors we must silence." The voice on the other side was muffled, but Henri knew the voice of his young brother as clear as a raven's cry.

"Come in, Michel. Be sure to lock the doors behind you," was all he could respond with. What madness was this? Henri only remembered glimpses of his conversation with Annabelle, of her coquettish ways—nothing of her death.

The doors clicked and swung open. Henri looked down at his hands and saw they were clean. Unmarked. Had he not felt the glass cut into his flesh? As the doors closed and the lock was bolted into place, Henri looked over at his brother. A steady gaze. A warning exchanged.

Michel registered the dried blood sprinkled down Annabelle's white neck—a crude resemblance of a necklace. Dried crusted rubies marred the bodice of her gown, her bosom static. Her slender arms were suspended above the sofa. Her fingers curled around an ornate fan, one she would never require again. Her legs were tucked beneath the soft folds of her skirts. The silence polluted by death now became heavier, darker, as tension sparked in the growing shadows of the room. The sun had set. Annabelle was dead.

"Wh—What have you done?" Michel's voice sounded pathetic, like a child's voice after waking from a nightmare. Michel hid his bandaged hand behind his back in a gesture of obedience. A movement Henri overlooked.

Henri looked at his younger brother. His younger brother who had been continuously nervous since he was a suckling babe. Skittish at the faintest of noises, anything other than the sound of the nursemaids' chatter and gossip. Michel had been afraid of the shadows that lingered in corners and down the dark halls. A perpetual state of fright is what Michel had cloaked himself within, jumpy and untrusting, ever doubting his older brother, the only other Geoffrey offspring to survive the nursery. Michel had been afraid of shadows from infancy until—apparently, this moment.

Henri gazed upon his brother as if he were looking at him for the first time with clear eyes. The pouty puckering of a spoiled youth, the anxious play of delicate hands, and the too-short nail beds scabbed and peeling. Weakness embodied within the slim figure of a young man. His brother.

"Where have you been, Michel?" Henri asked while he walked around the sofa, only stopping when he stood directly before the corpse, his gaze never leaving his brother's face. The question—an accusation—skittered across the floor between them. An expression of guilt appeared on Michel's once passive face.

"At the tables trying to get you a placement with the prince. We need to not be forgotten within his circle. My debts . . . our debts have increased tenfold within the last week, and now with the rumors beginning to circulate London . . . Henri, what have you done?" Michel whispered the response, his voice still frightened, still pathetic, but darkened with malicious intent and deflecting the question.

"Will you not even look at her?" Henri taunted as his fingertips brushed against the cold, too-cold cheek of the fallen Annabelle. "The very woman you swore to wed and to bed?"

"The people I am indebted to, they are dangerous. They have threatened to harm me," Michel began.

"Michel, do not whine as a sniveling child would into their nursemaid's skirts. Has your judgment been so impaired by gambling and sex?" Henri rebuffed his brother's childish remarks with a wave of his hand. A motion of dismissal. "Come, come. Why will you not look upon her one last time?"

Henri walked over to his younger brother and none too gently guided the youth to stand before the corpse. The red droplets half hid a gash across her throat as rubies might distract an onlooker from bruises (either from mishandling or misbehaving). Her auburn curls were still so perfectly placed across once creamy shoulders. The only thing truly amiss was a simple truth: she was dead. A lovely, lovely corpse still capable of stealing Michel's breath away once he finally looked at her.

Why was she so beautiful? Michel could still remember the sound of her voice, of her husky laughter as he read her love letters. Why was she so much more beautiful now that she was dead? His throat tightened as he fought against a sudden urge to speak. Instead, he focused on being timid before his brother and lowered his gaze from Annabelle's corpse. Why was she so beautiful?

"Now, dispose of her in the furnace. I will dismiss the servants for the evening to attend the local fairs." Henri walked toward the locked doors and undid the bolt as he turned to smile at his brother. "Remember, it is unseemly to bed a corpse. Do not repeat the offense a second time under my roof."

Click, click, and *boom.* The moment the double doors swung closed behind Henri, there was a roaring in the air, a crackle, and a hiss. It left the young man, now adrift with a lovely corpse, reeling and struggling to catch his breath. His entire body had begun to tense up as he stared, stared, stared at the faded blue gaze of his once-upon-a-yesterday lover. His lips were suddenly cracking; his mouth felt arid. One step turned to two, two turned to ten, and he was standing above her and before her.

Michel reached out to touch the creamy skin just above the bloody neckline. His fingertips grazing along the ridges of the laceration, which had so sweetly, so thoroughly killed Annabelle. A jagged breath was exhaled as he felt boundless perfect clarity.

"Your sacrifice will have been for not, as you were guilty of lust, corruption, and deceit. Why did you play the chaste façade for me? I knew you, and I know you still. You are as I am destined to be." His voice sounded off in the stillness of the room, his breath tickling the auburn curls floating about her face. "Come, come now, and let us dine together."

Michel lifted and guided Annabelle off the couch and into the darkness of the hall, humming a tune. It could have been a melody of love just as it may have been a childhood lullaby. *Swing my hands; swing my hands, ever near and ever far, from the flames of hell, from the flames of hell. Swing my hands, swing my hands, oh-ever love, oh-ever love, to the gates of heaven, to the gates of heaven.* No one heard this tune except for his brother, who lingered in an alcove as Michel and Annabelle strolled by. All were smiling, yet only one felt nothing.

One for the nightmare and two for the seer, three for the maiden, and four for the fear . . .

As the days trickled along, word of Annabelle's disappearance began to spread like wildfire through the social circles. Where was she last seen? With whom? Was the royal family going to investigate the disappearance of a mere countess?

There was speculation, and there were whispers, curious eyes, and accusatory glances. None of these mattered as the Geoffrey brothers continued with their social life without a hitch.

These two brothers knew what had happened to Annabelle on that fateful morning. Her lifeblood no longer flowing, her eyes no longer sparkling with mischief or glinting with malice. Her lips no longer smiling. Yet only one of the Geoffrey brothers knew what had happened to the body of the once countess and would-be lover. Even then, it was a question, so Henri kept a close eye on his brother after Annabelle's demise. A close wary eye as he watched his brother flirt and laugh with the young ladies. Would their secret be revealed with the slip of a tongue? Michel was a proficient enough courtier who also lacked the ability to keep his own mouth shut.

Henri kept himself under tight control, keeping to a rigid routine when at their residence and doing his best to ensure he appeared aloof, distant. He did not want to appear suspicious or openly grieve the disappearance of his . . . of Annabelle, for that would certainly add fuel to the fire just beneath his feet. Another scandal could not occur. Not when he had his eye on the marital market. *Ah, Annabelle, why did you have to be so persistent? So enchanting? So dangerous to the family, his family.*

It was for the better. It was also for the worse. Where was the balance to be found? Would her decayed corpse appear? Or was her name going to be forgotten as the whispers slowed and the days turned to weeks and weeks to months? She would be forgotten, correct? Annabelle had to be forgotten.

Henri had the intent to develop a plan to sway the court and society to overlook the extinguished flame once known as Annabelle Stanley. This plan included but was not limited to the pursuit of a wife, the pursuit of furthering his family's wealth, and creating a distraction for society. This way, the whispers and the teasing of Annabelle might be forgotten, faded away as if bleached by the sun.

"How could I have killed her? I do not remember slicing her throat . . . I do not remember wanting to harm her . . . I do not remember," Henri whispered to himself night after night as a mantra to conjure the memories of the day. No memories came. Not of the murder of Annabelle. Only of their conversation and her coquettish nature. Even until the end, she had been smiling and tossing her hair. Until she was only silent. So, so silent.

Then Michel was there within moments of Henri discovering Annabelle was deceased, her bloodied gown dried and her eyes so very lifeless. It was not a beautiful thing, death. Death was not a beautiful thing. Henri fought against the guilt as he sat at his desk, staring down at the sheets of paper splayed out before him. Lists and lists of names of eligible young women and their families, all recorded with a description of the family's connections, their assumed wealth, and their future prospects.

The plan had to begin in earnest. Even as he questioned himself: how could he forget the act of murder?

Late December 1790

I gave myself the best birthday gift this year. The corpse devotion of my love, my Annabelle. She belongs to no one else. ~~Henri thinks he killed her. I made him believe this lie.~~

Do I remember what her fingers felt like when they were warm? Not really. Do I care to remember? No.

Annabelle has never been more beautiful. She has never been this angelic.

She is mine forever. Forever and always mine.

-M.L.G.

CHAPTER FIVE
Dreaming of Your End

T HE ENTIRE PLAN WAS WRITTEN DOWN, BLACK ink on white paper, and meticulously sorted. Henri Geoffrey knew he was an eligible bachelor; he was aware his status in society had caught many a mothers' eyes. Despite this, the rumors circulating around him were ones of debauchery and disastrous. They were not entirely true, nor were they entirely false. As any young nobleman who had too much time on his hands, Henri had gone through a few years of wildness in his youth, more so in the years following his father's death.

The lord of the Geoffrey family had both freed Henri and burdened him. It had been dizzying to go from his father's caddy to his own master and the master of hundreds of staff members scattered throughout the city and the countryside homes. There was the matter of finances and checking on the accounts of the family fortune, where funds were being handled properly, and where there was a leak. It reminded him people were weak. They were susceptible to bribery and to deceptions.

This meant the family fortune had been managed but carelessly in the large picture. His father had forgotten how to micromanage the account books in his later years. The old lord had other priorities. Just another shame Henri was able to place on his father's grave and turn away from, laying the burdens of the past where they belonged—the grave. At least, he thought he could let the past stay buried. The burdens of the past were to prove themselves darker and deeper than even Henri had been aware of.

His primary focus, during the last few days, had been to complete the list laid out before him. Now came the task of narrowing down the list to the woman and future in-laws he could tame but not destroy; a family name capable of raising his own standing without lowering their own; a future wife independent of her family but not shunned by society. The task proved to be a headache he toiled over night after night, a back-burner priority Henri burned the midnight oil to focus on.

The list went from over a hundred young women down to twenty or so in a matter of days after several hours of research and elimination. The twenty women remaining came from prestigious families, and their names were not whispered or sullied in society's eyes. The families were wealthy and not known to be in any disastrous economic situations. Henri drummed his fingers along the wooden desk as his eyes roamed over the list of names repeatedly.

Now he had to begin the pursuit of each woman to evaluate her personal qualities.

This was tedious, but it was to be worthwhile, Henri knew. If it took effort and perseverance, it was worthwhile in the end; it was simply a matter of getting to the end. This was his mindset. The end was getting married to the woman he chose, and then he could move on with the next step of his plan. If the liabilities of his brother did not cause any further issues.

It was to be another few hours of Henri mulling over the information about every woman on his list before he narrowed the names down to three. There were numerous social gatherings set to occur in the next few weeks, and he was more than ready for them. Every gathering, his attention was to be focused on each of the young women still written down on his desk. What more did he need to do? There was the concern of where Michel had taken Annabelle's corpse . . . Had his younger brother listened to his order and burned her in the furnace? A clawing sensation at the base of his skull told him Michel had not burned the body. Henri chose to ignore this.

The first name on the list was Justine Ayling, orphaned heiress of Lord and Lady Ayling, left under the care of her guardian, Lady Rockwell. Twenty-four. Thoroughly unknown to society, as her guardian had kept her well-guarded and sheltered from scandals. Odds were in his favor that he would find the Lady Justine to be naïve and ignorant of the ways of the world. Perfection.

Such as it was, the Lady Justine was daydreaming about the day she could be married and truly run a household of her own. There was no resentment or ill will between Justine and her guardian, Lady Rockwell, but it was the simple itch for independence. Socially, Justine was aware of her wealth and that through marriage, her dowry and her family's fortune would go from Lady Rockwell to her future husband. It was not a real concern of hers as she had been raised with a golden spoon since infancy. Even with the sudden and tragic death of both of her parents, Justine had been shielded from the darker side of the world.

Justine knew grief, and she had known loss. She knew love, and she also knew consistency. Lady Rockwell had not wavered from day one when the weeping little girl had been brought to her doorstep, the skies dark and the heavens pouring down. Justine remembered it all but preferred to act as if she had forgotten. The vivid and detailed memory of watching her parents' deaths, seeing the life ebb from their eyes as they bled out. A burden of guilt and the blame for her parents' deaths sat heavy on her shoulders. As a child, Justine had convinced herself her parents' deaths were her fault; she had been the cause of the riding accident that had left both her parents dead. She had run away into the woods behind their country manor on that fateful Sunday . . .

The Harbinger of Death was the name she had gifted herself as an orphan at the tender age of nine. Even her mother's favored lap dog, little Charlotte, had perished at

Justine's feet. Justine had grown up telling herself she was a liability to all those she loved. The Harbinger of Death.

There was no point, in her own mind, to relive the past and to unbury the old memories. Especially those that brought her sadness. There was always a tomorrow, as she had learned. The sun continued to rise in the east and set in the west; the moon continued to turn and change as well.

Death was permanent for those who perished, but for those left behind, the days continued to drift on and on. Thus, she was soon an adolescent and soon a young woman. Lady Rockwell had held her back from her debut into society for one year, then two, and then three. Justine did not question this, as it meant she was able to continue her studies. She was well educated and highly intelligent, factors destined to be lost in the communication between Lady Rockwell and society, as Justine was to be viewed as a sheltered, naïve, and frankly, a fool.

It was not surprising her name and her identity were quickly marked by Henri Geoffrey as the prime candidate for his future spouse. He required someone who possessed a naïveté so fresh it could withstand the stains and the darkness of his home, of his brother . . . He required someone such as Justine Ayling. Henri had the bonus of knowing the young woman was a beauty with pale gold curls and eyes the color of sapphires—or so those prone to courtly love and poetry were keen to describe her while laughing over bourbon and cards.

"You will be the perfect bride, so long as you keep your head down and obey. Will your guardian, the formidable

Lady Rockwell, allow you near me?" Henri was saying to himself, softly chuckling as he drew circles around her name and drew lines through the other two names on the paper.

He reached out his hand and rang the servant's bell just above his shoulder. It was time to prepare for the banquet and ball where he was going to meet his future wife. There were many minute details to go over with his staff as they selected materials and ingredients. Henri was thorough when it came to tracking expenses his household was budgeted for. He knew how much the meat was to cost; he was aware of what the florist might try to up-charge. The shopkeepers at the markets knew Lord Geoffrey was not one to be swindled, as he would abandon a shop or its shopkeeper without hesitation.

A young woman appeared in the cracked doorway. She curtsied when his eyes lifted from the pages on his desk. She kept her eyes downcast. She kept silent.

"I need to see the quotes we received from the shops, as well as the menu Chef has prepared for me to review," Henri said.

The nameless young woman curtsied again to acknowledge the orders given by her master and quietly stepped backward out of the room. The door was left ajar. It was mere seconds after that another figure entered the doorway. This one was not so silent.

Michel sauntered in and immediately began to complain, his left hand idly placed in the pocket of his trousers. He was talking about some obscure gambling table where so-and-so had introduced him to another so-and-so with the promise of quick wins. All Michel experienced while gambling was loss, after loss, after loss. Then he whined to his brother about his pittance of an allowance.

"I do not have time for your nonsense, Michel. You are a disaster when it comes to your gambling addiction and your would-be womanizing," Henri bellowed out, thoroughly exasperated at the interruption.

"I am perfectly adequate at both, thank you."

"Why have you come into the study tonight?" Henri asked.

"I need your help with something. I did not listen to your instructions . . ."

"As you seldom do, brother. Take a seat."

Michel had begun to pace back and forth, back and forth. Two steps, pivot, three steps, pivot. Repeat. Until he heard his brother say to take a seat and his entire body collapsed into the chair conveniently located in front of the desk. It was a low-backed chair, difficult to slouch or recline in. Both brothers were forced to face the other as they sat in a silence for a few moments, each clearly focused on their own thoughts and their own priorities. At last, Michel spoke:

"The eight hundred pounds you gave me last week. I did not use it to pay down my gambling debt. I lost all of it and then some more on credit. I did not speak with the prince's secretary as you suggested. I slapped one of the servant's earlier today. I did not burn Annabelle's corpse. It felt too cruel. I preferred the idea of burying her. Proper. I need more money." It was all said like wildfire. The words may have blurred together if one was not paying close attention.

Henri had not been mentally prepared to hear the brisk summary of his brother's misdeeds and misfortunes. It had all been said in a monotone, which made it even more difficult to decipher one tidbit of information from the other. Had his brother done this intentionally? Again, brother stared at brother as Michel fell into silence again. The muscles in his cheeks worked as he clenched and unclenched his jaws to remain calm and believing Henri had not heard everything clearly. Such was the intent.

"I will not give you another penny this quarter. You will need to settle your gambling debts another way, outside of a duel. You know the prince has been harsher in punishing nobles caught dueling," Henri drawled.

Something subtle changed within Michel as he stared at his brother in shock. What did Henri mean, no more money? This was not going to go well with those he was indebted to. They had already threatened him with bodily harm if he failed to make a payment within the fortnight, and here was his brother telling him he was going to miss the first payment, thus facing the threat of bodily harm, if not worse. Michel's eye twitched as he fought the anger brewing within his chest, biting down on his tongue until he tasted blood. An all-too-familiar metallic tang.

He could not control his temper.

He never could.

"Oh, get off your high horse, you bloody fool! I am not the one who was caught up in the latest duel scandal regarding Annabelle!" Michel lashed out, spittle falling from the corners of his mouth.

Henri did not even blink when his brother used Annabelle's name as a weapon in this conversation, as it was a tactic he had gotten used to from their deceased father. It was nothing new for Henri, but it *was* new when it came from Michel, the weak little brother who chewed his nails to stubs. This was taken as a mental note, but he made no verbal remark about this shift in Michel's demeanor.

"You are the fool," Henri replied as his shoulders began to tense and his own posture changed to be more dominant.

"I want nothing more than to enjoy myself! There is nothing wrong with that! Absolutely nothing wrong! You stole immorality from me!" Michel had started to ramble, and his eyes lost their focus as his mind began to wander. Henri took careful note of the second change in Michel's behavior.

"Michel, settle yourself. Remain in our home for the next few days, perhaps a week. The debts you have will be paid in due time," Henri assured his brother as he stood up from his seat and slowly walked around his desk, his hand resting on his brother's shoulder. "Keep yourself well. I need you by my side."

It was the only flaw in his plan as it proved to be out of his control—Michel's behavior in the public eye. The erratic behavior had been more prevalent in their childhood and early youth; Michel had appeared to have calmed down since reaching his maturity. Henri had hoped. This hope was now in question as the same symptoms of earlier years resurfaced this evening. Had Michel been hiding it all this time? Henri did not want to be wary of his brother as he felt the pressures of everything else weighing down on his mind, but this was an important piece. If Michel were to have a break . . . Or had the break already happened?

Why could Henri not remember killing Annabelle?

Why was his brother starting to act erratic and unbalanced?

Would the Lady Ayling agree to be his wife?

A plethora of questions created a white noise in his mind as they all fluttered around and around. Henri had enough internal distraction to remain blind to other signs Michel was exhibiting, other warnings.

January 1791

I know that Michel is changing. I can see the edges fraying. Will he obey my command? I need to find a suitable wife. This stain from the duel and Annabelle's disappearance . . . I need to find a suitable wife to silence the hounds of society.

I need Michel to stay away from my future wife.

-H.L.G.

CHAPTER SIX

In the Darkness, You Scream

WHAT MORE NEED THERE BE? THE FESTIV-ities were scheduled to take place in two or three hours, which meant the party guests might start arriving within an hour or two. It was chaos within the servants' quarters and passageways as maids flitted about with last-minute tasks. A new dessert menu had to be rushed to the kitchens. The master did not want to smell the mastiffs. This butler was ill-tempered and wreaked of ale, but he was the only one who knew about the elite guests and their tastes. Chaos—an uncontrolled but tempered chaos—took place behind the scenes, hidden behind decorated walls and the sounds muffled by the simple tunes of a piano.

The musical notes circulated throughout the halls and whispered into rooms had a haunting rhythm. It faded and it rose, swaying and changing, yet it resonated in the ears of those who heard it. It caressed and it brought a sense of unease, of melancholy.

The older servants of the household knew this song. They knew it, and they knew the mood it reflected of their master. The song was a nursery lullaby hummed to the master when he was in swaddling clothes and in the tender years of a young child. Hummed by his mother as she fluttered through the Geoffrey homes. This woman was never spoken of, her name all but forgotten (forgotten by the ears of the family and the mouths of the servants), for gossip was a greater offense than theft within this great house. The old master had punished idle gossipmongers with seared tongues and ruined reputations as servants. Oh, but the woman had been so beautiful and so gentle! the elderly servants would murmur over their spiced ales when the fires ran low, and the halls barren.

The elderly staff acknowledged this house, as well as the other properties owned by the Geoffrey's, harbored secrets and skeletons and monsters in the dark recesses. The worst of these secrets were the events that had taken place within the light of the sun—for then the servants had to clean, scrubbing and scrubbing and scrubbing away the crimson before it settled and stained. They'd had to run a scalding bath for the mistress so she might make herself presentable before dinner. The cosmetics hid the bruises, and the waters washed away the blood, but the marks remained. The sounds of her whimpers echoed and haunted the memories of the staff. They knew, but they could not speak of it. Not even to each other, not even to themselves—even after the death of the old master.

The lullaby was one of sadness and of joy, a beguiling combination of something beautifully wrong. *Swing my hands; swing my hands, ever near and ever far, from the flames of hell, from the flames of hell. Swing my hands, swing my hands, oh-ever love, oh-ever love, to the gates of heaven, to the gates of heaven. Swing my hands; swing my hands, ever near and ever far, ever near and ever far. Swing my hands, dream and dream of love, of love. Swing my hands; ever near and ever far, from the dreams of love, of love, of love.* A lullaby able to calm the young master even as he fussed and raged at the misery in his mother's eyes. It calmed him; she was the only one who could calm him.

The staff knew he was mourning. They left him to his own devices as they obeyed his instructions, and if a question arose, no one was allowed to approach the master. He was remembering, and he was embracing the misery. It was his due. *One for the nightmare and two for the seer, three for the maiden, and four for the fear . . .* Little could be said to rouse their master from these dark moods, as they were of a depth few could be tempted to peer down into.

If he was disturbed in these dark moods . . . oh, there was a chill in the air, and the staff knew better than to seek anything. They did what they could with the orders from the butler. If a task went incomplete or a decoration was misplaced, a sharp reprimand took place, but then other responsibilities took precedence over a drawn-out admonishment as there was an event to prepare for, an event meant to be the highlight of society—if everything was perfect or merely appeared to be perfect.

And the flaws were there. The cracks beneath the polished surface crept along and through the foundations of the home. The blood had broken through the rushes, through the wood floor, and had seeped into the stone. It was too much blood; it was all too much.

The minutes ticked by, as did the hours. Guests began to arrive in intricate and ornate carriages, their great wheels crunching against the gravel of the driveway, a sound familiar and longed for by the footmen, who darted out the front doors of the house. They greeted and fawned over the wealth being displayed before them as they escorted each guest inside and through the beautiful halls to the grand ballroom. Thousands of candles flickered and glowed above the congregated individuals, who began to mingle and participate in small talk. Their voices escalated into a white noise that drowned out the lonely tunes of the piano. The festivities had begun.

Gideon, a gray-haired and antique member of the household staff, set himself about the task of alerting Master Geoffrey of his guests' arrival. Gideon had known the old master in his youth and had grown tattered when the old master married his first wife and she bore Henri. He had deteriorated further when the old master had married a second time and another son was born, little cherub-faced Michel. Gideon was haunted by the loss of the first wife as he strolled through the halls of the Geoffrey home. In each room, in each corner, in every step he took, he saw glimpses of ghosts and of horrors.

Gideon was partial to this master, as he was sensible and he was just. Not old-fashioned, but the young master appreciated and retained his staff, knowing the worth of loyal servants was more valuable than gems or precious metals.

Now, how was he to disturb his young master from his reverie? There was no fear of retribution or wrath for his interruption. This is what made it more difficult, because his young master had the patience of a—ah, Gideon caught himself in the age-old habit of gently wrapping on the door. It was slightly ajar.

"Have the guests begun to arrive?" came a murmured reply, the tunes of the piano fading off behind the words.

"Yes, sir. They have been mingling the last quarter hour. Refreshments will be distributed shortly. I thought to assist you in preparing for your introduction to the gathering. May I enter?" Gideon's voice was steady, albeit a bit weathered. His hand hovered near the doorknob but did not touch, waiting for the signal. It never came. Instead, the door slid open, and Henri stood before him with a smile.

"Gideon, you needn't ask for entrance. Am I not clear enough each time we have this conversation? No, no." Henri raised his hand to silence his aged servant. "I will accept a fresh overcoat and perhaps a glass of sherry before I make my way to our guests."

The two strolled through the halls toward Henri's chambers. They chatted about the running of the staff and the household accounts being tended to in the early morning. Planning and more planning proved a continuous demand in the running of a great house. This, Gideon prided himself on and was ever prouder of his young master, who kept an eye on his accounts and did not simply leave the task to his accountants and bankers. Who could trust a banker? They swindled and they flattered while lining their pockets with disloyalty and accumulated wealth.

They arrived at Master Henri's chambers and both paused as the double doors began to open. This was odd, as the doors were to be opened by Gideon, no one else, when admitting Henri into his chambers. As Gideon attempted to step before his master, a figure appeared through the opening. There was a flash of metal as the figure lunged forward, aiming high for Henri's throat with the high-pitched cry of a banshee. A nightmare.

Henri moved more quickly than Gideon because of his youth and practiced agility, shouldering the old man out of the way. Rather than blocking the attack, he kept his body's momentum going forward and slammed his shoulder into his would-be assailant's chest. The two tumbled into the chamber, and the clang of metal falling on the wood floor seemed too loud, too pronounced. A scuffle followed as the figure tried to wrestle away from beneath Henri, writhing left and right. Then all was quiet.

Gideon had bruised his shoulder on impact with the wall and had lost his breath. But he was determined enough to stagger back toward where Henri had fallen. Shaking and wheezing, he stood above the two, who were now sprawled across the floor. Others might have been shocked at the scene before him. Those who were newer, fresher, and unprepared might have cursed or fled. Instead, old wise Gideon merely extended two hands down to Henri and the figure—formerly known as Henri's mistress—in a gesture of peace.

"Mistress Percy, I had not received a notice of your appearance for this evening's entertainments. My sincerest apologies for not having you properly escorted," Gideon said, bowing low and keeping his gaze on Henri's shoes.

"Oh! The pox on you, Gideon. You should have known I was going to hear of this little party. And you!" The slim figure stood and pointed a well-manicured finger down at Henri, a pout on her face. "*You* did not bother to notify me of your return to London. I am bothered by your disrespect of my feelings and our history together."

"Are you quite finished?" Henri asked, still lounging on the ground with his arms behind his head, almost smiling.

"Am I—Am I what? Quite finished? You! You are an absolute ass," Percy retorted.

"I know that. You did not answer my question: are you quite finished?"

This went back and forth between the two. All the while, Gideon laid out new clothes for his young master since he had seen the gash across the white shirt and the scuff marks on the pants. Mistress Percy Brough was an old flame of Henri's, one extinguished more quickly than it had begun to spark. Yet Mistress Percy fancied herself one of the great lost loves of Henri Geoffrey's life and so behaved in unseemly and highly aggressive manners.

"Percy, sweeting, where have you been these last few years? I am not married because I choose not to settle for a plain Jane with a simple dowry. I am not with you because you—although you are beautiful and sophisticated—offer no fortune, no name. We were children when we loved. Are you quite finished being a child?" Henri was calm but pitiless in the way he handled Percy, for he no longer possessed the lust or the patience to deal with her ravings. And this was reflected in the detached way he spoke to her, his gaze hard and his body language reserved.

"I remember when you screamed. I remember the fear in your eyes when you awoke from a night terror. The fear was real. You screamed and screamed until I had to kiss you to make you shut up. Otherwise—Otherwise you would have awoken little Michel and sweet Elisabeth," Percy whispered, her gaze off in a faraway corner, her pupils dilated. "You screamed because you discovered the blood, the blood and the bodies. It was so much blood . . ."

"Percy, I need you to understand these memories that you have—they are not real. They did not happen. Do you hear me, Percy?" Henri offered a gentle touch to her cheek as he nodded to Gideon to undo the bed covers. "If you wish to dream of me, of us and our childhood together, lie down and rest awhile. I will return in a few hours. I promise."

Percy obeyed, almost as if in a trance. But she was calm, and she obeyed by allowing Gideon to guide her toward the bed. Gideon put the pillow beneath her cheek and pulled the comforters about her shoulders, and then he stepped back.

Henri looked down at his once love, once playmate before he leaned forward to place a tender kiss on her brow, whispering, "Sleep well, sweeting, and I will stay the night with you once everyone else has gone. There will be no screams tonight, I promise." He began to hum a lullaby. *One for the nightmare and two for the seer, three for the maiden, and four for the fear . . .* Gideon internally felt a chill at the eerie tune once sang by the lady of the house; externally, the old servant waited for his master.

Percy's eyes remained distant, but her thick lashes fluttered down over her cheeks once, twice, and then remained closed. Her breathing became consistent and heavy with slumber.

Henri straightened himself and glanced over at Gideon with a forlorn grin. He shrugged his way out of his ripped shirt and stepped out of his pants, and then he allowed his body to relax as Gideon dressed him in fresh clothes. It was done in ritualistic silence. The only sound in the room was the soft breaths of a sleeping Percy. No words needed to be said. The ghosts and the shadows were heavy, and they spoke volumes more than any mortal voice might. The demons were out to play, but they had to be held at bay. Just a few hours more. It was time to celebrate the coming of freedom, of serenity. Just a few hours more.

In the halls, the ghosts lingered and tried to reach for his hand as he strolled through. They were neglected, almost forgotten, and the shadows seemed to dominate the light of the lamps. It was a refuge where he had left Percy asleep, dreaming about what she might desire. Henri was almost saddened to have walked away from her. There was a tugging within his mind for him to turn around and crawl in between the sheets, curling his body around the warmth of childhood laughter and innocent bonds. Alas, it was not the course he was destined to take. It never had been.

There was no time to dream. There was no time to mourn. There simply was no time. Each step had to be directed, to be controlled. Each gesture, each phrase he spoke—it was all being assessed and evaluated. Society was a tangled web of courtesy and distrust, of smoke and mirrors, of beauty and deception. If he were younger, he might have been over-whelmed by balancing his family secrets against the public image, the knowledge of his family's sins simmering and rotting just beneath the polished image the world saw. Oh, if he were younger, he might be curled up with Percy, attempting to dream again . . .

February 1791

Percy is here. Why? I could not say. Not definitively. She doesn't belong here. Not anymore. Not after the death of Father, not after the death of Annabelle. Why does Henri do nothing to make the madwoman leave?

My brother is pathetic.

Henri is weak.

I am the one who knows how to handle the secrets of this house, of this family. I have guarded my own secrets well well enough.

-M.L.G.

CHAPTER SEVEN
YOU ARE MY REDEMPTION

S THE QUIET OF THE HALLS WAS ECLIPSED by the white noise of music and conversations, Henri's pace quickened. He was late. It was going to be remarked upon and spread throughout the gossip rings tonight and spread further by the morning. Oh well, he was late.

One mistake in two years of living for his own ambitions. No, not one mistake, for there were hundreds, even thousands of those in his private life. But this was his first public mistake. And it would resonate through polite society. Perhaps it was just what his name required.

"Ladies and gentlemen, Lord Geoffrey has arrived. Please seat yourselves and prepare for the evening meal," announced a booming footman just as Henri turned toward the entrance of the ballroom.

Let the entertainment begin . . .

"Have you heard of the Lady Stanley's disappearance?

It is quite shocking!" one older woman murmured as she fanned herself, eyes on the young Lord Geoffrey.

"I have heard tidbits and whispers. Is it true she was besotted with our own little Michel even after Lord Geoffrey spurned her? I thought she had him eating from her hand—she boasted as much!" replied the older woman's niece.

"If only I knew where she went. It is said that she was last seen at a social event with little Michel and was interrupted by Lord Geoffrey. It was quite the scandal."

"Hush, hush. Lord Geoffrey is coming this way. Smile, will you? I want to be in pleasant company when he sees me," hissed the young woman.

This minor reprimand left the older woman wanting to catch her composure, because Lord Geoffrey was indeed walking in their direction. She was not sure if she wanted her niece to be so intent on this notorious rake. Sure, he was wealthy, and he had the breeding. He certainly had the eloquence and the elegance to charm his way through society to keep his family name known and in the light. But the scandals!

"Such a splendid gathering you have designed for our entertainment, my dear lord. Thank you for remembering us."

"The pleasure is all mine, Marie—may I call you Marie, Lady Rockwell?" Lord Geoffrey took ahold of her proffered hand and bowed over it, brushing his lips across her knuckles as his gaze settled over her niece. Such a delectable little minx! The pouting mouth and the curious intense gaze utterly captivated him. "Will you introduce me to this lovely young woman who has accompanied you?"

I can see her beneath me. I can see her bruised and bleeding. I can see her screaming. I can hear her crying. I can feel her breath against my ear, her fears and her passions floating through my bedchamber. Pillow talk is the most vulnerable if you make the mistake. Let her be the temptation that she promises to be . . . His smile remained intact even as his eyes flickered out across to the other guests, who were mingling and talking over the background sound of an orchestra.

"Oh, oh, of course! How rude am I?" Lady Rockwell wrapped her fingers—talons truly—around her niece's forearm and yanked the young woman forward. "Lord Geoffrey, this is my beloved niece. Justine, this is Lord Geoffrey."

"Spoken like a true guardian, Lady Rockwell. I apologize for my boldness," Henri murmured as he turned to face Justine and bowed.

"It is a true pleasure to finally make your acquaintance, Lord Geoffrey. I have read about you in the papers. You seem to be quite the subject for scrutiny and speculation."

"Justine! Do not make such a horrible first impression with our host!"

The chastisement went without remark from the host as his gaze remained on Justine. Despite the way her gaze was ever so focused on meeting his own (often deemed rude and improper in a young lady), Henri found himself staring back. He maintained his courtier's mask as he listened to the tirade Lady Rockwell whispered none too quietly into the ear of

Justine— something useless about manners, about etiquette, about scandals . . . Ah, there his attention was piqued. There was indeed a smear of scandal across his family's name now with the disappearance of—no, he would not name her. Not in his mind, not in his memories, and most certainly not in the presence of this new little creature known as Justine.

The tirade was allowed to persist for a handful of minutes as Henri's gaze briefly wandered the expanse of the great room. Just a cursory glance, not allowing eye contact to be made with any other individual, as his focus was still on the two in front of him despite his detached mannerisms.

Suddenly, Henri raised his hand and cleared his throat. "Lady Rockwell, if I may? Mistress Justine . . ." His voice was steady, with a hint of honey to the low tones.

"Mistress? You demean her. She is a lady, born and bred, so you may refer to her as Lady Justine without the presumption of intimacy or knowledge of her guardians. As she is an orphan, I am her guardian tonight and until her marriage. Poor, poor dear . . ."

Another rambling of nonsense was in the making when Henri bowed to Lady Rockwell and extended his arm to Lady Justine. The shadow of the briefest of smiles flitted across his lips as he whispered, "May I have this dance, Lady Justine?"

Oh! The excitement was a wave of heat as it coursed through her—the excitement at being so singled out by such a grand and handsome man as Lord Geoffrey. It took a moment, perhaps two or three, for her senses to return, and she blinked away the fog of thoughts. The whirlwind of naïveté. Oh! She had to respond, as he was just standing there, so collected and so—

"If I assume too much, please allow me to ask for your forgiveness, as I often do forget the formalities required of new acquaintances when it comes to the more mindful . . . more *mature* society." His voice trailed off as his gaze wandered, rather languidly, in the direction of Lady Rockwell, who seemed to have recovered from the impudence of both Lady Justine and Lord Henri.

The older lady sniffled and nodded her head toward Henri, signaling that he could entertain Justine. "I will be off to greet an old friend of mine. My niece, do not be disturbed, as I shall remain close at hand." The last bit was said with her gaze locked on Henri, as clear a warning as any.

Henri chuckled softly and gave the briefest of bows to Lady Rockwell, an acknowledgement of what was said aloud and what remained unsaid. He was to be monitored, and the young lady was not to be without her chaperone. A pity, yet there was a need for a wife, and with the need for a wife, there was also the urgency to let society know about the courtship without any smear. Justine was to be kept pristine, as pristinely as she was displayed tonight in an evening gown befitting a . . .

"I will only continue to be in your presence if you desire it, Lady Justine, as you have not said a word since your admonishment. There was nothing impolite in your statement, only facts," Henri said, assuming her silence was out of embarrassment or shyness. How little he knew!

"Oh, I beg your pardon, Lord Geoffrey. I was lost in thought; it was rude of me. Yes. Yes, I do think a stroll through the art gallery would be most refreshing."

"Of course. Please do allow me to escort you and show you the prized possession of the Geoffrey estate." Henri emphasized the words *prized possession* even as his brow wrinkled.

Lady Rockwell had wandered a bit too far to hear this last brief exchange between the pair. Thus, she was left unawares as her young ward—her precious and prized niece—was whisked away by the scandal-ridden rake of the season. The pair made their way through the gathered party with few eyes being watchful of their whereabouts. Yet all it took was a single set of eyes to see the slightest impropriety for there to be a scandal. And a scandal could not happen, as it would only further complicate this new and blossoming relationship.

The stroll through the long and vacant hallways left little to be said between the pair. There was no need for the young man to speak, or so he thought. A quick glance, but it gave him more than adequate time to assess her appearance, posture, and her calmness. Was she not doubting her decision to wander the residence with him, alone and nowhere near a chaperone? This could so easily ruin her delicate reputation.

Society was truly odd in the way it viewed the two genders. Either way, he caught his thoughts before they wandered too much further down into the psychosocial system he had been raised in. The young woman beside him was lovely. Beyond lovely. She was truly exquisite.

"Sir, how much farther shall we wander before we come across this great treasure?" An inquiry, said in a softly spoken voice, brought his thoughts to a jarring standstill.

"Ah, madame, it is merely another turn. Just there, if you will, the treasure I mentioned to you . . ."

They had come across the library of the Geoffrey residence. The vast room appeared to tower higher and stretch wider than the great hall they had just left; even with walls and walls filled with books, the library itself felt airy and welcoming. Such a drastic difference from the halls they had just left. But despite the initial impression of welcoming and warmth, Justine sensed a more sinister undercurrent within the walls. It barely stirred as they entered, but she sensed the weight of this menacing ill-intent pressing down on her.

A few long inhales and exhales kept her calm as she looked about the beautifully decorated library, with her gaze finally resting on Lord Geoffrey. He had paused near the doorway and stood observing her. A detail she did not miss was the impassive look on his face. Was he truly as jaded and as heartless as the ladies warned?

"Have you grown callous to the wealth of knowledge being stored along the walls?" Her words floated through the air, then stilled and quieted. Curious there was no echo in such a vast room.

"No, not callous, my lady. I am merely enjoying the more exquisite sample standing before me."

"Oh, you are indeed a flatterer. Do remember, my lord, you mentioned a great treasure that belongs to the Geoffrey estate, and it is supposedly housed in this very library. My expectations have been set rather high, and I wouldn't want to delay too much longer for propriety's sake, as I am certain Lady Rockwell will notice my absence. Please, do indulge my curiosity so we might return to the gathering." Justine choked out the last sentence as she glanced up to meet Henri's gaze. Its intensity was unsettling. She had said too many words too quickly, and a warmth began to creep into her cheeks.

Lord Geoffrey continued to stand there, calm and collected, as he listened to her ramble. His gaze never left her face. His mind was mapping out the path to obtaining her as his bride, his wife, his prize. His. Then he stirred, in the most subtle of ways. His muscles merely tensed rather than remaining relaxed as his thoughts sharpened to the reason they had entered the library. Ah, she was not an idle-minded maiden . . . Excellent.

"Do forgive my self-indulgence in merely gazing upon you as if you were a statue, an artwork I might merely gain visual pleasure from. You are correct. I did lure you here under the guise of seeing my family's treasure. Come, this way." With that, the young lord pivoted around and began to walk down a darker part of the library.

Justine paused for a moment, a mere breath, before she chose to follow him, not knowing this was to be a turning point in her life, in her future. She forgot about the protocols and the precautions a young unmarried lady must maintain to keep a pristine reputation—one without rumor, without a whisper, without a smear or tarnish. It could mean the end of her suitors—well, an end to her *ideal* line of suitors, the eligible bachelors of wealth and impeccable breeding.

She had been raised to obey, to remember, to be demure, and it went against her nature and her inclination to indulge in being shown a private tour of the Geoffrey estate by its master. Her mind gave minimal thought to the fact her absence had already been noted and her chaperone, the overprotective Lady Rockwell, had already begun making a scene about her not being in the great hall. Those few who had witnessed her leave the social event with the Lord Geoffrey would begin to find their tongues, and such wagging tongues would find avid listeners to hear of the two young people disappearing for an assumed lovers' tryst.

Such scandalous whispers were kept away from the Lady Rockwell however, as those who spread such malicious and damaging rumors knew to not startle the older lady any further, lest she have an episode and cause further discomfort to those gathered. Lady Rockwell was quite beside herself, remembering her goal of keeping her precious niece well guarded and beneath her matron's wings, escorting her and showing her off to those most eligible, most desirable bachelors. Yet, despite her best efforts and most selfless of motivations, she was left standing alone with wild eyes and a racing heart. Her sister—God rest her soul—would surely haunt her dreams tonight if she did not locate her only child before the closing of the hour!

Again, this naïveté was so desirable in a young bride. It was what kept Justine walking a slow pace behind the lord of the house. Not speaking, as she sensed there was no desire for conversation as she was led through a maze of books and of statues and of priceless paintings. It took such great effort for her to not brush her fingertips across a statue of a shrouded woman, her shoulders hunched as she appeared to be frozen forever in mourning. Why was she so drawn to this piece? No time to process as she hastened her steps to stand beside Lord Geoffrey. Her gaze tried to find the great treasure, the mysterious object . . .

"There, just beneath the stained glass on the north wall. Be careful when you lift the cloth." His voice was once again passive, withdrawn even.

Why?

Justine blinked a handful of times before she stepped beyond him and gingerly approached a turquoise-and-gold-cloth-covered table. Silk? The fabric felt as smooth and light as air beneath her fingertips as she slowly moved it aside.

An audible gasp left her lips as she stared at the object. Seconds or perhaps minutes passed before Justine could look away from the marvel before her. She looked over at the man beside her and felt an acute shiver descend her spine when her eyes locked with his.

Had he been watching her this entire time? Perhaps.

"It is . . . It is . . . I do not have the words to describe this. Why have you entrusted me with this? This object is much sought after. Is not the Crown in want of this?" Oh, why was her voice a thread? Weak, tangled, fearful. Afraid. And why was he just staring at her? Why was his face so, so perfectly poised? Her heart began to beat harder, harder, and harder against her chest. The rushing noise of a great waterfall filled her ears. Had she forgotten to breathe?

"You will be my wife." He said it so easily, as one might sip on water.

"What?"

"You will be my wife. When we return to the gathering, all eyes will be on us, and I will announce our engagement. You will wear this ring." His hand opened to reveal a diamond ring. "Give me your hand." A simple command, one she followed with no resistance. The ring slid onto her finger.

"I . . . I do not know . . ." She was stumbling for words, no longer poised or eloquent. She felt raw, vulnerable, but why?

"It is a family heirloom. You will know the history soon enough, my sweet Justine." And then he smiled. It was such an apathetic upturn of his lips. His eyes remained distant, empty.

"I must speak with Lady Rockwell. I must return to the gathering. I must return . . ." It was then the panic began to form, flowing in a rush as her words ran together as fast as her heart pounded. Had she just snared the notoriously sought-after bachelor of the Geoffrey fortune? Was this what she wanted? Why could she not turn away from his aloof gaze?

"May we celebrate our engagement with the guests, Justine?" He had moved in closer to her, closer than propriety would've allowed between two unmarried members of the opposite sex. Yet he did not touch her. Respectful or intimidating? "Remember this feeling in your heart, in your head. Overwhelmed. Dazed. Remember it well," he warned. Then Henri spun around on his heels and extended his hand to her.

Why was she reaching out and taking ahold of his hand? It felt so unnatural, so dangerous.

"If you remember this sensation, if you remember to obey my word, you will thrive as my wife, my partner," he whispered each word precisely aligned with their steps.

This sent chills down her spine, shards of ice stabbing in a painful manner. Why was she suddenly so obedient to this man, this stranger who had declared they were going to be wed? Justine had not come to this social event this evening to become engaged. This was supposed to be a casual outing with her guardian to let society see her face.

The halls were dimly lit in comparison to the brilliance of the grand hall. Thousands of candles burned, or so it appeared to Justine's eyes as she made a reentry into the festivities with her hand in Henri's. It felt as if thousands of eyes were now staring at her. Judging. Assessing. Determining her worth as a subject of disdain or congratulation. The crowd was quiet, as if they were all simultaneously holding their breaths in expectation. Of what?

Henri paused a few moments after their entrance. His eyes were only looking upon Justine, gaging her self-control and weighing her strength to not show a change in her posture or her expression, even as he felt her hand quiver and shake.

"Ladies and gentlemen, friends and strangers, I have an announcement. It is with great pleasure that I announce my engagement to this woman, Lady Justine Ayling." As he said her name, he raised their joined hands into the air with a smile. His entire posture changed from that of the reserved aloof man from not a quarter hour before to one who was exceedingly warm and jovial. The crowd absorbed this display of geniality, and all at once, there was a thunderous roar of applause, of congratulations. There were a few who did not raise their glasses in a toast, nor did they clap or make declarations of joy. Those few surrounded the guardian of Lady Justine, Lady Rockwell—one who had not sought this union and one who did not want her niece to be married into the Geoffrey family.

Five for the dreamer, six for the sinner, seven for the corpse . . .

Mid January 1791

Oh! It is beyond all my imaginings, all of my daydreams! Lord Geoffrey, Lord Henri Geoffrey, has proposed to me! It is not a dream. It is not a dream. It is my reality! I am to become the Lady Geoffrey, Lady Justine Geoffrey. I will no longer be the ward of my aunt. A blessing that she has been in my life, but I will have my own home to govern. My own schedule to create and to maintain. My own life! Oh! Glorious day! Not even the snows can cool down the warmth of my cheeks or dampen my spirits. It is such stupendous news!

-Justine Ayling

CHAPTER EIGHT
Swing Me Softly, Away, Away

THE AROMATIC SCENT OF JASMINE TEA WAFTED through the warm air of the room. A crackling flame had been built in the centuries-old fireplace to keep the surrounding chairs and side table cozy. It was a well-loved and cherished setting for both women sitting in the armchairs, their hands curled around hot teacups as they gazed into the fire. Each woman appeared lost in her own thoughts. The older woman wore her lustrous, gray-streaked blond hair loose, and her shoulders were covered by an intricately designed shawl. Her nightgown was a soft lavender with lace detailing along the throat. The younger woman wore her blond hair coifed up and covered by a simple nightcap, her own nightgown a soft white with no added detailing.

Marie was the first to speak, breaking the spell of peace and quiet around them. "Justine, my dear, I am speaking to you as your aunt. I am speaking as the sister of your mother. Do not marry this man. Renounce the engagement." She was begging her niece as they sat opposite one another over evening tea. Her blue eyes were heavily hooded with dark circles beneath them since insomnia had become her companion.

"Aunt, you know my mother would have wanted me to be happy. Why can I not find happiness in marital bliss with Lord Geoffrey? He was perfectly polite and ensured his servant was nearby as we spoke. He guarded my reputation. He is handsome, and his family is older than our own by a century!" Justine enthusiastically recalled all the information she had gained about her fiancé and his family history. It was the ramblings of a young woman at the beginning of her fairy tale, a young woman who was about to turn the page of her story and begin a new chapter, eyes bright with all the possibilities before her.

"Your mother wanted better for you. Heaven knows. She may have been strict with you, but she saw your potential. Henri, Lord Geoffrey, is not the husband for you." *He will break you. He is a wolf in sheep's clothing, a monster hiding beneath the bed, a demon wearing false wings.* But these last statements were not said out loud, as Marie did not want to break her niece. Nor did she want to begin another argument with the blissful naïve girl. Oh, if only it were as easy as turning back time and never attending the Geoffrey ball!

The invitation had been peculiar to her as the Geoffrey family had not sought out the Ayling family, to which Lady Rockwell had been born, in decades. The older woman shook her head and leaned back into the armchair to gaze upon her niece with more care. There was a tender place in her heart where her niece was to remain, and her worries were unable to be eased at the thought of her beautiful niece being sent to the Geoffrey home. The decades old rumors had swirled and slipped through the cracks of doorways, as servants were idle gossipers when attending the young. Servants had also looked down upon Marie as she was a fresh widow then with no children of her own, so she stayed with her sister and tended to her niece.

Servants' gossip was ofttimes more accurate than the stories and riddles spun by the upper class in salons and front rooms. How could she bring this knowledge to her niece's attention? It did not seem feasible without also destroying the young woman's innocence and lighthearted mannerisms. Marie had worked so diligently to preserve her niece as best as she could, given the tragic circumstances of her sister's and brother-in-law's sudden deaths.

A deep breath in and a slow exhale out allowed for Marie to maintain her composure in front of her niece. The bright blue eyes staring at her were so terribly like those of her late sister! It was difficult to ignore the gentle ache in her chest. She reached out her hand and curled her fingers around her niece's cheek, a gentle and loving gesture often shared between the two of them. "I want you to be happy above all else. You are my family. I will do everything in my power to protect you," Marie was saying before she could stop herself.

"I do not need protection anymore, Auntie. I need your blessing for my marriage; otherwise, my heart will hurt knowing I lack your approval." Justine breathed out, curling her hands around her aunt's fingers.

"Justine. You met this man once. He is seeking to marry you in a month."

"And?" she innocently asked.

"It is not enough time to know whether this will be a healthy match, Justine. Marriage is complicated, and I want you to be . . ." Marie could not think of the correct words to say, as she did not want to expose her niece to the falsities men were, nor did she want to destroy the fairytale expectations Justine had. This would prove a disservice to them both.

Marie was married at a young age—too young—and her husband had already been twice widowed but remained childless. Her youth had been the solution Lord Rockwell sought. It was a miserable match and ultimately led to Marie suffering multiple traumas she was unable to disclose to anyone but God. Her sister had been suffering her own losses then, and her mother had been frigid. Marie did not know how to communicate this, any of it, to the young woman who meant so much to her. She felt tears forming beneath her eyelids, and she blinked a few times to banish them. No crying.

Justine started to chew on her lower lip with a worried frown on her face. It was not like her aunt to be at a loss for words. Lady Rockwell was held in high esteem by most of high society for her intellect and her quips. So, to hear her stumbling over her own words while sitting quietly before the fireplace . . . Justine saw the first cracks forming in the picture-perfect image she had carried for so many years—the

image of a happily-ever-after with her husband, a man beyond measure and someone who would treasure her. These
were minuscule fractures, but they had formed.

"Justine, promise me this . . . When you are married and
you become Lady Justine Geoffrey, always remember I am
here. If you need me for anything, be it large or small, I am
always here for you. Always," Marie said at last, a sadness in
her voice as she smiled over at her niece. This was the least
she could offer to Justine, leaving an open door.

"Of course, my dear aunt. I know you are here." The
reply was quick, but there was a hesitation near the end as
Justine truly looked at her aunt. There were wrinkles around
her eyes and a stiffness to her jaw Justine had often seen in
times when her aunt was stressed or angry. "I promise I will
remember to call on you." Justine spoke more deliberately
as she looked at her aunt. "If I ever need you, I will write.
I swear."

"I appreciate you saying so. You are so precious to me."

Her aunt's voice was thick and weighed down with emotion. This puzzled Justine. The promise was meant to ease
her aunt's concerns, not burden her further. So, why was her
aunt suddenly crying? It was rare for Marie to shed tears in
front of anyone, much less her niece.

One of the logs in the fireplace cracked and broke, star-
tling both women to jolt back from the other. The weight of
the promise was lost as they turned to observe the flickering
flame, and each said a quiet prayer. One was for gratitude,
and one was for safeguarding. Justine had pure intentions

when she'd made such a promise to her aunt despite the doubts she harbored, as her naïveté had placed Henri Geoffrey high up on a pedestal of chivalry and grace.

It was not going to be as simple a path as Justine was imagining, Marie knew this much, and she was sad to not be able to assist her niece with the truth of reality. Some social barrier held her tongue and kept her thoughts and her own memories to herself. It kept her truth hidden even as she wished to speak out loud for her niece's sake. Why were men so deceitful and cunning? Marie had been in love with her husband when she first laid eyes on him. He had been older but still handsome, with a confidence about his posture few could mimic. He had warm gray eyes when they first met, but within days of the wedding, the warmth had died, replaced with something cold and sinister.

Marie shuddered from the flashes of memories as she continued to stare into the flames, oblivious to her niece intently watching her. It may have been better this way, for Justine was lost in her own thoughts and her own imaginings. Perhaps she could have a love story as her parents had. Perhaps she would be cherished and beloved by her husband.

Perhaps, Justine dared to hope, this marriage might bring a new chapter for her life story. A turning of the page. A fresh start far from death and grief, shadows and tears. She did not want to envision herself as the Harbinger of Death whenever she saw her own reflection—the blackened wings of corruption, molting ash, and burnt feathers as her shadow.

ON THE OTHER SIDE OF TOWN, HENRI GEOFFREY was celebrating his engagement in a solitary fashion. It was a momentous occasion, a true victory in the grand scheme of his plan. Henri was glad his younger brother had chosen to remain idle in his chambers the evening of the ball. Then there had been no possibility of Michel creating a scene or a scandal—at least one larger than the chaos Henri had caused when returning to the gathered guests and openly announcing his engagement to Lady Ayling. Oh, the fury on Lady Rockwell's face could have shaken most men to their core, but it was a look Henri had long since become jaded to.

The history between the two families, Ayling and Geoffrey, was known to Henri as he had sought the information from Gideon, who had clear knowledge of the events from two decades before. It was a dark thing, a filthy thing brushed beneath the rushes on the floorboards, along with all other debris and impure remarks. The history did not deter Henri. If anything, it fueled his obsessive desire to marry the girl more speedily.

His plan had been meticulously written down and laid out over the span of years, and this marriage marked the first milestone toward change. The prince and his inner circle had entertained Henri here and there without future commitments or further invitations for smoke room conversations. It was a slight Henri did not take lightly, although he played it off well in the eyes of the court.

"I am nothing more than a puppet in his eyes, and though he may be right . . ." It was the beginning of a long monologue being murmured through parched lips. His breath was rancid, and his eyes were bloodshot and swollen. His figure stumbled back and forth through his study.

Henri was beyond himself. Celebrating and grieving. This was meant to be a joyous occasion. He was going to be a married man. He was no longer going to be a bachelor both desired and scorned. Yet there was an ache growing larger and larger in his chest, ever expanding until it consumed his entire being. A crashing of waves, a sensation of falling, an explosion of pain.

"I am more than you ever dared to see! I am more than you said I could be. I am my father's son more than yours. You are nothing to me but a memory, a shade. Begone!" More rantings and ravings as he yelled and pointed into the dark corners of the room, his blue eyes unfocused, his dark hair disheveled. Henri was lost in a world where no one could reach him.

"Swing me softly, away, away . . ." he began to sing, humming a melodic lullaby to himself as he lay on the floor. Blood was pooling beneath his head. It went unnoticed as he continued to sing to himself, his fingers dancing along the floorboards as he turned his head to the right and to the left as if gently rocking himself or slow dancing. "Swing me softly, away . . . away . . ."

Unsure of the passage of time, Henri woke up to a throbbing headache and a sharp pain in his forearm. There was the softness of a pillow beneath his cheek and the warmth of a coverlet over his body. He was still wearing the clothes from the previous night, but he was in his own bed. *Gideon.* Yes, it must have been Gideon who'd taken care of him once he had fallen asleep. A quick look around the room proved his intoxicated stupor of the night before had done property damage, along with a blood mark on his floor.

A groan.

"Good afternoon, my lord. There is coffee and some biscuits in the antechamber when you are ready."

"Yes, Gideon, thank you. Did I miss my meeting with the prince's mistress set for this afternoon?"

"No, my lord. The Madame sent her apologies and said she is going to be late. So, I thought it best to let you rest longer. Her carriage is still seen at the prince's secondary residence."

"Excellent." Henri breathed out. He took a few moments to gauge the severity of the headache.

Slowly, Henri sat up and moved out of his bed to take measured steps out to the antechamber, where he was assaulted by the strong aroma of coffee and bread, just as Gideon had told him. A chair was angled and expectantly waiting for him to sit. A few moments passed before Henri reached out and took a sip, then a second of the hot coffee. Gideon always managed to time these tasks flawlessly.

"Prepare the blue parlor for the meeting with Madame. I do not want her to see too much of my home as I do not trust her."

"Yes, my lord. Anything else?" Gideon stood ready.

"No, that will be all for now. I will ring the bell if I should have need of you or anyone else . . ." Henri paused.

"You have fresh clothing laid out in your bedchamber, my lord. I do hope it meets your standards."

"As always, thank you for your faultless execution, Gideon."

"It is my pleasure to do so, my lord."

Late January 1797

Do you think that he will love me? This man I am to wed soon . . . Henri. Lord Geoffrey. My aunt is concerned about his motives. Her fears are grounded in the mire of gossip and rumors. No man is above being discussed by the families of society. I still hear whispers of my own parents beyond their untimely demise—people are so cruel.

Will Henri be cruel to me? He does not seem to be the cruel type.

I hope and I believe with all of my heart that he will be kind and chivalrous. He has a younger brother. I think . . . I will have a family.

-Justine Ayling

CHAPTER NINE
THE PRIZED POSSESSION

THE SIMPLICITY OF THE GROUNDSKEEPING with the clean lines of the brick architecture was both stunning and calming to behold. Gideon had been the first to greet the Madame in one of his more dashing outfits as befitted the favorable visit being paid to the Geoffrey residence. Society only knew the prince's mistress by the nickname of "the Madame," as her identity had been hidden beneath layers and layers of intrigue and royal protection. The prince was covetous of what he deemed as his.

The Madame had been permitted a visit outside the palace for their meeting, an honor not lost on Henri Geoffrey. The woman was in her early thirties with only a few fine wrinkles around her eyes, clearly visible whenever she gave a dimpled smile. She had light hazel eyes, expressive and bright. As she entered the front doors of the beautiful home, there was a collective sigh of appreciation as the Geoffrey staff all bowed and curtsied in respect.

"Oh, this is too grand a welcome, Lord Geoffrey!" The woman's tinkling laughter filled the foyer as she looked about at the men and women lining the walls.

"Not at all, Madame," Henri replied. "Please, follow me this way."

The only sound traveling through the foyer and into the blue parlor was the click-clacking of the woman's heels. Habitually, Henri gave a cursory look over the sofa and the rushes when first entering the room. The servants who had been ordered to tidy the room had done a thorough job some weeks prior, yet there remained a haunting sensation whenever he reentered this room. Why could he not remember committing murder?

The prince's mistress took note of Henri's change in demeanor without openly remarking on it. This information, and all other knowledge gained in this visit, was going to be reported to her lover by the end of the night. She was a loyal creature. The doors quietly closed behind them.

"Lord Geoffrey, will you call me Genevieve? Only while we are enjoying this intimate visit, of course." The words floated through the stagnant air as she took a seat on the couch.

"Yes, it would be an honor." Henri felt queasy as a flash of Annabelle's corpse appeared in place of Genevieve. The horror of the memory surpassed the honor he had just been personally given to know and speak to the prince's mistress by her first name.

"Why is it you wrote to me, Henri? You have caused my darling prince too much worry these last few weeks with your erratic attitude changes." All pretenses had suddenly been dropped, and her voice lost its tinkling gaiety.

How was he supposed to answer? Yes, he had been earnest when he sent her a letter three weeks ago because of the shock at what he had done to his own lover. Henri had thought this woman might offer him advise on how to confess Annabelle's sudden demise, beneath his roof, to the prince. Then the harsh reality had settled in, and logic won. Henri could not disclose his heinous crime to anyone outside of his own home—even within his home. The knowledge of a blood-soaked couch, bloodied floor, and shards of glass in this room was a closely guarded secret. One of many.

"I am planning to take a wife—"

"Let me interrupt you a moment, Henri. I already know that you have the young Ayling heiress utterly in love with you. I know that her guardian, Lady Rockwell, is against the marriage, but she whispers this privately. Why did you write to me?"

"I need your assistance, in the future. When you . . . go into confinement, I request that you hire a woman named Katharine. She has a connection with Lady Rockwell that will serve me when my future wife gives birth," Henri said matter-of-factly.

"I will be going into confinement in the next season. Why this woman? You have not wedded nor bedded the Lady Ayling, yet you presume she is fertile. Tsk, tsk. You men are all the same in the self-worship of your own virility."

"Indeed. Think on it is all I ask of you. If you hire her, send me a note or token."

"Of course, Henri."

The agreement came with the arrival of tea and crumpets. They both sat peacefully as a few servants had come in to arrange the trays of tea and the dainty snacks. Any other individual may have been put off by the sudden change in Henri's posture as the younger servants came through the doors. He appeared more . . . dominant, then slowly seemed to deflate as the doors were once more closed and they were left to themselves. Why were men so simple and yet so complex? The silence continued as Henri poured the steaming tea into two porcelain cups.

"Why are you pursuing Lady Ayling, Henri?" Genevieve asked.

Henri set down the teapot and gracefully grabbed one of the teacups and its saucer, carefully handing each to Genevieve as he stared up at her. The sudden change of expression on his face startled Genevieve, causing her teacup to clank on its saucer as she worked to compose herself again. What had she just seen race across his face? It seemed a combination of anger and caution, with a shadow of something else—something more dangerous.

"It is beyond time I took a wife, and Lady Ayling is the most adequate candidate. She is educated, with a pristine reputation of chastity, and she is an heiress to the Ayling fortune. Why would I not pursue her?" There was an edge to his voice as he answered, his words short.

Henri was struggling with anxiousness at Genevieve's open questioning. It was not wholly expected, and that is where he had miscalculated the woman before him. He had assumed she was just another beautiful face the prince had taken for bedding.

"Why not indeed."

"Lady Rockwell has raised enough alarms for the engagement to become the talk of town these last few days. She is making a spectacle of herself, even casting a shadow of doubt over Lady Ayling." Henri was talking more than he should have been, rambling on before he caught himself and cleared his throat.

Genevieve took a slow sip of the jasmine tea and observed the young man who sat across from her. He had been a continual favorite of her prince the last decade or so. *Be careful around him and his brother . . . They have deplorable taste . . . At this one party, they drank the blood of a servant and laughed . . .* Another slow sip of the tea and she was calm once again. There was a shadow in those light eyes of his—something Genevieve was unable to identify, and it continued to bother her.

"Henri, I do wish you a successful and blissful marriage. Perhaps you will become a father within the year." Genevieve raised her cup as if to gesture a toast.

"Aye, Genevieve. That would be grand."

A lull in the conversation followed, during which only the gentle noise of the porcelain cups being set down disturbed the quiet of the room. As the silence built and built with heavy expectation, an answer lingered just beyond reach. There were numerous strings playing out between the two of them, strings that were meant to lead and to restrain, to ensnare and to harm. Strings of words left unspoken. Strings of thoughts and opinions.

Genevieve had turned her head to face away from Henri and was trying to figure out the patterned design of the gardens, as the cobblestone pathway was an oddity to look at. It did not take long for her to forget she was in the middle of a social visit with Lord Geoffrey, for congratulations and for information. Information was an asset a person could possess, especially if she could be the firsthand informant to the prince. Henri had become notorious in court and in society because of the combination of his family, his wealth, his dark reputation, and now his engagement to the Ayling heiress.

A gentle knock on the door came shortly before a voice announced the arrival of Michel Geoffrey. Genevieve felt a pique of interest as she looked at the young man who stepped into the parlor. She saw nothing spectacular or exciting about Michel today, so she became dismissive in her attention to him. The dark rumors circulating around Henri included the young Michel and deep depths of debauchery and sin. Just how dark did they truly go? She supposed there *was* something curious, something unusual about the brothers.

"It is a pleasure to see you, Madame. You are radiant today as ever." Michel began to bow, but his brother's fingers were tightly curled around the back of his neck, yanking him to stand. A brief scuffle broke out between the two men as Michel struggled to stand apart from his older brother.

"Tsk, tsk, gentlemen. No need to batter one another. Come have a seat, Michel. It has been a while since we last spoke. Are you heartbroken over Lady Stanley's sudden departure from our circles? My prince has been asking about her whereabouts, but no one seems to have an answer," Genevieve casually said while one of her hands curled softly around Michel's forearm, pulling him to sit across from her.

Henri was the first to wear the courtier's mask again—an empty expression able to hide the inner turmoil upon hearing Annabelle's name suddenly spoken by Genevieve. Not many had the nerve to speak about the missing woman in front of Henri. Henri had tried to give off the impression that he did not care, yet something in his mannerisms gave others the impression that they should not speak about this topic because it bothered him.

Although he was preoccupied with thoughts of marriage and fulfilling the first step of his plan, Annabelle still haunted his dreams. She still caused his skin to crawl and chills to splinter down his spine.

Michel was less adept at making his expression change on demand—at least this was what he wanted the world to think. So far, Michel was perceived as the weaker of the Geoffrey brothers, and not only on the fact that he was the youngest.

"I . . . uh, yes. I do miss her company. Annabe—Lady Stanley was a remarkably witty woman," Michel said, his lower lip quivering as his gaze slid over to his older brother.

"Lady Stanley was often a guest in our home. We are sorry that we have not seen her these last few weeks," Henri said calmly, an attempt to end the discussion of the woman he had supposedly loved, the woman he had been rumored to be courting until Annabelle had been seen with Michel more and more throughout town, attending both public and private events together. Scandal. Shock.

"I did not mean to cause you distress, Michel," Genevieve crooned, her fingers still curled around the younger man's forearm. It was a blatant lie, as a smile soon revealed. There was nothing the two men could do or say to contradict Genevieve as she was the prince's mistress and held great power in court, albeit in the shadows.

"Will you choose to stay and dine with us, Genevieve?" Henri interrupted the intense exchange happening between the woman and his little brother. There was too much friction and raw emotion beginning to surface, and that was not beneficial to his family. Too much could be lost.

Why could he not remember committing the murder?

"Oh." Genevieve's attention was removed from Michel as she turned to face Henri with a forlorn expression. "I must decline your invitation for today. This visit was not scheduled to be too long. My prince has another appointment, and he wants me in attendance with him this afternoon."

"A pity. Perhaps next time we might all dine together. Send my regards to the prince, will you?" Henri said as he stood up from his chair. It was a disrespectful gesture to show Genevieve the visit was concluded by standing up before she did.

Genevieve arched an eyebrow at the sudden change in Henri's demeanor but did not remark on it. Rather, she took her time to stand and glanced over at Michel with a more critical eye. The younger Geoffrey was hiding something, and it was intriguing for her to witness the unspoken currents between the brothers. She was going to provide a feast of information to her prince about the state of the Geoffrey home.

"Until next time, my dears." Genevieve did not hesitate to walk out of the parlor and through the front doors of the Geoffrey home. She did not wait to call a servant, and she did not care to look back to see the men's reactions. Instead, she went immediately into her carriage and rang the bell to alert the driver that she was ready to depart.

Henri remained standing in his place, even at the hasty departure of Genevieve. All his senses were on high alert, and he was on edge. What had the woman unearthed in such a short span of time? Curses flowed through his mind as he stared over at his younger brother. The fool was the one who had created the need for secrecy and continual lies. The fool!

"You do not make any further commentary about Annabelle, do you understand? Not to me, not to anyone. If you do, I will cut out your tongue," Henri threatened.

"I hear you, brother. The minx knew what she was doing. She commented about Annabelle so suddenly . . . It caught both of us off guard," Michel began to explain but was cut off.

"She commented about Annabelle because she has heard the rumors, such as anyone on the street corner has. Annabelle was last seen entering our home!"

"Rumors are not evidence!" Michel roared, defensive.

Henri inhaled sharply as if his brother had thrown cold water on his face. The doubts and the fog of his own mind had continued to fail him as he tried and tried again to remember the details. None came but for the facts: Annabelle had been in the blue-and-gold parlor. He had discovered her corpse. Michel had been quick in arriving, to his dismay. It was indeed a misdeed, nothing more. Nothing less. He missed her laughter and the merriment in her eyes as she looked at him from across a room. They had ruthlessly flirted with one another for months before any true actions were taken.

"Michel, I will cut out your tongue if you speak Annabelle's name again," Henri repeated.

Such a magnificent woman she had been.

February 1791

Annabelle is mine. She was always meant to be mine. It was only a matter of time.

Henri could not handle her. Henri could not appreciate her.

Her depth. Her beauty. Her silence.

Henri was wrong to keep me away from her, away from you.

Annabelle, you know that you are mine. My one and only. There can be no others. No, not this time.

Annabelle, you are mine.

-M.L.G.

CHAPTER TEN
ONLY YOU KNOW MY HEART, MY INTENTIONS

THE SKIES WERE DARK, HEAVY WITH CLOUDS and rumbles of thunder, as the two figures leaned against the windowsill side by side, looking out the open window. Streaks of lightning skittered across the skies, followed quickly by the claps of thunder. It meant the storm was nearing, edging closer and closer to where the lovers stood. Neither of them stirred as the rumbling grew louder to the point that the window frame shook with each rumble. Unbound cascades of curling auburn tresses could be seen during the brightest flashes of lightning and a glimpse of a man's fingers twirling the ends. The man and a woman were spending time together quietly as the storm broke out before their eyes.

The room behind the two was simply furnished. It possessed a beautifully carved wooden desk, a simple bed, and two ivory chairs facing a bare hearth. Other items were strewn about the room in a manner of disarray, a side table in two corners with knickknacks scattered about. It was not a peculiar space. Nothing about it was threatening but for the air. The air in the room was heavy with frankincense and cinnamon and sesame oil, bowls and bowls of which were laid out across the floor in a pentagon.

As the lightning continued in the chaos outside, the man had stepped away from the woman and left her to stand by the window in solitude. He was humming a soft tune, his posture placid, content even. He continued to hum as he knelt on the ground a few feet behind the woman, resting his hands on his knees and simply staring up at her back, admiration in his gaze for her lustrous locks and the silhouette of her figure illuminated by the storm outside. A gust of wind swept through the open window and caused the woman to sway a little. Despite this, she remained perfectly still.

"Why are you so rigid, my love? My brother did not mean his threat. He could not bring himself to physically harm me. Henri is jealous." Michel was murmuring more to himself than the woman before him. Michel was the one who was able to benefit from more worthwhile time with Annabelle. It just confused him why she was so stiff, so unaccommodating to his affections.

"Swing me softly, away, away . . ." Michel sang as he stood up, took slow steps to stand behind Annabelle, and wrapped his arms around her waist. He buried his face into her auburn hair and inhaled once, twice. "You are so intoxicating, my Annabelle. Annabelle."

Tears were flowing down his cheeks as he continued to hum and then sing into her hair. His body began to sway side to side as he embraced her quiet form. He was grieving. He was placating her silence, her anger. Why else would she be so silent, so rigid? If she were not angry at him, Annabelle would be smiling and laughing with him or at him.

Those rosebud lips were parted, but no breath flowed. Those blue eyes were open, but they were clouded; they were unseeing. Michel was allowing himself to grieve her loss.

"Yet I still have you here with me. You will forever be with me, as you promised. You swore that you would be my wife. You swore we could have eternity together as man and wife. You swore. And so, you are mine, forever. You will never become ashes, because ashes drift away at the slightest breeze. You are eternal," Michel was saying as he turned his head to stare out the window once more. The thunderstorm had already passed overhead, and the clash of thunder was quieter now, the lightning less visible, dimmer in the distance.

"We could have been more discreet. Then Henri would not have discovered our love as quickly as he did. I am disappointed in you for being so wanton with your affections, displaying them so openly, yet I loved it." Michel said.

Michel's hands began to wander up and down the sides of her waist, idly tracing the seams of her gown. He was so obsessed with her beauty, with everything about her. It was maddening to not touch her, to not be near her. It was through this proximity that the voices in his head were able to be quieted, that the demons gnawing and clawing at the back of his mind could be calmed. It was only Annabelle who brought this semblance of internal peace, and before Annabelle, it had been Elisabeth, but Elisabeth was a decade gone, and Annabelle was the perfect successor.

Michel quickly stepped back and away from the still figure, turning to face one of the side tables, and walked over to it and rummaged through the bottles. His hand grasped a dainty bottle of perfume, and he was once more behind Annabelle, spraying the perfume on her hair and then down along the curve of her back. His mind soon became overwhelmed with the sweet scent of orange blossoms, something he was to always associate with Annabelle.

"So sweet, so tender . . ." he whispered into her ear, his teeth grazing her earlobe as he tossed the perfume bottle to the floor at their feet. It was a gentle clatter. As the thunder was no longer resounding through the room, there was a sense of peace in the space around them—an artificial peace, but it was one Michel cherished.

Masterfully, he contorted his body to where he was able to pick up Annabelle and hold her against his chest. A fresh wave of orange blossom filled his senses as he closed his eyes and took memorized steps away from the open window and back into the depths of the room, only pausing once his knees brushed along the edge of the bed. Slowly, ever so carefully, Michel laid Annabelle down on the coverlet and soft pillows of the bed. She was so beautiful! She was so peaceful! It was a shame her throat had been marred by the laceration, but a lovely diamond necklace was draped across her slender neck.

"You are so beautiful. You are so precious. Do you feel my love for you? Do you know I cannot breathe without you? You are imprinted in my mind; you are the keeper of my heart. My soul is yours, just as yours is mine." His voice grew husky, burdened by desire. Michel had become lost in the feel of her hair. It was silk between his fingers. He had become lost in the sweet orange blossom scent of her too.

Michel's light gray eyes were closed as he began to imagine another person with him, his mind wandering backward in time. It was the same room; they were the same smells of cinnamon and frankincense. Despite this, he was imagining someone else who'd felt cold beneath his touch, someone else who had been so very silent. It had always been like Elisabeth to ignore him, to never speak to him. Elisabeth had preferred to admire Henri; Elisabeth had preferred to speak and play and be happy near Henri. Michel felt a rumble forming in his chest as he growled out in frustration and shoved himself up and away from the bed where Annabelle lay.

"Why am I not enough for either of you? Am I not adequate?" Michel yelled, spittle forming at the corners of his mouth. His eyes had darkened, and he stormed over to the wall and punched it. A sickening crunch followed, and he cradled his hand to his chest, growling out the pain rather than crying again. No more! There was going to be no more rejection. Annabelle needed to love him as she had promised repeatedly. The woman had no choice now. She could not slip out of his grasp to laugh and smile with someone else. Ha!

"You are mine alone now. You cannot escape to Henri. You cannot run from my embrace to laugh about my love behind your lace fan. You cannot leave me. Not ever again!" Michel still raged. His entire body was taut with tension as he did not know how to release his anger. He did not dare to harm Annabelle, because then . . . then he could not fix her, and he could not love her beauty.

Michel's eyes became unfocused; his vision blurred as he became transfixed on another time. *Michel, you said that Henri was going to meet us in the gardens. Where have the servants gone? I do not hear Mama,* a soft voice had said, laughter intermingled with the words. His memories began to overlap, and he closed his eyes, Michel was able to see Elisabeth in her white housedress as she spun in circles over the cobblestones of the garden. The garden had been the pride and joy of their dear mother. *Do you think they will surprise us with a tea party? Mama . . .* And the little voice was suddenly distorted as a sickening crunch vibrated through his memories. Then the silence. Then the splatters of red, sprayed across the white roses and the cobblestones.

Why had she been so disrespectful? Why had she continued to speak, repeatedly? Why was she so annoying? Michel saw the smears of red as he dragged her body through the flowers. He saw the emptiness of the gardens as he hid her corpse behind the rosebushes. It was summer; the bushes were full and lush. Her little body could not be seen. Michel had been too young (only ten!) to know the heat of the summer sun was going to cause the body to rot—a stench more powerful than the roses. Michel had not given his little sister a second thought as he walked out of the gardens and continued with his day. Elisabeth had only returned to his thoughts when a scream, feral and keening, later filled the entire house. His stepmother had found Elisabeth . . .

Michel blinked again and again before he roughly shook his head. Why had such a thought come to his mind right now? Elisabeth was nothing like Annabelle—a little girl, a pathetic sister, compared to the prized beauty laid out before him now. Perhaps Elisabeth might have grown into something beautiful, but there was no knowing for certain. He had taken her hopes; he had robbed her of growing up. A smile, twisted and dark, curled along his lips as he looked down at Annabelle.

It was no crime to end another person's life.

It was no sin to continue to love, to cherish, to care for the dead.

It was a sign of respect, of love.

"Swing me softly, away, away . . ." Michel began to sing aloud to Annabelle's deaf ears. He leaned over her and combed his fingers through her auburn curls. Truly a remarkable woman, truly a beauty—in life and in death. Then the spell was broken when the peace of the moment was shattered by a banging on the locked door. *Why? WHY?* The question roared through his mind as he fought the rage, sparking and burning hot.

"WHAT?" Michel shouted, imperious and enraged.

Silence was his answer. Silence and then another knock, knock, knocking on the door. It took a few seconds for the rage to subside and the more rational part of his mind to regain control. Who would bother to knock on the door after being yelled at? Gideon. It must've been Gideon on the other side of the locked door—the old butler who had been in his life from day one. A sneer took over his expression as he hissed out a few curses while pushing up and off the bed. He did not bother to cover Annabelle's corpse behind him before he sauntered toward the locked door.

A few clicks of a key, already placed and kept in the door-knob, and the door was swung open. Michel bit down on his tongue to keep from spewing out further curses, an attempt close to failure as his entire body tremored with tension.

"What is it you need?" he spat out.

The older man, who stood in the hallway, peered over Michel's shoulder into the darkened room and clearly saw the body on the bed. The scents of cinnamon and orange blossoms wafted through the open door; the potent mixture would have been enough to turn anyone's stomach. Gideon was immune, as it was a mixture of scents he associated with Michel, the younger brother of his lord and master.

"Your brother asked me to send you word: The wedding ceremony is going to take place within the fortnight. Your brother commands you behave and that you keep yourself locked within the house. At most, you can walk through the gardens. You are not permitted to leave the Geoffrey estate until after the wedding takes place," Gideon murmured.

Michel blinked and blinked again. He was commanded. By his older brother, who saw himself as superior to every-one. No, it was Michel who was the superior one! *I am God. I am the one who is in control of everything!* he whined in his own mind.

"Inform my brother . . . I will obey," Michel simpered.

A pause followed, then the pause extended into a few moments of silence as both men stood on opposite sides of the doorway. Annabelle was clearly visible to both, only Michel's back was turned to her as he worked on maintaining a watchful eye on Gideon. The older man did not bother to look at Michel; he held no respect for the younger Geoffrey brother. No, Gideon was focused on the woman's body on the bed. Even in the faint light of the room, Gideon was able to identify the auburn curls and the pallid skin. No words were exchanged until Michel moved his hand to the doorknob and started to close the door.

A foot kept the door open, a foot belonging to Gideon, who had moved a step into the doorway, into the darkness of the room.

"What is it you think you're doing?" Michel hissed.

"Do not let your brother discover her. Henri would not forgive you if he knew you had blatantly ignored his order to burn her."

"Henri does not dare to enter this room. This space where his mother was murdered, and my own mother perished. This room frightens him too much because he is weak."

"Do not let Henri discover her corpse, my lord."

"Fine, fine, fine. I will be discreet with her. I swear," Michel acquiesced as he stepped closer to Gideon, fitting his lean body into the doorframe to prevent the older man from stepping any farther into the room. This space was his sanctuary; it was his temple. No one else was allowed to violate the space. Not Henri, not Gideon. Even his father—God forsake his departed soul—had not dared to enter this room once Michel had claimed it.

Mid February 1791

Do you hear the sounds? The sounds of crying, of singing, of choking? Do you hear me when I whisper your name? Do you feel my hands in your hair, my Annabelle? My lovely angel. Mine only Annabelle.

Do not take this news as a betrayal. Henri never cared for you. Not like I love you. Not like I have protected you, making you mine forever. MINE!

Henri is going to be married within the week. Her name is Justine. She is younger than you, younger than me. A naïve little lady. Henri might be able to handle her. Henri might be able to control her. I need him to. No one new was supposed to enter our house. You and I, we have a beautiful thing.

Do you know that I love you?

-M.L.G.

CHAPTER ELEVEN

ARE YOU, MY KEEPER?

THERE WAS A TENSION IN THE AIR. IT WAS tangible to Justine as she walked into the church for her wedding ceremony. There were smiling faces turning to stare at her, a thousand eyes observing her walk down the aisle. The last hundred steps she would take as a maiden, as an unmarried woman. What else could she do but take in a deep breath and slowly, slowly exhale it? This was not the time nor the place for her heart to start pounding, for her mind to start racing. The tension increased with each step she took.

It took a few seconds for her eyes to adjust to the world around her plunging into shadows. Justine still steadily took each step, holding the gentle smile on her lips in a relaxed and expectant expression. Lady Rockwell had been concerned about the rush of the engagement, the inevitable race to the altar, but even through that concern, she had spoken kindly to Justine about what to expect during the wedding ceremony, how all eyes would be on her and every guest would be assessing her. Also, Lady Rockwell had spoken about the expectations of the wedding night and every obligatory night Justine was going to owe her husband. Obedience.

Justine inhaled shakily. Her gaze focused on the priest standing near the altar ahead of her. The weight of her wedding gown was slowly becoming heavier and heavier as the thousands of beads glistened in the candlelight with each step. Her shoulders were bare and felt the cool air. Her hair was braided and coiled around her head as she was no longer going to be a single woman when she walked out of the church. The slippers on her feet were softly padded and allowed her to feel the coolness of the stones below her. Every sensation was heightened.

"Why do you think the wedding is so swift?" It was the first murmur she heard.

"It must be a child in her belly. Shame on her for ensnaring Lord Geoffrey in such a scandalous way."

Not true! It was not true! Justine wanted to turn and scream the words of denial at such a harsh and false accusation. Were these the rumors now circling around her?

"Does she know about Lady Stanley?"

"I thought the Lady Stanley was to be the bride for Lord Geoffrey, not this unknown lady. Shame on her." It was the last of the whispering voices Justine allowed herself to overhear. Instead, she focused her attention on the rustling of her skirts as they dragged along the stones beneath her. She focused on the roaring in her ears.

The last month had been a whirlwind of events, of faces, and of planning. In Justine's mind, she had sought a way to speak gently with her fiancé. A word said behind a hand for them to ease up on the speed with which their union was approaching. Despite her every intention to request a pause, a reining in, there never came an opportunity to speak privately with her intended. Henri was always preoccupied with one task or another, both personal and more urgent dealings of his estate or political matters.

This momentum had also obstructed Justine's opportunity to learn more about Henri. The courtship was so swift; any anticipation or expectations she may have previously had were whisked away. But that did not mean these women, these guests attending her wedding, could speak so disparagingly about her.

One more step, then another, and another. Again, and again. Justine felt dizzy. She could no longer hear their slanderous lies but rather began to hear more disturbing tidbits about her soon-to-be husband: He was a thief. He was a womanizer. He was lecherous. He had a temper. He was dangerous. The Geoffrey family was cursed when it came to its brides. At last! Her steps had finally carried her to the base of a brief stairway, on which her fiancé stood at the top near the altar and the priest.

Why were her legs suddenly weighed down, unresponsive? There was a flair of panic as she looked up toward Henri with a pleading expression on her face, knowing only he and the priest could see her face now. Had he smirked? Why would he smirk when she was seeking his assistance, his strength? She frowned.

The rest became a blur as she felt her hand being held by someone else's fingertips and her feet proceeded up the stairs. Then she was left with only Henri and the priest. The vows were said, and the pledges of fidelity, of honor, of love were uttered by both parties. A cool kiss was exchanged, and then they were turning to face the gathering of people in the pews.

"Now we are one. Behave yourself, and do not mind the malicious ones when most are willing to celebrate any festivity for a distraction from their own insipid lives," Henri whispered.

Justine was smiling, too overwhelmed by the cheering and the beautiful flower petals floating down around them. A quiet life was what she had led before this engagement, and this was a whole new chapter, a whole new book for her to begin now that she'd married into the Geoffrey family. The earlier whispers were locked away in her subconscious, where they could plant themselves and fester, causing a future itch. But today, she was the bride, a newlywed escorted on the arm of her dashing new husband. The smile on her face was genuine; the glow in her cheeks was the warmth of expectation and the blush of innocence. Justine was beautiful, and she was beguiling in her open display of gratitude and delight. Those who had come to tarnish her reputation were contrite in their judgment, and they were quick to make amends.

"You are such a lovely bride, dear one, such a blushing modesty..."

"Keep her close, Geoffrey. Her naïveté is fetching . . ."

Justine denied any wine and only partook of water or tea. She did notice her husband also abstained from becoming drunk with the gentlemen, who were quickly becoming belligerent. A loud voice broke through the revelry of the crowd.

"My wife and I thank you for your support and your love as we celebrate our union today. However, it is time for you to go home to your own families, your own beds. Seek out your own entertainments if you must, but it will no longer be under my roof. Good night!" Henri boomed as his hand hovered and then gently curled around Justine's shoulder.

How many hours had already elapsed? Justine was exhausted, and it hit her rather suddenly, sinking into her bones and making her quiet as the obnoxious crowd filtered out. The couple was now standing at the doorway, shaking hands and smiling to words of congratulation, rude remarks, gestures. Henri shielded his young wife from many of the lewd remarks made by the sloppy men as they were leaving. He was quickly becoming impatient and thus more disgruntled by the behaviors of his departing guests.

Soon, although it felt like years to both, the two of them were alone—albeit the shadows of servants fluttered through the background as they began to clean up the ballroom. The servants were utterly silent as they were trained to be.

Justine looked up at her husband. How odd a thought! Her husband. A distinct sense of unease snaked through her head as she looked over at him. This man who was now her husband, her guardian . . . her keeper? Had she truly been passed from one gilded cage to another?

"Are you well, my lord?" she asked.

The way he looked at her was breathtakingly fierce. Justine fought every inch of her body to not step back or put her hand up. It was difficult to concentrate with the flood of emotions pulsing through her; every sense was now on high alert. Why was he looking at her in such a way? As if he were assessing her, judging her.

It was not necessary. There hadn't been any fault in her actions throughout their wedding day. She had practiced over and over for too many hours to have made any mistakes.

"Yes, dear wife, I am well. I return the question: are you well?" he replied at last.

A startled look must have crossed her face, for Henri's expression seemed to soften and change completely. It went from borderline malicious to concerned. Did he truly care for her, then? She saw a glimpse of tenderness.

"I am tired as it was a long day, my lord," Justine whispered.

What more could there be to say? What more could there be to do? Oh! Oh . . . A warmth spread across her cheeks as the realization dawned; tonight was their wedding night, and he had dismissed all their guests. Thus, they were left alone—and it was frightening. She was officially frightened of what was to come. Justine was not prepared.

Henri immediately sensed the change in her demeanor and sought to remedy it. There was a bit of a distance between them, and he closed it with a few steps. His hand reached up to touch her cheek but landed on her shoulder instead. She flinched. Why was she flinching?

"Are you, my keeper?" came a soft voice, barely audible to his ears.

Was he . . . what? Her keeper? What did she mean? Henri paused a few moments to allow his thoughts to sift through the many layers such a simple question might entail, might imply. He was her husband. They had said vows to be faithful in sickness and in health, but nowhere in there was the mention of a keeper. Henri was frowning down at the floor. They were both frozen, her face turned away from Henri and his hand on her shoulder.

"My lord, are you, my keeper?" Justine asked again.

"Yes," Henri answered.

A sense of peace began to move through her body, an ease she had not felt since the agreement and announcement of their engagement. It was relief, an immense relief. She was going to be taken care of, provided for, and guarded. Henri, her husband and her lord, was going to be her keeper. What more could she need?

Henri observed his wife (such a strange realization). He watched the emotions move in waves across her face and through her eyes. Fear. Gratitude. Tension. Peace. There was a blend of others, but he did not observe happiness. This was purely a marriage for politics, for financial gain, and for prestige. It had been his luck that Justine, this new wife of his, had not heard the rumors of his family's past—not before it was too late. There would always be the gossipers who sought to create chaos and drama for society to feed on; these were the ones whispering about the decades-old rumors continuing to circle the Geoffrey family. *Two brides dead within five years. A third missing, supposedly a runaway.*

It did not surprise him to see she was not happy, nor did she feign happiness. Henri did not question her chastity, but he did judge her naïveté as only superficial. This seemingly delicate flower of a wife was stronger than most assumed. Henri was not going to underestimate her. It was not in the plan.

Justine was to be the wife who raised the Geoffrey family higher than Henri had already risen in society. He had worked hard to establish himself at court. He had gone countless hours over ledgers and reports to assist the king's council. Was he boastful? No. Was he resentful? Yes, to a degree. A calculated degree. After the death of the late Lord Geoffrey, his dearly departed father, Henri had taken the mantle of responsibility with dignity, with self-loathing, with hauteur.

This wedding had been only a single step in the path to Henri's goals, goals he had designed in his youth. There was to be no mercy, no patience, no shame. No mercy even for the young woman who had never known a world such as his. No patience for a young wife who did not have the knowledge of running a household, much less of the official duties she was to assume in the morning. Henri was afraid of losing more than he had gained through this marriage. This fear was persistent; this fear was tangible. It was fear that stirred his thoughts and hardened his heart against his wife as she looked up at him with pleading eyes doe eyes. She was just another target, just another step in his plan.

One for the nightmare and two for the seer, three for the maiden, and four for the fear.

Justine was startled when there was nothing. She was left alone in her room without so much as a message or note sent to her from her husband—the word still strange and foreign in her mind. Why was Henri not coming? Rejection was something new to her, and it burned. It burned so forcefully through her chest and spread as a wildfire through her thoughts, searing the memories of this day, leaving behind a blackening, a scarring never to be removed.

February 27, 1791

Oh, I am a fool! I have been nothing but an utter fool! My husband does not touch me. It is my wedding night, and I am alone. Utterly and devastatingly alone! I was afraid of the pain that would come with the consummation of my marriage . . . but that also meant our union could not be annulled. I need Henri to hold me as a man holds his wife.

I don't need to be alone right now.

I don't want to be alone right now.

I hate being alone.

-Justine Ayling
-Justine Geoffrey

CHAPTER TWELVE
Are We Dancing in Circles?

I T WAS THE THIRD MORNING AFTER THE WEDDING. Last night had been the third night she had spent in the Geoffrey house—her new home. It was the third morning, and Justine felt more a stranger than when she had first arrived. Her husband had failed to introduce her to any of the staff. Well, there was Gideon, the older butler. Henri had told her Gideon oversaw the entire household and its staff obeyed him. Her husband had failed to consummate their marriage. For three nights she had sat up waiting, nervous and expectant, to ultimately be left disappointed and bitter. This was not how marriage was whispered about between the young women. This was not the expectation. Be it nightmare or fantasy, she was not supposed to have been abandoned like this!

Three days she had stayed in the confinement of this bedchamber, memorizing every detail of the tapestries hung on the walls, learning every crack, and taking note of what needed to be touched up. How many years had it been since this chamber felt a feminine touch? Justine could not remember the entire summary her aunt had explained to her about the history of the last two generations of the Geoffrey family.

The old Geoffrey had been married three times, widowed twice. The third wife had simply . . . vanished. The new Lord Geoffrey, Henri, had become the head of the family at a rather young age. He had never married; neither had his younger brother. Thus, it must have been at least a decade since a woman had overseen the household.

Boredom had started to sink in. She no longer felt restful doing needlepoint or watercolor painting. This was not what she had imagined the first few days of her marital journey would be. Isolated and bored. The door to her chamber was not locked, but there was a servant on the other side of the door, a servant who scowled at her whenever she cracked open the door to peer out. Justine was timid enough to feel chills splinter down her spine at such a scowl. The fear was tangible.

Was this some wicked prank her husband was playing on her? A dirty welcome, a disenchanting beginning to slowly poison her hopes and her aspirations? Justine began to assume her husband was putting her in her proper place within the hierarchy of the household. The servants sneered and ignored her whenever she opened the door. They did not speak to her, nor did they outrightly forbid from her leaving the room. It was a tension; it was an unspoken rule. This triggered Justine into childhood memories of being locked and hidden away in the nursery, in the closet.

It was while her mind was in this dark rift that the bed-chamber door opened and her husband stepped in, closing the door with a click behind him. Henri paused in the door-way to assess the scene in which he had left his young wife for the last three days. There was no disarray to the room. This meant she had self-control, or she simply lacked a temper. Good. He next focused on his wife and took careful note— she was well-groomed, her hair brushed and beautiful. Justine was in a simple gown with a light shawl about her shoulders, but she was dressed for the daytime, not wallow-ing in self-pity or sadness. Also, good.

Henri cleared his throat as he hovered near the door. "Good afternoon."

Justine was startled by his voice. Clearly, she had not heard him enter the room. Henri wondered why her at-tention had been so diverted, but then he brushed it off as happenstance since he had left her alone the last three days. It made sense for her to be skittish.

"Oh, uh . . . good afternoon, my lord." Justine scrambled to do a curtsy in proper greeting of her husband. She had omitted using the title *husband* in this greeting as this was the first true exchange they'd had as man and wife. There was a part of her, however small, that felt a spark of indignation at the way he had abandoned her the last few days. Despite this, she held her composure, remaining still.

"Will you sit with me?" Henri took confident steps far-ther into the room and half turned toward the window seat on the other end of the room. "We have a fair number of things to discuss today."

Justine responded promptly to her husband's invitation, and she moved swiftly over to the window seat and stood beside him. He towered over her by a good half a foot. It was a detail she had not noticed in their whirlwind courtship and wedding planning, as they had only spent a handful of minutes together. This realization caused her brows to furrow as she worried the tender flesh of her lower lip.

"What is it we need to talk through, my lord?" She kept the formalities as best as she could, unintentionally using them as a shield.

"First, we need to discuss your role in this household," Henri said as he sat down on the cushions of the window seat. One of his hands patted the spot beside him as he looked up at his wife, his expression neutral and rather distant.

Justine was less inclined to sit beside her husband thanks to the look on his face and the chilled tone of his voice. Why was he so cold, so aloof? In a defensive gesture, she sat down where he had motioned, making her posture stiff and formal. Her hands were primly placed in her lap as she curled her feet closer to her, and she angled her body to be slightly turned away from Henri. She did not speak. Rather, Justine looked at her husband with an expectant smile.

"This evening, you will be assigned two maids to act as your personal attendants. In two days, you will sit down with Mr. Gideon to go over the details of the household and its staff. You will need to become proficient within the week, understood?" Henri only paused to glance out the window behind them. "You must be mindful of your time for the remaining hours of today as we are going to have a meal as a family."

"Yes, my lord."

"Explore your new home. Get to know each hallway and room at your leisure. You are forbidden to enter two rooms: my personal study and Michel's study."

"Michel . . . your brother?" Justine was perplexed for a moment.

"Yes, my brother. He remains unwed, so he resides with me as this is our family's primary residence."

"Of course, my lord."

Henri felt his impatience growing; she was so elusive with calling him *my lord* throughout this one-sided conversation. Was she truly this complacent? No, there had to be something brewing beneath the surface. Something she was guarding from him. All women, to his knowledge, hid a part of themselves from the world and from their husbands. It was a way they could feel in control of some part of their limited worlds. This is what Henri had learned from the secrets his mother kept, the secrets Annabelle had kept . . .

"Within the week, I will come to your bed," Henri said nonchalantly, seeking a reaction from his wife—a crack in the armor she was displaying to him. Ah, there it was. The flicker of self-doubt, of clear hesitation at the idea of Henri coming to her bed. This gave him two notes of information, both of which were pleasing. One, she was flustered in the way a virgin would be. Second, she lacked confidence when it came to the thought of sharing a bed with her husband. This is where her true vulnerability existed. Excellent.

"I—will you send a note before your arrival?" Justine asked in a quiet voice.

"Your maids will be notified when I am ready. They will know to bathe and prepare you for my visit," Henri crooned, his voice oddly warm in contrast to the way he had addressed his wife earlier. This was intentionally done.

"Yes, of course. You said I could explore the house; does that include the grounds? The gardens? I noticed the intricacies of the western gardens, and it would be—"

"Explore all you want, with the exception of the two rooms I said before." Henri reached out and placed a hand on her knee. It was the first intimate touch between them as man and wife, excluding the chaste kiss they had shared at the altar. The simple gown she wore was of fine thin material, which allowed his hand to feel the warmth of her skin. He slowly inhaled and closed his eyes to savor the sensation. The warmth felt amazing beneath his fingertips.

Justine had not noticed when she'd relaxed in his presence, but the moment the weight of his hand was on her knee, her entire body went rigid. Frozen. Her body as well as her mind all froze. What could bring this reaction out of her? The answer was simple: her husband was a stranger to her, completely unknown. It felt wrong to feel his touch, but they were husband and wife, so it was not wrong. There was conflict growing within her heart. That conflict was starting to fracture the image she had created about what married life was to be like.

This was not what she had imagined, but there was no space for complaint, as her aunt had taught her. Marriage meant loyalty to her husband; marriage meant bearing the cost of joy and of pain. The last three days of isolation had not been joyful, nor had they been painful. Merely lonely. Loneliness was not a crime.

"I will need to have a bath drawn for me if I am to be ready for our family meal this evening. Is there anything else we must discuss at this time?" Her voice was far calmer than she felt.

"Indeed, there is."

Henri answered her question but stopped there, creating a drawn-out pause during which he watched her with cold eyes. He had noticed her entire body grow tense mere moments after he touched her. His hand was still resting on her knee. There was no movement between the two of them. This intimate meeting between them felt wrong, which was not what Henri had anticipated. This young woman was his. An object he now possessed, an object he neither cared for nor thought to console.

"You are not allowed to contact anyone outside of this house, not without my approval beforehand. This includes your aunt, Lady Rockwell. I am a private person, and I intend to keep the matters of my household guarded. If you violate this, you will be locked inside this room."

"Similar to the last three days, or will I not be able to open the door?"

Henri smirked at her remark. His hand withdrew from her knee and settled on the cushion between them. His fingers curled into a fist even as he chuckled.

"The door and the windows will be locked," he said after a few seconds.

Was he amused by her question? Or was he upset by it? His curled fist gave the opposite impression of his smirk and throaty chuckle. Justine bit her tongue to keep from making another quick remark as she tried to gauge her husband. Was this going to be her relationship with him? Tiptoeing around him to ensure he remained content, if not happy?

"I will obey your command, my lord."

"Excellent, Justine."

The way he drawled out her name sent shivers down her spine. Justine did not know how to respond beyond a subtle nod, and she brushed an invisible piece of dust from her skirts. It felt odd to be seated so close to a man without a servant or a chaperone in the room. It felt odd that, when she looked up, she looked into the darkening eyes of her *husband*. Why were his eyes darkening? Had something gone amiss?

"You may expect my next . . . visit to be four days from now. I must attend to business at the court beginning tomorrow morning. Continue to rest and to explore my home— your new home, dear wife."

Henri reached up a hand and stroked his fingertips along her jawline and down the side of her neck, his thumb gently pressing into the hollow of her throat. The touch did not last long. Henri stood and walked toward the closed door. In his mind, there was no further time he could waste as he had preparations to make. Other matters required his attention, and dallying with his young bride was not a priority.

He gave a curt nod in Justine's direction before turning the doorknob and opening the door. There he paused, ever so briefly, to look across the room at his wife.

Justine was poised as if she, too, might stand. Her hands hovered above her stomach as she lost her breath. Why? The casual touch from her husband had sent her inwardly reeling. Her heart had begun to pound, and her head pulsed. Why? It was not improper for her husband to touch her. It was a gentle caress, but it had startled her.

"Good night, wife," Henri said before the door closed behind him. His intention was to let her be alone for those four days to recover, to explore, to accept they were married. Henri had observed his father's hastiness in wedding and bedding two wives, each younger than their predecessor and each just as scared. Let her have time to understand this new chapter in both of their lives.

Therefore, due to her husband's neglect of his marital duties, Justine was left to her own devices for a string of days. It was the early days of spring, so the days were becoming longer, and the nights were shorter. Justine had the curiosity and the wish to become knowledgeable about her new home and the household she was the mistress of. Lady Justine Geoffrey—she was going to own the name and ensure it was carried with pride. The Geoffrey estate was unobstructed from Justine's whim for exploration as she went from room to room, forgetting the warning from her husband: do not enter the studies, neither Henri's nor Michel's.

March 1791

Do I need to get rid of Justine?
She is getting in the way.
Henri does not seem to see anything wrong with her.

-M.L.G.

CHAPTER THIRTEEN
Do You See Me or Do You See Through Me?

IGHT FOR THE TRINITY . . . NINE FOR THE blasphemy . . . On this day, of all days, was when Michel wanted to sanctify his memories of Annabelle, his sweet, sweet Annabelle. Today was the day they would have been—the day they could have been—married in his delusional mind. There was no better time than when the parishes were chiming their bells and when the nuns and monks were praying, fasting all day and all night. This was when his connection to Annabelle could be immortalized. The powers above would absolve him. The powers below would condone it. This was a holy act; this was a loving act.

"Do you think I relish in this, my love? Do you think this is enjoyable for me? Well, you're wrong. Oh. So, so wrong. I miss your laughter; I miss your hands holding mine as we danced through the night. I miss your expressions as you spoke so animatedly with me, with others. I miss watching you. I miss being near—no, I am near you now. I own you now. But where has your soul gone? Where has the light gone? Your eyes are so sallow." Michel was whispering into the ear of Annabelle, his hands running through her hair—carefully, so carefully to prevent his fingers from getting tangled and pulling strands out.

"Why are you so pale, Annabelle? You were so beautiful. You are beautiful still, don't be offended. I didn't mean it . . . I meant you are an eternal beauty, yet you are no longer thriving. You are rather pathetic now. I miss your vibrance. I miss your passion. What do the French say? C'est la vie. Not your life. Not any longer. My life."

He was looking at her, memorizing every inch of her face and her neck and her shoulders. Her lilac gown was still stained and ruined, but the blood no longer dripped, dripped, dripped down. It was a grotesque dried patch, crusted over and over, as was the slash on her neck. It had grown. It had become more mutilated each time Michel had reached and touched it. Annabelle was barely recognizable. Michel had failed to embalm her correctly, and he blamed his brother and his new wife.

His hands clenched into fists, and he buried his face into Annabelle's neck, inhaling in the hopes of smelling her perfume one more time. It was of no use. Flesh and bone. Annabelle was only bone and flesh. Why not ashes? Why not tears? Why not more? Why was there never more below the surface? Why was there never more when there was no longer breath?

Why was Annabelle not different? Why did love not make it different? Why did his obsession with her not make her different? It was all so disappointing. It was all so aggravating as he recalled his brother's discovery of Annabelle in their blue parlor. Henri had gone comatose. Was it the shock of her dead body upon the chaise? Why had his brother reacted in such a way?

Michel did not understand then, and he still could not comprehend now. Those emotions were foreign to him, unknown and dark. Out of reach. Michel had placed the shard of glass in his brother's hand carelessly and thoughtlessly, only knowing he could not be blamed by his own brother for the death of their lovely Annabelle. Henri had to be implicated, even if in his own mind. Michel smiled now, his lips curling upward.

"I loved you with all of me, but it wasn't enough to make you more. You were too weak. They have all been too weak, too beneath me to be more. I thought you were different. You acted different. You accepted the death." Michel was still whispering to her as his hands trailed her shoulders, fingertips dancing across the decomposed flesh.

Michel had taken Annabelle's body into an abandoned, less traveled part of the Geoffrey home. Her corpse had to be hidden better; Gideon had found him too effortlessly. He had taken her into a place of his own creation, where the walls were dark and the floors were hollow. Peeling back the wooden panels revealed his secrets, his keys, his skeletons.

One for the nightmare and two for the seer, three for the maiden, and four for the fear . . . There was no fear in this room. There was no life in this room. There was no light in this room. It was not hell, and it was not heaven, as it was barely on earth. Or so Michel felt. As he walked through the doorway and closed the door behind him, something about crossing over the threshold changed him into a god. A holy being, powerful and powerless. It was so wonderful, so debilitating.

In his haste, Michel had left the door ajar on this visit, on this day of all days, when he had most longed for the scent of Annabelle, the smell of her.

Justine was wandering through the halls, seeking some unfamiliar path and some amusement. Henri had left her with little to do, little to oversee, so she often wandered the Geoffrey home for hours and hours in between the meals and the teas. Today was to be another day of such wanderings, tepid and mindless innocent wanderings. A door ajar was out of place as she glanced down the dark hallway. It stood out. It caught her attention, and she was fixated on the discovery of it.

Five for the dreamer, six for the sinner, seven for the corpse . . .

The smell was what first shook her to her core. Something rancid, something sweet—it did not belong with the other scents of oak and old things. No, this should have been her warning to stand still and seek justification for following an empty hall toward an open door reeking of . . . what was the aroma? It was unlike anything she had smelled before. Curiosity became overwhelming rather than deterring.

Michel would later believe the blame was to be placed at her feet, her curiosity an infestation. Quietly, carefully,

Justine made her way through the doorway with her fingertips curling around the doorframe. Why was she trying to be silent? It felt as though all her instincts, all her urges and her curiosity were suddenly screaming to turn around, to turn around and run. Fast, faster. Justine's entire body went cold as if she were suddenly submerged in a thousand snowstorms, shards of ice splintering against her skin and scraping along her bones. What was she seeing?

Two bodies contorted. The sickly sweet smell burned into her nostrils, the faint scent of orange blossoms whisking through her mind. This was not real. This was not true. This had to be a nightmare. A waking dream. She was watching two bodies collide and disconnect, one fluid and beautiful, while the other was rigid and empty. What was this? Why could she not turn away? She was watching two silhouettes dance around the floor; one was graceful and flowing, while the other was stiff and disjointed. What was this? Why could she not turn away?

The sickeningly sweet stench was death. The orange blossom was perfume coming from the corpse. The room was dark, but the atmosphere was black, bleak, forbidden. Sinful. Detestable. Repugnant. Justine could not feel her body as she tried to move her hand, tried to move her feet, as she tried to move anything, anything at all. No, no, no! Why could she not turn around? Why could she not leave this accursed room? No!

Five for the dreamer, six for the sinner, seven for the corpse . . .

"You are my love, my one and only love. You are my own. My own sweet, sweet creature of beauty and of..." The words carried through the quiet of the dimly lit room, so quiet, so very quiet. Yet there was noise. Noises unlike any she had heard before: a grinding of bones, a slithering of ash on skin. A demon. A demon was what she must've been witnessing. A demon had come to haunt the halls of this home, this damned home where she was now confined, imprisoned in her own castle.

What were these demons saying? It had gone quiet. It all had gone silent. Her heart felt as if it had stopped, and then suddenly there was a rushing, a roaring in her ears and a knot in her throat as she registered panic. The demon had seen her. The demon was watching her as it coupled with the skin, with bone, with ashes. The form beneath the demon was draped in a soft purple fabric, no longer a gown and no longer a body. Its arms were contorted into shapes. Its legs were... Its eyes...

"Dear Heavenly Father..." she whispered, the words slipping into the silence before she could stop them. Justine inhaled sharply. The eyes. The demon was above something. It had eyes, it had a nose, it had a mouth with such a twisted waxen smile. There was a gash across the throat. Oh God, oh God. The demon was now moving away from a body. There was no blood. There was no sign of a struggle. This body was not... It was a corpse.

The demon was now directly in front of her, its claws scraping along her cheek and its eyes boring into her soul. Its breath was foul. Its talons were—they were fingers! Justine jolted backward and fell back into the wall, a scream forming in her chest. The scream got trapped as the hand went across her mouth, and she suddenly could not breathe.

"Why did you find us? Annabelle promised she did not tell anyone. Elisabeth said she could keep a secret. Can you keep a secret? No, I doubt it. *Oh, Heavenly Father . . .*" he mocked her. It was a familiar voice. Those eyes looked as if they were bottomless pits straight to hell. They were burning, yet they were empty dark voids.

"Why are you here? You are not supposed to know. No one is supposed to know. We were having such a grand time, my love and I. We were about to try for an heir, but my love prefers to dance. An heir to make my lord happy, an heir to make my lord happy, an heir to make my lord happy. Happy, aren't we happy? Annabelle, tell her . . . We are happy here. Tell her you are happy now. You're with me, forever and only mine. Mine, all mine. No one else, no one else. Aren't we happy?" His voice was quiet but rousing as his words kept flowing out. Louder and louder and louder as he began to shout into Justine's face, spittle spewing from his lips.

"Aren't we all happy? The three of us could be happy, the three of us . . . Justine, don't you agree?" He spat out her name, his fingers curling around her throat as he shouted. Justine was frozen. She could not breathe; she could not move; she could not think.

Then, oh, then there was a thundering boom as the door smashed into the wall and the room was filled with light. Such a blinding light, but it gave truth to the corpse. The body was lying on the couch, clad in a violet gown, stained. Stained! Justine sobbed. The demon shrunk back, hissing and howling and incoherent as a body stood before her—blocking her, shielding her. But then there was a blow against the side of her head, and the world faded to black.

"Do not dare touch my wife again. I will kill you, brother or not, if you touch my wife again." The whisper resounded through the blackness, echoing repeatedly. *My wife.* The body of the woman, the corpse. The name. Annabelle. The blackness saved Justine from retching, from writhing about in pain as the truth formed in her mind. Searing itself there, never to be forgotten.

Seven for the corpse . . .
Eight for the trinity . . .

March 1791

She found me. She found us.
She saw us. Annabelle and me.
Henri had said the woman would be contained,
that she would be on a tight leash. And yet she
walked into MY study. MY territory, and she
intruded on Annabelle and me.
Henri's wife is a fool. Henri is a fool.

-M.L.G.

CHAPTER FOURTEEN
Why Did You Disobey Me?

THE WORLD HAD GONE BLACK. DARKNESS cloaked her mind as well as her senses. Justine was only aware of the nightmares as corpses danced around her, as demons weaved in and out of those dancing rotted bodies. Each with a garish grin, each with pits of despair where eyes should have been . . . There was no escape. Her body had become unmovable, weighed down with fear, with revulsion, with shadow. *An heir to make my lord happy . . .* The voice, as it echoed through her terrors, became mangled in such a way as to sear itself into her mind.

As a terror worse than horror, worse than dread.

It was the binding. It was the chains locked and heavy around her wrists, around her ankles, and around her neck. Heavy, heavy. There was no blood. There was no life. There was a corpse and a demon. Over and over, the images played through her mind. Over and over, she heard the wicked voice. *The three of us could be happy.* The disgusting sound of flesh on bone. It was the stench she could not shake. It was a repugnant reminder every breath she took. It triggered the memories, the images of the dead corpse being . . .

Justine could not handle the foul smell for much longer, but she knew she could not cease breathing. As time continued to move sluggishly, she became aware that the heaviness around her wrists, her ankles, and her throat was not chains. The heaviness was nothing tangible, only a burden placed by her own mind. Cobwebs and fog started to clear from her mind as she became more aware. Her eyes were closed, and her breathing was shallow. Once she had gained the courage, she tried to reach forward with her right hand, and it hit something solid. A knock sounded. Why did a knock sound? It was more of a dull thud.

The spindly legs of panic began to creep up the back of her neck as Justine tried to turn her head. First left and then right. She could turn her head. Another shallow inhale, another exhale. Then she leaned forward, and immediately, her forehead rammed against something solid. Confusion splintered through the panic. *What?* At last, Justine had the strength to open her eyes, and she instantly felt regret. Were her eyes open? One blink, two blinks, three. Nothing changed, eyes open or eyes closed. The world around her was pitch-black—a depth of darkness she had not encountered in over a decade.

What was this?

Where was she?

Why was everything so, so dark?

Why could she not move?

Justine reached out her hand a second time, and her palm met the rough surface. Her fingertips curled against the . . . wood. The texture was too distinctive, too familiar. The panic mounted higher and higher as she pushed outward and nothing budged. She attempted to swallow but was met with the pain of her throat, dry and parched.

She stretched her arms upward and felt more wood, the texture grazing her skin. Hot tears began to fall down her cheeks as her breathing hitched, becoming more and more uneven. *The three of us could be happy* . . . The voice of the demon ricocheted through her mind as the reality of her enclosure dawned. One last test as she stomped her heels and was rewarded with the dull thud of wood.

"No. No . . . No, no, no. NO!" Justine screamed again and again.

Why was she surrounded by wood? Her fingers felt above her once more, then to her sides. Why was she . . .? A scream, primal and petrified, tore through her throat.

A coffin!

"No! NO! NO!" Justine was screaming, louder and louder.

She dug her nails into the wood in front of her. Repeatedly until it began to hurt, until she felt her nails curl backward and felt the drip, drip, dripping of blood. Survival had sunk its talons into her mind, and she continued to try to gouge out the wood.

Her throat burned.

Her fingers throbbed, ached.

As her mouth opened and closed, as her fingers clawed and dug at the paneling before her, Justine felt her body become numb, and she allowed her mind to collapse in on itself. Sheer terror and exhaustion enveloped everything—mind, body, and soul. Who could have done this to her? Had it been the demon she'd caught coupling with the corpse? A wave of nausea burned the back of her throat with bile as she tilted her head back and back until she felt the wood behind her.

A coffin. This wooden enclosure around her was a coffin. An ache pulsed along each of her fingertips as she stared and stared at the blackness. It was suffocating her, drowning her senses in its terrified muteness. Justine's throat burned; her head pounded; her hands throbbed. It was in this moment she began to doubt her own sanity. She began to doubt if she would survive this . . .

It was in this moment of breaking that the brilliance of sunlight poured in and blinded her. A hiss escaped her mouth at the sudden pain caused by the bright light, and then she felt her body being pulled forward and then dropped onto cobblestones and moss. Where was she? Disoriented, suffering waves of pain, Justine was not able to open her eyes for another few seconds. Precious time when she attempted to scream again, but the only sound made was a hoarse whimper. Did she hear a chuckle?

"Open your eyes." A cold command.

Justine pushed her hands against the cobblestones and began to stand up, swaying side to side as she fought to maintain her balance, eyes still bleary as she forced them to open, fighting against the sharp pain ripping through her head. She was outside. A cool breeze floated across her perspiring face, and with it came the scent of roses, of jasmine.

"Where am I?" Justine rasped out, one of her hands curled around her throat, as if she could force the pain, the burning to leave her throat.

"I brought you out to the gardens so you could recover from your nightmare." The cold voice again.

There was a gentle touch on her shoulder, and the silhouette of her husband appeared before her. Her eyebrows furrowed as she stared up at her husband's face, so handsome and so cold, as his words rang through her pounding head. To recover? From her nightmare? What nightmare? What about the coffin? Justine pivoted around and gawked at the white coffin leaning against the brick wall. It looked so out of place and yet so perfect.

"Why did you lock me in a coffin, Henri?" she screamed at him. Justine took a step backward, then a step to the side, avoiding her husband and the coffin. The smile she saw form on her husband's face was answer enough. It was ludicrous. "Are you entertained by this?"

Henri was slow to answer as he watched her with an amused smile. He took in every detail of her appearance, her posture, the fear dilating her pupils. Henri saw a ripple of annoyance in her as he looked at her. She'd raised her voice at him. An offense to be remedied. It was quite a long list of tasks he had to train her and break her for.

"You disobeyed my direct order, wife. Did you forget?" Henri took a casual step toward her, his hands in the pockets of his pants, seemingly unaware of the fear radiating from her body. He paused mid-step and decided to reach out to close the lid of the coffin. The hinges screeched in protest until there was a thud and the lid closed. His gaze never left Justine's face.

"No . . . I did not forget . . ." Justine whispered.

"Think again, dear wife. Think harder."

Justine opened her mouth and then closed it, opened and closed. The cool trickle of sweat fell down her spine as she took a small step to put more distance between herself and her husband, more distance between herself and the closed coffin. Why had he closed her into a coffin? Panic spiked again as she began to worry the flesh of her lower lip. Harder and harder she pressed until the metallic taste of blood shot through her mouth. She yelped.

"Did you—Did you lock me into the coffin because I broke a rule?" Justine sputtered out.

"We are not playing this game. Answer me. Why did you forget my order?" Henri calmly said as he traced a finger along the outside of the coffin, tracing circles and swirls. Idle and relaxed. The exact opposite of his wife, as she was tightly wired, and he saw the invisible fractures continuing to form in her mind.

Justine did not answer him. Instead, she turned and tried to run. The escape failed as she slammed face-first into the thorns of a rosebush, her legs tangled and burdened by heavy skirts she had forgotten. In the panic, in the fear of being caged in the coffin, Justine had not remembered the dress she was wearing. The fresh slices of pain on her cheeks caused another whimper as she slowly pushed herself up and out of the thorns' clutches. Was there no escape? No longer was she surrounded by darkness and solid wood, but she could not walk away from the silent wrath of her husband.

"I became tired of idleness, constantly waiting and waiting with no directions, no expectations of me . . . for days. I wanted to become familiar with my new home, so I began to explore the house. Step by step, hallway by hallway. I had no ill intentions as I wandered, I swear," Justine attempted to explain. Her throat continued to burn, and her voice remained hoarse.

"You swear?" Henri crooned, his body arched into a predatory pose, eyes on her. Hands curled and uncurled from fists at his sides. His legs carried him to stand right in front of her. His frame blocked out the beams of sunlight. It blocked out the cool breeze of roses and jasmine.

"You . . . I did not mean to pry, to witness such . . ." There was a crack. Her voice cracked and splintered as she took a hesitant step backward. Justine could not focus on where her foot went, as every instinct within her was screaming for her to run and to run fast. The monster before her was a lethal predator.

Henri said nothing. He did absolutely nothing as his wife began to search for another escape route, fully and keenly aware of every angle her head turned, of every hitched breath she took, of every minuscule step she tried to hide. This was not the way he had planned to bond with his new wife. Today was meant to be more pleasant than this.

"I am sorry, my lord. I will not break your rule again. Please forgive me for trespassing," Justine whimpered as another step was taken backward and away, another subtle attempt to get farther from him. What part of the gardens were they in? In all her wanderings, Justine had not focused on being outside. She did not know where they were in the gardens, on which side of the home these gardens existed . . . Realization dawned. Justine was not aware of a way out. She was not aware of an exit.

The three of us could be happy. The words echoed through her mind, and she was not able to distinguish when it had been said. They echoed and echoed throughout her thoughts in a repetition. Over and over again until it hurt. The voice that had spoken those words was not something she could forget either. Why? Oh, she should not have asked why. The images came in flashes, overwhelming her instinct for survival, overwhelming her to the point of freezing. To not being able to move another inch, to move at all. The demon and the corpse. The whispers and the slithering sounds of flesh and bone, ash and bone.

And she collapsed.

Only to awaken to see glimpses of the cobblestones beneath her, to see a doorway, to see the shifting of light and shadow as she floated through hallways. A faint sensation of being held, being cradled in strong arms and cocooned against a hard chest. It felt more like another trap, another cage she could not escape.

Little by little, the world shifted and changed, difficult to navigate. Her head rested against cool stone. Her body curled into itself as she stared into nothingness.

Mid March 1791

I am so full of laughter. Henri is punishing her! His precious Justine, his delicate wife. He is punishing HER. HA! The little fool saw us. Annabelle, she saw us and thought to get away with it! Her violation of my privacy, of my—of our—little sanctuary.

Henri was upset with me, yes.

But I'm not the one in the coffin! Not today!

-M.L.G.

CHAPTER FIFTEEN
Remember When You Cried, Remember When You Wished to Die?

IT WAS CALM, TRANQUIL IN THE LONDON TOWN-house. The last of the servants had turned in for the night with just a few hours left of the dark. It was beyond midnight but just hours before the sun was due to rise again. The moon had been shrouded by clouds, which obscured the stars and left the little garden in darkness. No one was awake within the residence. No one heard the piercing scream, but it shattered the tranquil night and sent a flurry of panicked birds into flight.

The scream was of agony, of despair, and of fear. A fear that death lingered just behind one's shadow, just beyond the borders of this world. It was short-lived. But it had existed.

Did no one hear her scream? Justine had clapped her hands over her mouth when she heard herself cry out. It was when she knew her life was forfeit. There was no returning to the safe nursery walls of her aunt's countryside manor. There was no escape to the skirts of her guardian. She had ensnared herself in the web of the worst kind of beast. And there he stood. Not looking at her. Not moving. Not seeming to breathe in the cool night air.

She was shivering. Aware of her bare shoulders and her bruised feet, aware of her tangled hair and broken nails. It had been hours of struggling, hours of agony to break free from her coffin. Coffin! He had placed her inside an ivory coffin. Bile rose in the back of her throat as she held her hands tightly over her mouth. Willing herself not to breathe too loudly. Willing her feet to remember the path they had just taken. Willing him not to have heard her.

"Scream again and it will be the last sound you ever make," came the threat. Henri's voice was threaded with malice, with wickedness.

Her body began to shake uncontrollably, and she bit her tongue until she tasted the sharp metallic taste slide down the back of her throat. This was not the man she had married. This was not the composed man who had asked for her hand. This was a monster. This was a murderer. She had seen the bodies!

"Justine, my sweet, come closer so I might wrap this blanket around you. You are utterly naked against the cool air. Do you wish to catch a cold?" The voice was still detached, deceitful in the honey of concern dripping from the words.

Justine felt her feet begin to move as she took one step backward and then another. He had not turned to face her. She could hardly breathe, let alone go near him again! She had made it six steps backward before she felt the ground shift beneath her, and her legs crumbled. Sobbing, she began to crawl away from him. Too slow to not see he was staring down at her. A glint in his eyes: madness, pure madness. She could not get away.

"I—I'm sorry for everything. I did not mean to disrespect you."

The words fell out. Round and round, she crawled as tears clouded her vision and her heart hammered against her chest. Could he hear her terror? Of course, it was in the tremor of her voice. It was in the cool sweat dampening her palms and coiling at the base of her neck. He knew. He knew and he did nothing to abate her terror. It seemed to feed him. It seemed to attract him as he slowly stalked her about the room, their room.

At last, Justine was too exhausted to keep up this charade of escape, and she laid her burning cheek against the cold floor. Her body ached. Her head throbbed. And a gentle whisper of a touch grazed the back of her neck as she took in a deep unsteady breath.

"Justine, we are husband and wife. I could not wish you to be anything more nor anything less than you have been born and bred to be—an esteemed lady who runs a smooth household. Our household . . . it is . . ." He paused as his arms slid beneath her, and he effortlessly lifted her stiffening body from the ground. Henri cradled her against his chest for a moment as he thought about his family, about his household, and about the thousands upon thousands of skeletons lingering in the shadows and the secrets cemented within the brick and mortar of this home.

"Our household is a nightmare. You will learn of its secrets, and you must harbor them, for they are yours now. You witnessed a terrible scene. One I had hoped to keep from you until you were old and beloved on your deathbed. But now it is this one nightmare. It will haunt and terrify you, yet you must keep it locked away." His voice had warmed, bit by bit, as he chided her for her outburst at the dinner table. It had been a maddening scene, where she had thrown wine at his brother's face and accused him of acts worse than heresy, worse than murder.

Justine sobbed as she felt the cool soft touch of a pillow against her cheek. Her eyes could no longer open. Were they swollen shut? Oh, she wished to open them and not see the glossy stare of the corpse her brother-in-law had . . . A muffled cry erupted as she turned her face into the pillow.

Henri crooned and petted her hair as she cried. "Little Justine, my little lamb, you will become accustomed. It is truly not so horrid as when you first see it. You will become accustomed. I dare not say jaded because you are too precious, too innocent of heart. My Justine, my sweet Justine, he will never lay a hand on you, for he knows your value to me. If you fear him, consider him banished from your sight—in everything but our family dinners, as they are a display of our solidarity. Our strength."

The trickle of the tears had ceased. Her breathing had slowed. Her body still shook, but now it appeared to be from exhaustion rather than emotion. Henri pulled the coverlet about her shoulders.

"If your guardian had not agreed to have us wed, it would have been you upon the table. Michel lusted for you, but not in the way I cherish—no, no, do not cry again. You are protected because Michel fears me more than he dares to ever admit. For he knows what I . . . he knows what I am willing to do to protect the things I covet."

Justine tried to keep her body still, even as her heart fluttered and pounded in irregular rhythms. The back of her throat burned with bile. What was this twisted fairy tale she was living in? Her lips were cracked. Her throat burned. But she could not let his monologue continue as if she were nothing but a rag doll. No. Nothing but a porcelain doll to be petted and displayed upon a mantle.

"Henri, your brother is damned for what he has done. It goes against—" But she could no longer speak for her airway was cut off. Fright turned to instinct as she thrashed and clawed at his fingers. They were laced too tightly about her throat. Constricting, crushing . . .

"Be quiet! You do not know the half of it. You—You do not have the authority to damn my brother. You do not get to judge him. Are you suddenly God? Are you suddenly a judge to say such a malicious lie? Hold your tongue and be warned, if you speak such things again, you will regret it." It all came as a hiss. Then Henri released his grip about her throat and rolled across her to the other side of their bed. Calmly, he began to unbutton his shirt.

"I had thought to take the carriage to the exterior gardens in the morning. It will sit well with the servants if you were to accompany me. Perhaps you might consider wearing your lilac gown, as it becomes your complexion."

Justine gasped for air, trying not to spew vomit across their bed as wave after wave of bile rose in her throat. How could he? How dare he? Fear and anger boiled together in the pit of her stomach as she listened to his plans for a stroll about a garden that had been neglected for half a decade because the family had suffered losses. Sorrow had kept them away from the maintenance of the grounds.

The lilac gown with the high neckline—a neckline designed for modesty but would now act as a culprit to hide the bruises about her throat. The lilac gown she had first worn when being introduced to the Geoffrey brothers. After tomorrow, she would see it destroyed or ruined in some irreparable way. Damned gown!

"Justine, it is rude to not answer your husband." It was a harsh whisper, as if there were unsaid words constricting his throat. "I need you to understand something, my sweetheart. Are you aware of the responsibilities of a wife?"

"My lord husband, I am aware of the expectations of the role you have given me. My guardian explained it to me well. Honor, obey, and provide an heir. Is there anything further you, personally, will require of me as my lord and husband?" she asked.

Henri stood there a moment. That moment turned from seconds and thrummed into minutes. Or was it hours? The intensity of his gaze and the stillness of his posture were both predatory and defensive, as if he might seek her demise while slipping into the shadowy recesses of their chamber. Henri's jaw worked as he sought to control himself, sought to conquer the rage as it still burned throughout his body. His fingertips tingled, thirsting to be around her throat again.

He wanted nothing more than to frighten her into docility and muteness.

Instead, oh instead, Henri took measured and quick steps toward her once more. "One, two, three—come back to me. Four, five, six—close your eyes. This will be . . ." The childhood rhyme spilled forth.

His hands began to slowly, slowly unlace her nightgown in a way so tender, Justine began to shiver. How was he capable of going from hostile and wrathful to soft and placid? Goose bumps rose along her arms and up the base of her neck as she listened to his breathing, willing herself not to move, not to flinch, not to escape.

"Justine, Justine, my sweet Justine, I require your loyalty. Above all else, I require your loyalty. For you see—or perhaps you will eventually see—this family is damned in ways and blessed in others. There are phantoms and skeletons allowed to see the light of day, as there are those cursed to remain in the shadows. Deep, deep within the shadows. When it comes to my brother, those skeletons are best kept unheard. Do you understand, my sweet Justine?"

Where was her voice? It had fled as the last remnants of his wrath flitted from her mind. She was quickly losing focus, and the events of the day were blurring together into something foreign, something frightening. Or had it not been Henri who'd frightened her? Where was her voice?

"I swore obedience in our marital vows, and obedience you shall have. Loyalty is another . . . is another thing you cannot tame." Ah, was it correct thing to say? Justine felt her heartbeat quicken as he grew still and quiet, as if he'd become a statue.

"I see. I shall count on your obedience when I command your discretion when it comes to keeping hidden under lock and key the secrets of the Geoffrey estate. My name is now your name. You do not want society to frown on *our* atrocities, do you?"

"No, no. After all the—" An unintended pause as she warily watched her husband, this man who could transform his mood from poised and warm to detached and bestial.

Henri was calm. He was humming. *Swing my hands, swing my hands, oh-ever love, oh-ever love, to the gates of heaven, to the gates of heaven. Swing my hands; swing my hands, ever near and ever far, ever near and ever far. Swing my hands, dream and dream of love, of love. Swing my hands; ever near and ever far, from the dreams of love, of love, of love.*

What was he humming? Justine had never heard this tune before, but it seemed to calm her husband, this stranger who was both her rescuer and her jailer. She stood.

"My lord," she whispered, her fingertips reaching out and brushing along his stubble-lined cheek. There was no response, no flickering of recognition to either her voice or her touch. Had he withdrawn into himself? Justine willed herself to look up into his eyes, and she took a sudden step backward. His eyes! They were cold. They were empty, empty pools reflecting her look of horror back to her.

"Henri! Henri!" With a raised voice, panic and concern blending, she stroked both of his cheeks while saying his name. "Henri!"

But he was far away. Someone else was crying out his name, someone dearer to him than his own life—Elisabeth, she was crying, crying, crying for him. Alas, he could do nothing to find her, to rescue her. *Henri! Henri! HENRI!* It blurred. The memories and the face before him were blurring together. Who was the young woman standing before him? She certainly was not Elisabeth.

Justine could not identify her own emotions as they swirled and chased one another: the need to flee, the urge to stay, the desire to comfort, the demand to scream. Scream, again and again. Scream, again. There was nothing left to do but to remain by his side, her fingertips brushing along his cheeks, softly caressing away the pain and the fear. And softly, the memories began to ebb away. Henri was exhausted. His entire body refused to move, to twitch, to feel anything. He was not cold, but he was not . . . he was not alive. Why were his eyes closed?

It must have been hours because as his eyelids flickered open, he noted the darkness of outside. The utter stillness, the blackness of the room. Yet he was not cold. He was not lonely—correction, he was not alone. There was soft breathing against his cheek. Inhale and exhale, inhale and exhale. It was a steady breath, soft and sweet.

Henri knew who it was. No memory, no ghost, nothing could haunt him, as he was already a damaged and broken being. No, it was his wife. One finger twitched, and then his hand was able to be lifted, up, up. Why did everything feel so delayed, such a struggle? Why was Justine sleeping so near to him? No, he was the one curled up against her. Curled in the fetal position, curled into the warmth of her, into the comfort . . . Suddenly, all his muscles tensed and spasmed. He jolted away. No.

"Get away," he hissed through clenched teeth.

Her body moved more quickly in response than her mind as she pulled away from him, all senses on high alert as she struggled with the flight response. Justine tried to focus on her breathing, in and out, in and out. This was nothing compared to how her father had beaten her. Henri was reacting. He was in survival mode. Right? No, she peered over at him and glimpsed clarity in his gaze.

One, two, three steps she took backward and away from this man, her husband. When had she stood up? There was no recollection of the jolting movements her body had taken moments before when he hissed into her ear. It had broken through the calm, through the tranquility of her mind and her dreams and shattered it all. She blinked.

"You were screaming out. I thought only to soothe you. I did not mean to fall asleep near you, much less in the same room. Forgive me, if you must." Her voice was calm even as her heart pounded in her chest, and she felt as if she had run up a hundred steps. Calm was easy; calm was the defense. If she was calm, perhaps he would remain calm.

"None of this is your concern. Your duties do not include

consoling and coddling me. Your duties are to be a feminine figurehead beside me in public and to bear an heir. One you are capable of; the other is lacking."

"We have been wed for less than a few months, my lord husband," came her reply.

"Four months. Over four months and you show no signs."

"I beg your pardon, my lord, for not fulfilling that particular duty to date."

Henri made a *tsk* noise in dismissal of her reply. There was no urgency to what he was saying to her, the production of a child. Did he truly want to pass on his family name? Its wealth, its status, its secrets . . . the burdens? There was no way to fathom the depth of the loathing he felt for his own father once the weight of the household had been leveled on his shoulders. It was too much for one soul to be burdened with. What did this have to do with the conversation he was having with his wife, in this moment? Ah, yes, a child.

"Be sure to keep yourself well, my Justine. This is what I ask of you. A child will come when it is willed." Willed by who? By God? Did he believe in a god?

"Will you take a glass of wine with me in the study, my lord?"

"No, not this evening. There is much to be done in preparation of Michel's announcement. Ah." He held up his hand to pause what Justine was about to say. "There is no need for your hand in this. Michel and you should be kept apart a bit longer since you still bemoan your nightmares to the staff."

Yes, yes, the staff are not your confidantes. I am sorry to say. This was never said aloud. Justine had to know this household was run by its master, and that was where their loyalties stayed.

It was cumbersome to see the crestfallen look flit across her features, but it did not last long. This young woman before him was quite adept at keeping her composure. It was one of the qualities he had chosen her for. Her self-control was exquisite.

"Good night, dear wife. I will see you for breakfast," Henri half whispered as he stepped away and toward the doorway. It was said half-heartedly as an endearment, but it was not received kindly.

Justine did not bother to look back at her husband when he said his farewell. There was no need to. No response, no reaction. It was best to let things rest between them. There was too much brewing beneath the surface to be drawn into another argument. Her fingertips curled around the chilled doorknob and turned it ever so slowly. She opened the door and slid through the narrow opening. The door was closed just as quietly behind her, and at last, she exhaled. Her shoulders heaved with silent sobs as she bit into her knuckles, trembling, shaking. What kind of life was this? What kind of marriage was this?

This could not be normal. This could not be deemed as "happily ever after" as the fairy tales would have led her believe. There was some naïveté when she had entered this marriage. This felt ugly. This felt filthy. Appearances were more important. Family came before self. Image came before emotion.

The shaking had subsided enough for her to be able to breathe, to focus as she walked away from the bedroom door. *May we never conceive . . .* It was a fleeting thought, but its impact was felt within her heart, coursing through her core.

"I want a child of my own, Henri. Not one born only to belong to you or this house. I want . . ." Justine's words were said to only the air surrounding her as she walked down the hall. Or at least she thought she was alone.

There was a shadow lingering in one of the many alcoves. A shadow heard her words and took them as a vow, as a threat, as a curse. A pale hand was lifted to form the sign of the cross to ward off the evil doings as the woman walked away. "Witch . . ." Percy hissed.

Henri did not look up when the door opened again. He had moved to a chair with a handful of papers all due for review and feedback before the dawn. There was continued quiet as the door clicked shut again.

Why were women so predictable? It was a nuisance, such a waste of time to keep entertaining Percy this way, but what else could he do with her? He could not wed her, as he had Justine, for Justine was a thousand times more qualified to be his wife. He could not bed her, as he had made a vow of monogamy to his wife. Henri could not cast her aside, as she would be ostracized as a cast-off mistress by society, unwelcome in all parlors. The few that allowed her entrance now did so only because of her connection to him out of courtesy for his continued patronage to the salons.

He sighed. "What is it, Percy? There is much I must do in the few remaining hours of this night."

"Were we ever meant to be happy?"

"Happiness is a thing of childhoods and fairy tales, my dear. Happiness is not what I desire in this life."

"But what of my desires, Henri? What of my happiness?" came her whine, the voice no longer melodic as she wrapped her arms around his shoulders and rested her forehead against his neck. "What if I desire to be happy with you? Were we ever meant to be happy?"

"You are selfish, Percy. You are selfish and do not see the world for what it is. There is—"

She silenced him with a kiss. A kiss of desperation, of anxiety, of longing. He left her feeling so empty, so unwanted, and yet she could not leave, for Henri held her above all others. Or so she believed. There was no love. There had never been love, not in the way she knew could exist. Percy knew Henri could not give her any type of warmth. He was cold, very cold.

"I want us to be happy, Henri. You deserve to be happy. No matter how you dismiss the notion as fanciful and wasteful, you deserve happiness—happiness that will not come from that wom—" A resounding noise, like that of a wounded animal, cut off the last of the word as Percy gasped in pain.

Henri's hand was tight around her wrist, his eyes ablaze with rage as he stared down at her. Slowly, ever so slowly, a smile began to form on her lips, and she reached up to kiss his chin.

"Do not speak of my wife with such words or in such a tone, Percy."

"You will forgive me, my love, as you always do forgive my trespasses. Will you not kiss me for my folly? I am jealous. She does not—oh, yes. Your *wife*." She puckered her lips and furrowed her brow, creating a picture-perfect pout as she stared up at him. He was still angry. Had he ever become so angry in defense of her? Only once, a thousand lives ago, he had been angry over her bleeding. It did not happen again, for the cost of his temper had been too great.

She had never seen him lose control as he had that one time, and she would never see it happen again. *More's the pity*, she thought. It was the hidden rage, the chained monster within him that Percy found herself attracted to.

This beautiful man standing before her with his eyes suddenly cooled, his lips in a firm line, and his expression withdrawn. Oh, she had offended him. Percy knew better than to touch him or even attempt to touch him as this point, so instead, she chose her next words carefully.

"Henri, *your wife* does not understand you as I do, for she does not see you as I do." Her voice was tender, her eyes pleading as she stood there waiting for his response. She anticipated and hoped for warmth, acceptance, or an embrace as the seconds ticked by, turning to minutes. Percy began to feel something akin to cold. It crept from her heart and slowly consumed her entire body. She swore it felt as if daggers were tearing her open from the inside out.

"Do you love her, this wife of yours? You dare to love?"

He was still withdrawn; he was still so distant.

Percy began to cry, an abhorrent noise that changed into hysterical laughter. Sobs pummeled through her body. Her cold, cold body. But Henri was gone, the door left ajar as he left without a goodbye. The door left open was a symbol that she was dismissed. She'd been discarded.

July 1791

Henri punished her. Once.

Henri did not punish me. He has not bothered to speak to me again over the last several months, even when we sit down for family meals in the evenings. My brother, his insipid wife, and I. Percy lurks in the shadows. Why do women seem to become besotted with my brother? He is nothing.

Henri favors Justine now. Justine is a problem in my life, in our life.

I am afraid that my brother no longer loves me . . .

But I heard her screams. I saw the bruises on her skin. I saw the chafed redness of his knuckles. I know that he hurts her. And you know what? That makes me happy.

-M.L.G.

CHAPTER SIXTEEN
WHERE IS MY SANCTUARY?

NOTHING FELT BALANCED IN THIS HOUSE-hold. There was absolute silence when the couple was served their meals. There was no shuffling or coughing. Only silence. Even at her father's dinners there had been some banter, some laughter and comradeship between the servers. This was not right. Justine felt as though she, too, ought to tiptoe around her husband even as he read the newspaper at their brunch. Every Friday and Saturday, they had brunch. It was an un-official display of their union as the curtains along the front windows were thrown wide open and the morning light was allowed in. This was a home of shadows, of fallen things and horrible dreams.

How could she raise a family here? How was she to tell her husband she was, in fact, carrying his child when, for the last two months, she had deceived him and her maids with bloodied sheets?

An alarm would be raised with a doctor, and she might be placed on bed rest, and then what? Her every action would then be placed under even further scrutiny. Justine tried not to visibly shudder as the thought—no, as the truth slammed into her conscious. Was there to be no sanctuary, no safe place to shed her tears and rest her burning cheeks? Was her aunt so far lost to her? Could she return to her old home? Unlikely.

"Justine, I was hoping for your insight on something . . . has begun to . . ." Henri stopped speaking as he glanced up at his wife, quickly realizing she was not present. Physically, yes, but mentally, she was elsewhere. He had become familiar with her expressions, her body language. "Ah, my dear, you seem exhausted this morning."

No response was given by Justine until Henri moved as if to stand from his seat, the feet of his chair scraping along the floor. Suddenly, Justine recovered herself enough to not stare agape at her husband as he leaned in toward her, his fingertips a moment's touch away from her cheek.

"Did you not rest well, my dear? It seems a pattern is forming," Henri surmised.

"Oh? I want to apologize, my lord. I was merely daydreaming about how to decorate the front parlor. You briefly mentioned you were tired of the blues in the room. Forgive me. What were you saying before?" Justine replied with a brief smile, adjusting herself in her chair as her fingers wrapped more tightly around her fork, the prongs fishing through the custard tart set before her.

"Hmm, yes, you have been more idle since the close of the season. Do you wish to decorate the parlor? You may make calls to the vendors in town. They could use the business at this time of year." He was ready to comply with her apparent distraction and subtle request. Permission was granted. Henri slowly sat back in his chair and observed his wife more closely. Nothing was openly amiss about her, but she was not quite . . . not quite the same.

"Thank you, my lord. Ordering decor and speaking with the vendors, as you suggested, will give me more to focus on. It will liven our house as well." Perhaps the last bit was too much to have said aloud as she eyed the servants standing along the walls. Did they move?

Henri did not respond, as he seemed focused on a piece of dessert. He slowly placed it in his mouth and chewed, his gaze never leaving his wife's face. But she had grown accustomed to his stoic quiet, and it no longer unnerved her to be beneath his stare for so long. *Excellent, she is learning,* he thought. *But what is she learning and what is she hiding?* A daily account was given to him about her habits and her movements throughout the house. He had declined to invite her previous servants to follow her into her marital home as he needed to have the loyalty and trust of those who served her. Trust. Such a powerful word. *Trust* was the incorrect term. Henri needed to *command* the few allowed to surround her, this wife of his.

"It does not explain the fact that you seem more tired during our brunches together. Should I call the doctor?"

He asked this over the rim of his glass before he took a sip of water.

Justine physically jolted at the idea, her self-control cracking as he kept prodding at the subject she had so carefully been avoiding the last month. Justine's composure was so simple, so fragile. She had lost hers, and this bothered her as she stared at her husband and attempted to baldly lie to his face. "No, I am not tired, my lord. As I said earlier, I was merely daydreaming about the blue parlor—" Something in her voice cracked, and her facial expression changed, and she was aware her husband saw it.

"Do not lie to me again, understood?"

An all-too-familiar chill shot up her spine and landed as a razor's edge at the back of her skull. Fight or flight, fight or flight. Rather, her body chose to freeze. Their eyes locked as she tried to think of something to say, some retort that might disarm him and his cool demeanor.

A memory of a conversation she'd previously had with Michel came to mind as she stared at her husband. What else could there be to say? The truth? Justine laid down her fork next to the plate filled with untouched food. Her appetite had decreased over the last several weeks. Finally, after what felt an hour, her throat did not feel dry and constricted.

"I am with child, my lord." She said the words slowly, carefully pronouncing them in a calm manner. Neutral. Nothing could have prepared her for the sudden rush of her husband's body encircling her in a tight constricting embrace. Was it laughter she heard? Yes, oh dear God, yes. He was laughing. It was laughter that surrounded her and thundered through her head as she tried to compose herself.

Justine had imagined a thousand scenarios, a hundred responses, but none of them had included this.

"Oh, I am pleased! An heir for the Geoffrey's, a child of our own. Well done, wife, well done!" Henri enthused as he released her from the overpowering embrace. His eyes were warm as he looked upon her anew, as if she were a stranger all over again. "This explains the exhausted state you've been in, your pallor, and your lack of appetite. How long have you suspected—no, how long have you known?"

The happiness and joy he had possessed mere seconds before was gone, destroyed by the mirthless realization: she had hidden this from him. How long? Henri was still close to her, ever so close as he put his fingers below her chin and tilted her head back, once more forcing his dominance over her and her life so easily, so quietly.

"How long have you known, Justine?"

"Am I not allowed to hold some piece of my life to myself? Am I not allowed to harbor a joyous secret for a bit to enjoy it, to savor it? Am I not allowed sanctuary? Where is my sanctuary?"

The words spilled forth without her being able to stop the overflow, the questions, and indirect accusations. She was tired, beyond exhausted with having to compose herself all day and even at night. She was allowed no respite from the eyes of the servants, the stares, and the blank faces. She repeated the last question, more quietly, more submissively: "Where is my sanctuary, Henri?"

One of the servants moved, his fingers curling into a fist. Was this a display of a hidden temper? There was life within these servants; well, at least one had dared to display something out of the usual nothingness. The gesture had not gone without Henri's notice, but it was not to be dealt with at this time. No, instead his focus was homed in on the young woman before him as she stood so still, so quiet.

Where was her sanctuary? What kind of question was that? Her sanctuary existed in the parlor, in the privacy of her bedroom. Her sanctuary came from the carrying of his family's name and the wedding ring on her finger.

"I am your sanctuary." *I am everything.*

"I need more. Henri, I need more than you. I need a—"

"You need me and nothing more. Now then, you will redecorate the blue parlor as well as the nursery since having one is a necessity. Those two tasks should keep you occupied for the foreseeable future. I will have the doctor come by this evening or in the morning before breakfast." His voice meant there was no room for discussion. What he said was final. Justine felt her heart plummet into her stomach, and she suddenly felt ill.

Justine leaned over the edge of the table and lost the little bit of breakfast she had forced herself to eat. It was at this most ungraceful moment that her brother-in-law, Michel, walked into the room. *Oh, for all that is sacred . . .* Justine thought as she felt her cheeks. They were warm, and she was most definitely in a disheveled state.

There was an immediate undercurrent of friction formed between the trio. Michel seemed to exude a restless energy; Henri was on edge; and Justine was lightheaded.

A servant stepped forward and pulled back a chair for Michel, while another began placing dishes on the table, and yet a third served pastries to the young man. A world of entitlement for all of them. A world her child was to be born into.

Oh! But she had not dreamed the horror of the vision. She had not dreamed her brother-in-law beside the decayed Annabelle. Another wave of nausea overtook her, and she leaned over again and dry-heaved, as her stomach had already emptied itself.

Justine was panting by the time she sat back upright, droplets of perspiration on her upper lip and across her brow. Michel was a monster. She could not have her child in the same house as such a creature, such a demon. Her eyes flickered between Michel and Henri, back and forth, back and forth. Why was her heart racing? Why could she not clearly hear what they were saying?

"Michel, how kind of you to grace us with your presence. Where have you been these last few weeks?"

"Hmmm?" Michel drawled; his clear gaze focused on his sister-in-law.

"Where have you been?" Henri repeated, setting down his utensil as he kept his focus on his brother, ignoring the fact his wife was not well, and thus the rest of the room ignored it.

"I have been visiting with an old friend." The words *old friend* were said with an edge, which curdled Justine's stomach all over again.

"You are a monster," she whispered toward the floor.

A monster. A demon. Something she wanted nothing to do with but nonetheless had to dine with. Henri had heard her clearly enough and was irked she would say such a thing out loud. Justine did not know how to comport herself in the presence of the servants, not yet. His young wife would require a lesson, perhaps two. There were subjects never to be said aloud at the dining table.

The servants knew better than to repeat anything said throughout the house, whether at a meal or during a simple sitting in the library. The consequences were severe if they were to dismantle the fortification of silence Henri had worked so hard to maintain. If he discovered a servant had spoken a shred of gossip about him or his house, the servant was released from service and their name was tarnished to such an extent that they could never gain meaningful employment again. If they were ever even heard from again.

"Gideon, take Mistress Geoffrey to her chambers. She is clearly too exhausted to be in polite company. Send in Nanny to care for her." Henri snapped his fingers and was finished with the care of his wife.

Justine was seen from the table on shaky legs with a continued pallor to her complexion. She avoided the gaze of both her husband and his brother, not bothering to say a word to either. Michel was not disturbed in the least by what she had said, seemingly consumed by the deliciousness of the pastries, crumbs across his lips and his fingers.

"Michel, you must be more . . . attentive to your surroundings when you visit this old friend of yours," Henri said into the quiet room before returning to finishing his meal. The servants had begun to clear Justine's place, finally addressing the mess she had made.

No one spoke. No one dared to breathe as they hurriedly cleared the space. Then all returned to the walls and held their breath. Their master's voice had a new sting to its words as he addressed his younger brother.

Michel continued to inhale the pastries easily within his reach, oblivious (or seemingly so) to what his brother had said. Even of the fact that Justine had left the room. Henri observed a change in Michel's posture as he continued to eat; the nervous energy from before had subsided, and contentment was clearly expressed on his face.

"The chef outdid himself this morning with the desserts. They were delectable. It is a pity Justine could not stomach them," Michel said with too loud a voice.

Henri slowly set down his fork and lifted his napkin to his lips, pausing as he assessed his brother's mood. There may be a display of temper; just as effortlessly, there could be peace. Michel was becoming more and more unpredictable. Such a nuisance. Could he be resentful of the responsibility placed on his own shoulders? Then there was the reality of his sick attributes.

A deep breath in, a deep breath out, and Henri stood up from his chair and swiftly walked to stand directly behind his brother. A flash of movement and his hand was clenched around the back of Michel's neck, shoving it down onto the table.

The dishes clanged as Michel's head hit the table with a loud crack. There was a tussle between the two. Michel struggled to sit upright, twisting and thrashing, but his head remained pinned against the table. He licked his lips and tasted the metallic tang of blood. His blood. How tiresome.

"Henri, this is not necessary. Henri, this is not necessary. Henri, this is not—" But his words were cut off as his head was slammed against the table a second time. Michel flew his hands up to wrap around his brother's arm, an attempt to stop a third blow.

"You will not disrespect my wife. You will not mistreat her. You are nothing. You have always been a nothing, a nobody but for the secondhand son of our forsaken father. Nothing is what you shall remain if you dare to exploit my wife any further. Watch yourself. Watch yourself closely when you wander these halls and visit your old friends. I will not warn you again," Henri nastily said into his brother's ear as he slammed Michel's head down a third time.

"Yes, sir," was all Michel replied with as he tasted more blood. How tedious. Michel loosened his grip around his brother's arm and appeared to become pliant, even relaxed. "May I suggest a scent for your wife? I think *orange blossoms* would be perfect for her . . ."

Silent. The silence of the room was destroyed with a thunderous storm when Michel was flung backward, his chair and body crashing onto the floor, dishes shattering around his fallen form.

"You dare to imprecate my wife? You dare to suggest orange blossoms! Of all things . . . of the things you've said and done, this is by far the most foolish! You bastard, you pathetic little bastard!" Henri bellowed out curses down at his brother, spittle falling from his mouth.

One for the nightmare and two for the seer, three for the maiden, and four for the fear . . . Fear was what shook Henri so deeply, fear his brother might seek to harm his wife, his pregnant wife. When there was nothing left to throw, when the last of the dishes were shattered and the body of his younger brother was lying still on the ground, only then did Henri force himself to inhale a deep breath.

Michel opened his eyes and blinked once, twice, three times. He felt a stinging along his face, his hands, and even in patches along his back. What an unpredictable response from his older brother. Henri was normally the calm one, yet he had exploded as he had only once before when their dearest Percy was around. Or shortly after Elisabeth's demise. She was an angel not meant to be corrupted by his mind, by his actions, by his words. Oh, little Beth. . . *I miss you, sweet sister.*

"I was merely saying the scent would suite her nicely or even bring a new image to society since the last person who wore orange blossoms has so untimely . . . disappeared, as they say." Michel spoke rather tranquilly despite the blood oozing from his forehead, his cheeks, and the lacerations scattered across his body. Slowly, achingly slowly, he began to position himself upright and cracked his neck.

"Do you want society to build a connection between my wife and my former paramour? Truly? What else is your intention, Michel?" came the brisk reply.

There was no answer as one brother stood still and the other casually stood up, brushing the broken shards of porcelain from his clothing. The servants still had not moved, even though some had been struck by the broken jagged edges of dishes. Michel took a few steps to be closer to his brother, crunch, crunch, crunching until he finally came to a standstill. Henri did not move as his gaze focused on his head butler, Gideon. He then lifted his chin.

"We are finished here. While I have your company, brother, let us go over the stipend I give to you as your spending . . ." The last of the sentence faded off as the two Geoffrey brothers walked out of the dining room, leaving behind a costly scene of chaos and fury as was oft the habit of the Geoffrey's.

Five for the dreamer, six for the sinner, seven for the corpse . . .

August 1791

I have been unwell these last weeks. At first, I thought it to be a side effect of the shock I experienced. But then I realized the incident took place back in March. My nausea and discomfort did not begin until late June.

The first week, I blamed the nausea on the brutality my husband had inflicted on me. The injustice of it all. I am the one being continually punished and berated over the faults of my brother-in-law.

The second week, I could hardly sleep at night. The insomnia returned to haunt me as it had throughout March and April. The terror of being confined in a dark space, in a coffin. Henri is a cruel man! A beast!

These last several weeks have proved to me that I am with child. I have not bled since May. I am terrified. I told Henri that I wanted a child of my own, but . . .

-Justine Geoffrey

CHAPTER SEVENTEEN
WE WERE NEVER MEANT TO BE HAPPY

ERE WE EVER HAPPY, PERCY? TRULY happy, truly carefree as children ought to be when they play through the halls and through the gardens. Happiness. It was such a fickle emotion, so trivial and yet so powerful as so many lost themselves in its pursuit. Henri contemplated Percy's question for far longer than he had intended to allow himself to. It had crawled under his skin and coiled around his heart, constricting it in a way he had not felt for . . . he had not felt in a long, long time. Guilt.

Guilt for Percy. Guilt for Michel. Guilt for Elisabeth. Guilt that he had not done enough. Guilt that he had not fought hard enough.

It had been weeks since Henri had last spoken with Percy. He was aware the woman remained on his estate, as was her due. Despite himself, Henri had heard the last question Percy had thrown at him. *Love.* It held no meaning for him as he had not known the love or the affection of his mother's gentle touch or even from a nurse.

It was the iron fist of his father he remembered most, as it had scarred distrust and rigidity into his childhood. The earliest memories he had were of screams, of shattering glass and broken bones. So why did this sudden mention of the word *love* from Percy resound through his head as a headache, as the forming of something new? No, there was no time for new things. It had been weeks! Why was this possessing him now?

There was hardly time for the old; there was only what was before him. Today was where his focus was. Today was his. The worst . . . the worst had already happened, and it was forever in his history. How much had Percy been exposed to? Had his father harmed her in any way?

It began as a soft buzzing in his head as he continued his overview of the household's accounting. Henri tried to stay attentive, but his head began to ache—a dull ache at first, but then it festered, and the numbers began to blur together on the page. Why was this happening today? This was a most inconvenient time for the headache to manifest itself. A thousand curses on Percy for igniting this!

The woman was a nuisance in his life, as she was a perpetual reminder of his past, his history better left buried six feet beneath the ground in a rotted corpse no one thought to pray for as the soul of a deceased man. A soul surely burning in the eternal flames of hell.

A hell is what Henri believed in, a hell intended for the soul of his omnipresent and domineering father. A hell beyond . . . beyond any of the memories beginning to slip through the cracks of his mind. The screams. The crunching of bones. The red, red floors. The silence.

It all began to circulate behind his closed eyelids as he fought against both headache and memory. *Damn it, Percy!* This was not supposed to have been the way his day was spent—chasing away demons and embracing the shadows. It was arduous to sift through one's history and seek out the what-ifs, the imagery of happiness of a content child or a joyful scene. None of these came into his mind's eye as he sought to remember a time of happiness, even of ease.

Nothing came to mind, not in the definition Percy had surely meant as she tossed out the word to him, even as she questioned him. "Damn her," he hissed.

Not knowing what else to do with himself, Henri walked over to the window of his study, then pressed his cheek against the pane of glass—it was cool, chilled against his skin. As cold as Annabelle had been. As cold as Elisabeth had been.

Steadily, his eyelids drooped. He allowed the gates around his memories to swing open; the floodgates had been unleashed. The memories came in waves, crashing and ebbing, crashing and ebbing. An ache began to form at the base of his neck as the tension filtered through his limbs.

> *It was all too much, overwhelming him as he ran through the halls and took corners at a too-fast pace. The screams were no longer muffled. They were escalating, intensifying. Who was screaming? Running, running, running . . . It never seemed to end,*

until he came to stand before a set of double doors. Dark, enormous, domineering. There was a shriek, a wailing. It sounded as if an animal were being slaughtered. The pain, the immeasurable depth of pain in those shrieks . . .

"Elisabeth! Elisabeth, my baby, my sweet girl . . . Elisabeth!" Words weaved through the cracks of the dark doors. Hell had opened. The shrieking continued. The doors swung open and a monster—a shadow-demon—stood in his way. A crooning, a sobbing . . . Large hands wrapping around his neck . . .

Dreaming. It was all a nightmare . . . The screams were intense, burning into his mind as he felt his body slam into the walls, into the furniture. Someone was yelling, "Stop! Stop! You'll kill him too! Stop . . ." And then silence as the shadows overtook him . . .

Henri shivered and shook, the realization dawning in his mind that his father had blamed *him* for Elisabeth's death. Henri had almost died at the hands of his own father. His entire body began to convulse as the memories overwhelmed him, the waves building higher and higher in his mind. Suffocating him. Drowning him. There was no escape. There was no waking up because these were not nightmares. Henri knew that he was awake.

Michel was standing there, hovering over the broken body. The broken body was cradled in slender arms, fragile arms. Tears sprinkling the little face . . .
Michel was standing there . . . hovering . . . touching the lifeless Annabelle . . . whispering to

her, soothing her. Michel was standing there, but it was not Michel who felt the blows, who watched the world through flashing lights and darkening corners. It was not Michel who felt the pain . . .

Henri had little control of his limbs. His hands and his feet felt heavy, leaden. Why was Michel so close to the bodies of Elisabeth and Annabelle? *One for the nightmare and two for the seer, three for the maiden, and four for the fear . . .*

Michel was holding a shard of glass, blood dripping from his hand. There was nothing else . . . silence and the faint scent of orange blossoms. When Michel had walked into the parlor, he hid his hands . . .

Henri was running again, running again, and again, and again . . . escaping the screams, escaping the pain, escaping the accusations. Running faster, faster, farther, farther . . .

Henri opened his eyes. His vision blurred as he looked out the window at the beautiful garden below. It had been a design by his late mother, completed after her death. Ah, the memories were receding now. One thing remained in his mind; one detail could not be shaken loose. It failed to retreat with the rest of the shadows.

Michel had been there, for Annabelle and for the little girl. Michel. The echo of his younger brother's sneer, the eyes feverishly bright and the glacial expression on his face. Michel had been there. Michel had . . . Henri took in a deep, deep breath and forbade himself from completing the final thought. It would be a declaration of war, of murder, of dubiety.

No, the truth was too fanciful for Henri to acknowledge what he had just remembered. He knew about his brother. He knew his brother, correct? Michel was the second son, the spare where Henri was the heir. Michel was granted the second best, the leftovers, the residual efforts of his father when Henri was not enough. A rift between the two brothers—a rift stretched greater than the years between their births.

Michel had a sweet mother, a young woman who knew little of the world and even less about how to be a stepmother. But she was imprinted in Henri's mind as those haunting screams echoed once more through his head.

The memories had not been completely locked away like they had been before. Locked and stored safely in the recesses of his mind, falling into his subconscious. No, this time they lingered, and Henri could feel them slithering along his spine and crawling beneath his skin. Why could they not disappear? Why could they not be contained? The room surrounding him was quiet, isolated from the rest of the residence in such a way that the smashing of a vase did not alarm anyone, for no one heard it.

No one heard Henri start to yell and curse, throw a wooden chair against the wall, smash the glass of wine on the floor. Screaming, screaming, screaming until his throat was raw. Screaming until it felt as though his throat might bleed. Screaming until he could no longer make a sound.

"Get out of my head! Father, you are dead. You are dead. DEAD! Cursed to burn, cursed to ashes and dust. Let the worms devour your heart—it deserves to be rotted." He screamed it repeatedly, a mantra. It no longer relieved him of the memories. Of the truth. Of the nightmare.

Michel was above Annabelle. Michel was above the corpses, laughing and dancing. Michel was destroying the beauty. Michel was burning.

Elisabeth was laughing. She was dancing. She was playing. Golden curls bouncing as she peered over her shoulder at her eldest brother, her blue eyes twinkling and merry. She was saying something . . . He could not hear her, but she was happy, so happy . . .

Henri clenched his hands into fists and dug them into his forehead, pounding his head against his knees, curling into the fetal position as he tried to tear the images from his mind. It was not working. The images of Annabelle and Elisabeth were blurring together, blending in a deteriorating way. The childish face of his sister and the face of his lover. They were morphing together into a horrendous mask of atrocity. Innocence defiled by sin.

Why was this happening? Not today, not tonight. It should have stayed buried. It should have stayed hidden behind the smoke and fog of disbelief, of denial.

The truth. It shattered the fortifications he had built around himself, dismantling the lies one brick at a time. There was to be no returning to the false reality he had dwelled in. Yet what was he to do with this resurfaced knowledge? Henri knew his brother was of questionable ethics, wretched morality but this went deeper.

This was a truth Michel had kept hidden away, shrouded by smoke and mirrors of other half-truths, other scandals, other distractions. Who was Michel? Did Henri truly know?

Despite the atrocious state of the room and his own disheveled appearance, Henri stood up and walked over to the wall nearest to him. He pulled the red cord twice. Then he waited, turning around and facing the scene of his rage, his confusion, and his emotions—they had overwhelmed him and overtaken all sense as he destroyed the room once constructed as his refuge.

A knock sounded from the door. Then silence. Seconds passed, then minutes. The silence continued as Henri collected himself to a point that he could walk to the door and turn the knob, opening it to Gideon's passive face. Henri knew no one else would see the state of the room nor hear of the state of Henri himself. Gideon slid into the wreckage without letting his gaze move from his master's feet.

"How may I be of assistance, my lord?"

"When my father was the lord and master of this house, did you keep his secrets as you keep mine?" Henri asked, his voice low and empty.

"Yes, my lord. I will continue to do so until I die," came a quick reply.

"I am not questioning your loyalty, Gideon, merely asking to solidify my own demons."

Gideon did nothing but stand there fully composed and watch his young lord's feet. It had been a long, long service he conducted for the old Lord Geoffrey. A lifetime of unquestioning, unblinking employment during which he had learned silence was always the best solution.

The old man had gained a job in the Geoffrey household in a time when there were few options: the factory or the military. Back then, Gideon had to provide for his young family, a wife and two little ones, along with his sickly parents. Back then, Gideon had thought it would be a temporary employment, but it was direly necessary, so when he witnessed . . . horrors, he kept quiet. The quiet was far better than the screaming, far better than the pain.

The dependency was what had ensnared him into his old master's web, for if he misspoke or reported what he'd witnessed, then his family starved. The years had trickled by as the secrets worsened, and the silence ensued. *Quiet, keep quiet and look down.*

Look down, down, down and maybe hell would forget his misdeeds as he failed, time and time again, to protect those innocent souls from the depravity of the old lord Geoffrey. He became an accessory to his lord. The cruelty, the abuse, the skeletons. By any means necessary, Gideon had earned the trust of his former master, and the same trust had been transferred to the new master, the young Henri. The young man standing before him now with the imploring eyes so like his mother's.

"Your demons are also my own, my lord." At last, Gideon spoke, his voice calm and his posture upright. Despite his age, despite the burdens he carried, despite his own losses, he was proud of his status within this household. This cursed godforsaken house.

"I need you to look after my wife, your mistress, more carefully around Michel. He seems to be on the border of another episode, and I do not want my wife in the crosshairs."

"Understood, my lord. Anything else?" the servant asked.

"Assist me in getting ready. Tell me something about my mother." It came out of nowhere and left Gideon bewildered for a moment—a moment Henri took note of. Ever since his boyhood, the subject of his mother had been a forbidden one. Henri now possessed the authority and the curiosity to ask, but why was he asking now?

"Yes, my lord. Your mother was a lovely lady. She was kind, courteous, and saw the world in a beautiful way. Her intelligence was unmatched . . ." Gideon went on, his voice calm and monotone as he recited the script his previous master had given him. *Never was the boy to know the truth of his mother. Never was the boy to know the truth.*

Henri as a boy . . . The boy had already been aware of his mother's misfortune, her darkening soul. It was not the boy's fault his father was abusive, and his mother had begun to lose touch with reality.

"Gideon, the Lady Justine must be kept safe," Henri whispered. His voice was empty, foreign as it floated through the air once Gideon had fallen quiet. It was nothing unusual.

"Yes, my lord," Gideon replied, bowing his head and placing his left hand over his heart.

August 1791

The bitch is pregnant. Annabelle, she has done what you were not able to do.
What you will never be able to do.
I suppose this is your failure.

-M.L.G.

CHAPTER EIGHTEEN

WHERE DO YOU REST YOUR HEAD?

HAT HAPPENED TO HER, HENRI? WHAT happened to Annabelle? Tell me honestly, accurately. Nothing less. Otherwise, I will report her disappearance as hostile rather than convenience." It was a bald-faced lie, a trigger meant to grab her husband's attention. Hostile meant murder, convenience meant mistake.

There would be no benefit to her if Henri or Michel were arrested or charged with the death of Annabelle Stanley. Yet she could not bring herself to carry her child to term in such a household as this. Not without knowing the truth.

What other dark secrets lay nestled between the floorboards? What other skeletons might surface in her nightmares? She had spent countless hours of restless nights tossing every which way, as she dared not close her eyes and see the grotesque smile of the corpse—the once notorious Annabelle.

Was that to be her own fate after she gave birth to a Geoffrey heir? *No, no*, she told herself, for it felt as though Henri might care for her in his own twisted corrupt way. Justine looked at her husband, warily watching him for any subtle changes in his demeanor, in his posture. There was nothing, absolutely nothing.

"Henri, my lord, my husband . . . Our child cannot be raised fatherless, tainted by this . . ." She whispered the last, having seen her cousin's attempt to atone for her uncle's scandal. It was a generation past and thus was not fodder for recent gossip. But it still affected their family. Justine could not allow such a thing to happen to her own child. The Geoffrey name was now her own. It was her child's name.

"Henri, please. Say something," Justine implored. The distance between them was more than physical. The mental abyss she saw her husband falling through was dark.

It was dark, and it was treacherous, and she did not dare to reach out to touch him. Even if the very touch might assure her he was alive, his flesh warm beneath her fingertips, she knew better. By now, she knew better.

"Where do you rest your head?"

The question was asked in a disjointed voice, one she could not fathom came from her husband. It startled Justine, and she could not respond, not right away, as she fought a sudden wave of nausea. The back of her hand went to her mouth as she fought the urge to vomit.

"I asked, where do you rest your head?" Henri turned to face his wife, and he observed her, distant and assessing.

"I—I rest on the pillow of the bed you gifted me. I rest my head under the roof of our home. The Geoffrey estate is where I rest my head."

"Excellent answer, wife, but where do you rest your head?" he asked again.

Confused, growing wearier, Justine swallowed the acidic bile burning in the back of her throat. Her hand slowly lowered down to her lap. The way he was watching her was like the look of a predator, an animal. It lacked emotion. It lacked anything resembling the gaze of another person, another human being. Why did he shift between such extremes? Why did he act the way he did? Why was . . . Why were both Geoffrey men the way they were?

Justine's own upbringing had been isolated, and her every move, every word had been under scrutiny, yet she had developed the social skills for both public appearances and private meetings. She had remained balanced. Anxious and hypervigilant, but balanced.

Did Henri feel out of control, out of his power when certain events took place? If she knew the answer to that, it might have provided some answers about the majority of the shadows and ghouls surrounding her husband and her brother-in-law. Yet nothing could explain the ghastly obscene acts Michel had done with the corpse. It was a sin, a double or triple sin. Surely it was condemned beyond any redemption. The dead were supposed to be laid to rest, their souls prayed for, and their bodies left to the earth. Not what Michel had done. Not what Henri had allowed to be done.

Where did she rest her head? Justine continued to watch her husband as she maintained her silence. Weary and a bit subversive, Justine did not want to simply submit to her husband's will in this matter.

"I will be going to town to shop this afternoon, as I need a few new gowns for the upcoming months of my pregnancy." She said it softly, lowering her gaze to the floor. Justine changed her demeanor into that of a timid young woman, hoping this might shift his attention back to the child in her belly. His child, his heir.

"Where do you rest your head at night, Elisabeth?"

"Henri, I am not Elisabeth. I am your wife. Justine," came the soft answer.

"Elisabeth has gone to bed, Lord Father. Please allow her time to rest. The loss of our mother was hard on her. No, no, you are right. Mother was a fiend; she was the worst sort of woman, but Elisabeth needs to rest, regardless of what still needs to be done. She is only a child." The last sentence was spoken with a sob, a sudden shift of emotion. Henri began shaking. His shoulders heaved, and his face contorted with grief, and yet no sound left his mouth as his body crumpled into itself.

Justine was lost. She feared a repercussion if she were to touch him. She feared a melancholic or even catatonic state if she did nothing. It felt as if there were only two options for what she could do for her husband, who was now curled up on the floor. No sounds came from his trembling lips as he shook and shook with a grief of profound depth, a depth she could not fathom. What happened to him? Who was Elisabeth? It was a name she had heard Michel speak of as well.

Quietly, dreadfully slowly, Justine stepped away from her husband and prayed she was heading in the direction of the servant's bell. If she rang it, her husband might punish her. If she rang it, he might stay in his current position. The risk of punishment was outweighed by the concern she had for his mind, for his body, and perhaps even for his soul. Groping, groping, groping . . . Where was the damned cord? Panic began to clamp around her heart as she reached backward and sideways for the red cord. Finally! She felt it slide along her wrist, and then finally her fingers were wrapped around it, and she tugged, and she tugged, and she tugged.

Deep down, Henri heard the chimes going and applauded his wife for her insight. Gideon was to be summoned, Gideon who knew what to do to retrieve his master from this darkness, this abyss. He could not speak; he could not move. Why did this have to happen in front of Justine? What had triggered this episode? Henri whirled round and round in his own mind as he was forced to listen to his wife plead with the old servant, faithful and loyal to a fault.

Warm leathery hands curled around his shoulders, and Henri felt himself be hoisted up and over Gideon's shoulders. His eyes closed as he sighed out of relief, out of exhaustion. Justine . . . Justine. Let her go and rest in her own rooms. Let her lock the doors while he was torpid and could not ensure her safety from his corruption. Henri's body jolted and twisted, but Gideon held firm to his young master and said not a word.

Justine followed closely behind, her fingers curling and twisting around themselves. Her teeth worried on the flesh of her lower lip as she watched servant and master. What was she witnessing? What had she witnessed? Elisabeth.

Elisabeth was not a name associated with the Geoffrey house beyond the mentions by Henri and by Michel. Could she ask Gideon who this Elisabeth was? Justine tried to remember the ramblings Henri had said. Mother . . . the loss of their mother had caused Elisabeth to go rest?

Gideon laid Henri down on the giant bed. The bedchamber was dim, poorly lit. Justine fought her urge to flee, to turn and seek out the light of the hallway. All the wall sconces lit for the evening hours meant brightness, safety. Panic was still grasping her heart, a pressure deep in her chest as she stayed along the perimeter of the room.

Gideon ignored the presence of the young woman, his sole focus and his only concern the well-being of his master. Slowly, tenderly, he took off Henri's boots and took off the overcoat. He did not fully undress his master. No, he left him comfortable but still presentable as he had been trained to do.

"There now, my lord, you can rest now. There is nothing urgent for you to see to just yet. I will light the fire and let you repose." Gideon spoke in a soothing melodic tone as he backed away from his master, who was now reclining on pillows and covers on the bed.

Henri stared up at the ceiling, a familiar thing, a costly thing. His body was no longer clenching and shaking, yet he still could not mobilize himself. Where had Justine gone? Gideon was still nearby, as he had not been dismissed, and Henri knew he would remain in the room until told otherwise. A deep breath. He struggled to inhale as he closed his eyes.

"It was a relief to watch the life ebb from his eyes and feel his heartbeat slowly fade. He was a monster—a true spawn of the devil—and his reflection is imprinted in my mind. His death was both a release and an imprisonment," Henri confessed.

It meant there were no more answers, no more lessons, and no more secrets to be revealed—for they had been taken to the grave. Well, the secrets the old Lord Geoffrey had not divulged to his eldest son and heir. Sinister secrets. Truths and half-truths lost for eternity if they had been possessed by only one owner. Oh, the truths should never have been.

"Ah, yes, my lord," Gideon replied, remaining perfectly composed even as he heard a sharp intake of breath from Justine. The young lady had stayed. A pity she had overheard his master's ramblings. "I shall leave you now. The lady of the house is here to see to your needs. Rest well, my lord."

Justine watched the old servant glide from the room. Was he not nearly sixty, if not closer to seventy? Yet his gait could have been one of a younger man. She felt her own body weaken as the tension, the anxiety, and the panic finally eased.

What had she married? What type of family? What type of legacy was her unborn child to inherit? Had her husband just confessed to murder? Justine felt faint. Ill. Useless and pitiful. Emotions churned within, shifting and changing as she tried to comprehend what her husband had uttered. Gideon had not reacted nor responded in an alarmed way; the old servant was quite neutral. No, not neutral. The old servant had been lax in his response to his master's words. This was not something new to the old man. It was not something new.

It was this realization that sent chills throughout her body and had Justine kneeling on the ground for longer than she had intended, longer than she realized. Her feet had gone numb, her legs tingling.

"Water." It was a single word, a command rather than a request.

"Yes, my lord," Justine replied promptly.

Justine realized Gideon had returned when she turned to get water for her husband. Gideon stood in the shadows of the room, quietly attentive to both master and mistress but offering no assistance unless spoken for. Where had such a servant learned this level of diligence? She had asked the other staff and gathered tidbits of responses, all revealing a snippet of detail: Gideon had been in service of the Geoffrey family for over thirty years. He had lived his youth and his best years as a servant for the old master. Gideon had stayed on during the death and inheritance transferring ownership and lordship on to Henri.

Gideon knew things others did not—knowledge Justine wanted to understand.

"Gideon, that will be all," Justine said.

"Yes, my lady," Gideon replied and let himself out with a gentle click of the door behind him.

"It is not your place to dismiss Gideon, wife." It was a petulant voice, pained and irritable.

"Contrary to what you may believe, my lord, I am in a place of authority within this household. You seek to keep me powerless, isolated even, but the staff take heed of what I say, although I seldom speak." She caught herself, demurring backward as if in deference of his authority, when truly, she sought to protect the servants who had sought her advice, sought to please her on minute details of the running of the house.

"It looks right on you," Henri murmured.

"What does, my lord?"

"Confidence. Confidence looks right on you," he repeated. Exhausted now, Henri felt the throbbing between his eyes as he touched the side of his head.

There was not much else to say or any further actions to take between them. Despite this, Henri hesitated in dismissing his wife. The beautiful young woman standing before him had changed. She had shifted from the fragile and malleable maiden he had first met. What was he to do with her? Had pregnancy altered her such a great deal? No, it was not the pregnancy, not altogether. Henri knew what had changed her, what had altered her.

Henri felt the same as he had when he first began to court her. When he first began to seek out information about her, her family, and her upbringing. There was no doubt she was of impeccable stock—meaning her line was free from scandal. It was imperative nothing might mar the birth of his heir. Thus, the knowledge his wife had witlessly stumbled upon about his brother's . . . torrid affairs was a gash.

"How have the renovations come along for the nursery and the blue parlor?" The sudden inquiry startled Justine into an upright position. Henri glanced away from her to look across the expanse of the room, his gaze drawn outward to the gardens. They were barren, the branches lacking any blossoms or leaves.

Justine felt her stomach become unsettled, nausea once more burning the back of her throat. Where was the flask of water? She spotted it and quickly moved away from her husband and poured herself a glass, then sipped it. It eased only a little of the burning, the continuous burning. Was it to leave a scar, a constant pressure in the back of her throat?

The burn in her throat felt like the ache of guilt, of shame, of complicated matters. Unspoken matters. The knowledge of who her brother-in-law was, what possessed his mind . . . Was that what was truly burning the back of her throat? So then why was she irritated when her husband asked about decorations and renovations?

Trivial matters, womanly matters. Things not otherwise occupying the thoughts of her husband until he wanted to keep up with his wife and what might assist her in keeping busy. Busy meant she could not examine the dangerous waters surrounding Michel, surrounding the servants in a shroud, and kept the demons hidden behind a veil. Henri maintained such a delicate balance, such a delicate thing, this veil, that held his family together.

"I have drawn a few sketches," she whispered, "but I have lacked the ambition to travel to the shops. My energy has been lacking these last few weeks. The doctor says it is a positive sign." She added the last bit when she saw her husband rouse, as if concern might enliven him again.

"You need to rest. Will you stay with me awhile?" Henri surprised them both with the request and even further with the depth of emotion those words were tangled in, drowning in.

"I—Yes, yes, I will stay."

And so, Henri moved himself out of the center of his bed and reclined back against the headboard, his gaze fixated on his wife as she stood rooted to the floor, her body language giving off uncertainty. He cleared his throat and looked down at his hands, suddenly feeling unsure about his own impulsive request for her to stay with him. Only for a while. Not for the night. Why was this so awkward of him to ask of his wife? His wife was still a stranger to him. However, she was carrying his child, his heir.

Justine hesitated for a few moments, weighing every potential outcome, every option laid out before her even as she had already verbally confirmed she was to stay. Would he chase her if she fled? This unexpected request had sent her already frayed nerves into a frenzy, whirling round and round in her head. Despite this internal confusion, Justine was soon resting beside her husband with her hands folded demurely across her slightly rounded stomach. Her gaze was locked on the mural painted above the bed.

They were as still and as quiet as two corpses with a chill settled between them. Justine could not forget the brief glimpses her husband had shown her by mentioning Elisabeth's name. It was not the first time she had heard the name whispered from Geoffrey lips. Michel had been the first to say it aloud to her and now Henri. Who was Elisabeth? A sister? Throughout the years, the Geoffrey brothers had remained the prime bachelors. There had never been whispers of a sister—wed or unwed, younger or older.

Justine could only presume Elisabeth was dead. She could only work to put the pieces together for so long before exhaustion began to creep along her limbs and became a heavy weight in her chest. Complete exhaustion.

Since Justine had witnessed Michel and Annabelle, tonight was to be the first night she slept peacefully. No nightmares. No fits. Even as her mind wandered into the fear that Henri might attempt to harm her as the shadows of his previous anger flashed through her mind's eye. Before Justine could fall asleep, it felt like an eternity had passed. Henri tracked the time. It was mere minutes before his wife was breathing slowly and evenly, her features softening in the dimly lit room.

Why had she come? Henri was ashamed his wife had seen that side of him. Gideon had been the only one aware of these demons, these guilty emotions still clinging to him.

Percy was aware of his nightmares during their childhood and youth, but Henri had feigned they had ceased. Could he trust Justine to keep this information to herself? *Yes.* The answer came without hesitation.

There was no deep love story between them. There never would be, and he was the one who had manufactured their relationship to be this way. He had been violent toward her, angry and hurtful both physically and emotionally. He felt no guilt, no shame as he recollected those early nights when she had been utterly alone in her rooms. It had proved Justine was trustworthy, as she had not written to her old guardian to complain. Why? Henri reached out and traced the delicate jawline of his sleeping wife, the mother of his future, of his unborn child. The cost to keep her protected was going to be a high one, and he did not think he could pay it.

Michel had to be kept in check.

Percy had to be kept away.

Justine had to be hidden back in the shadows, returned to the darkness of naïveté. Was it possible? She had been exposed to far too many of the secrets within the Geoffrey home. The ghosts were dancing along the corners of the room, and Henri felt their stares, their judgment.

"You will not possess her, Mother. You will not touch her, Father." Henri was mumbling as he stared off into the darkness, his hand resting on Justine's shoulder as he stared and stared. "Elisabeth, you would have loved her. I think she could have been the sister you always desired. She would have been better to you than I could have ever been. I am sorry, Elisabeth."

Justine had woken enough to hear his apology to Elisabeth, but she kept her eyes closed. She kept her breathing calm as tears pricked her beneath her closed eyelids.

September 1791

Maybe I have misunderstood my husband? Maybe I have judged him too harshly?

No. I need to keep my unborn child safe. Safe from Michel.

-Justine Geoffrey

CHAPTER NINETEEN
You Are My Sacrifice

PERCY HAD CONVINCED HERSELF JUSTINE WAS a witch, a wicked sorceress who had stolen Henri from her. How else could Henri so suddenly, so savagely turn his affection from her to this other woman? He had not spoken about the woman ever throughout their time together. It was as if their years as childhood companions and adolescent love had never existed. Percy felt herself forgotten, cast aside as if she were a used and tarnished doll. *I am better than this. I know I am!*

This was the second encounter Justine had had with Percy. The first had been a few days before, during a passing introduction made by her husband. Henri had been dismissive of the other woman; thus, Justine had not given Percy a second thought. Not until this morning.

Justine had sat down in the dining room with the expectation of having another breakfast alone. The solitude was no longer bothersome to her, as it had provided an opportunity for her to reflect on her life as a married woman.

"Henri is my husband, Miss Brough. What do you mean I am to leave him alone?" Justine was utterly confused by the confrontation she was now facing. Who was this woman to cause drama and conflict within *her* home? This other woman was claiming Henri as hers, and apparently nothing else mattered—not marital vows or the hundreds of witnesses or the God-fearing bond she, Justine Geoffrey, was now bound by.

What else could there be to say?

Percy shook her head to clear her thoughts; she must have misheard the witch. *What do you mean I am to leave him alone? Henri is my husband . . .*

"No!" came the scream. Percy barely kept herself in check. Her impulse was to lunge toward the witch before her with an urge to scratch out her eyes and mar her flesh. "Henri is mine! He has always been mine. We were promised to one another at a young age—"

"Miss Brough, you are incorrect in this. Otherwise, Henri and I could have never been married within the walls of the church, nor could our engagement have been publicly declared. Henri was not promised to anyone prior to our engagement and our subsequent marriage."

More words! Percy felt tears pricking beneath her eyelids as she shook her head back and forth, back and forth. Why was this witch speaking more words, more falsehoods? Henri had promised to marry her. Many, many years ago, but the words *had* been uttered between them. There could be nothing more clear-cut than the exchange the two youths had whispered. Of love, of cherishing, of protecting.

Percy Brough was twenty-six, and she felt utterly hopeless in her love for Henri. He was everything to her, and he had always been everything to her. There had been conflicts, and there had been joy. Such was life! She was capable of gifting Henri with laughter, with love, and with tears. Who was this witch to say otherwise? Percy was the one meant to make Henri happy. Percy was meant to be the one for Henri! The woman standing before her was a witch, a lying and conniving witch.

"You do not know Henri as I do. And you never will, wife or not. I have his heart and his mind," Percy loudly declared, unable to hold her temper.

Justine controlled her own flaring emotions as she took in a slow breath and counted to ten within her mind. There was the familiar acid burn rising along the back of her throat, burning, burning, burning. Slowly, she exhaled and focused on inhaling again. What more could she say to this delusional woman? There had been women before her, Justine knew; she was no longer a naïve bride. She had aged tenfold in the months following her marriage into the Geoffrey household. Nothing more could be said, yet she did not want to allow Percy Brough to keep the upper hand in this argument.

"Henri made a vow, an oath before man and God. He is my husband and I, his wife. Nothing else can be held in higher esteem than that." Justine spoke calmly, trying her very best to keep a monotone as she said the truth. Blunt. Trying to reason with Percy.

But there was no reasoning. There was no logical approach.

Percy closed her eyes. And she screamed, louder and louder, until her throat began to burn. Her hands tangled into her hair as she shook her head. "I am the one who loves Henri Geoffrey! Not you, not Annabelle, not Elisa—" A look of panic flashed across her face, but there was no taking back the names she had spoken aloud. Percy had to remind herself that Justine was not supposed to be told the names. Not on repeat. Not within this house. Those names were not supposed to be said within the Geoffrey home.

"What do you mean?" Justine asked.

"Nothing! You mean nothing to Henri. That is what I meant to say," Percy tried to correct herself and ignored the truth of what she had uttered.

"No, you meant something more. You intended to hurt me by saying the names. Annabelle and Elisa-who? Elisa*beth*?"

"Stop it. Do not say those names again! If Henri or Michel were to hear them said aloud in this house, there would be hell to pay. I cannot fall any further out of their favor. I cannot fall any lower in their eyes. You have already ruined so much!" Percy spat, each word said more angrily.

"I have heard the rumors about Henri and Annabelle. I have not heard any about Henri and Elisabeth. Why did you say those names to me only to recant them seconds later?"

"Be quiet!" Percy cried.

"Annabelle. Elisabeth. Who are they to you?" Justine persisted.

What more could be said? Percy had already violated the pact the three of them had made: she, Henri, and Michel. Her focus was the terror mainly derived from the pact between her and Michel—a pact Henri remained ignorant of. There was not going to be any forgive-and-forget if Justine kept saying these names on repeat like the chimes of church bells.

"No one. They are no one to me, just as they are no one to you. I only meant to warn you that Henri is mine and mine alone. You may be his wife, but I am his love. I am the only one who could ever make him smile in the dark years. You will be forgotten." Just as all the others had been forgotten, while Percy remained. Faithful and true, as true as a young woman in love and in pain could be.

What more could there be? A husband and a wife, a man and an old flame. Justine frowned as she looked across the dining room at Percy, almost pitying her, as there was nothing else to be said. Justine had repeated the same thing twice, perhaps three times by now, and Percy was only getting more and more agitated. Justine was beginning to lose control of her own temper, and her calmness was evaporating as swiftly as the morning mist under the rising sun.

"You are of the past, Miss Brough. You are not in the future of this house nor of my husband. I will ask you this once and only once: leave my home and do not speak to me in such an aggressive manner again." Each word was clipped and enunciated with a simmering anger. Justine was taken aback by the look of pure hatred and spite Percy shot at her.

"You are a witch! A foul creature of hell to crawl into the bed of my Henri and taint his love for me!" Percy screeched. It felt as if the Furies were propelling her forward with a swift justice.

There was a blurring of hair, a flashing of eyes, and a contact of nails on flesh. Both women howled on impact, one out of rage and the other out of astonishment. They both felt the floorboards as they fell down, down, down. It was faster than either had anticipated, and there was a sensation of igniting a flame. All the confusion, all the frustration, all the fears came pouring forward through the floodgates of Justine's mind as she stared up at Percy above her. She felt the other woman's fingers trying to curl around her throat, and she began to fight back.

"Get off of me!"

"You do not belong with Henri! You do not belong here at all!" Percy yelled.

Their skirts fluttered around them, chaotic yet yielding, the fabrics tangling legs and arms in the unfolding fray. It was not a quiet skirmish, but it seemed to draw on for far too long as each woman endured flashes of pain and labored breathing. It must have been an hour, thought Justine, as she made continual efforts to deny Percy contact with her throat, with her eyes, or with her face.

"ENOUGH!" came a booming voice so loud it rattled the fight-or-flight daze both women were held fast in. Four eyes blinked and gazed upward to the silhouette of a man in the doorway. It was Percy who first responded with a hasty retreat from being above Justine. It was Percy who began to babble some maimed excuse for their tussle.

"I do not care, Percy Brough, about the reasoning behind this pathetic display of temper," came the terse reply.

Percy cowered and fell backward into a chair not so far from where she and Justine had just been fighting. Her hands were scraped and bruising, tender as she folded them across her lap. "I do apologize for the disruption, Gideon. Please do not report this to Henri."

"I am required to, Percy Brough, as the mistress is with child. I would not be fulfilling my duty to my master if I did not report this incident to him." Gideon spoke calmly, each of his words having a visual effect on Percy. Her expression changed to one of dismay. Her shoulders began to slump forward, curling into herself.

Justine was still on the floorboards with her hands just now falling to cover her eyes. Her breathing was still ragged and her emotions too raw. Why had Gideon revealed her pregnancy to this mad woman? Had he not just witnessed this scene?

Gideon cleared his throat and took a few short steps in the direction of his mistress, his hand extended out. "Mistress, if you will, please be seated in the chair. Percy, remove yourself from this room, and if you are wise, you will remove yourself to the gardens until the moon rises this night."

Percy was gone. No further sounds came from her as she fled from the room as a criminal might from the scene of a crime.

"T-Thank you, Gideon," Justine uttered aloud, her voice hoarse as her stiff body rotated from floor to chair.

"You do not need to forgive Miss Brough, Mistress, but have pity for her. She is a lost soul without a home or a family of her own. This house has been her sanctuary and her prison the last two decades," Gideon explained.

"There is more beneath the surface of what you are saying, is there not?"

"Yes, Mistress, there is more."

"Will you not enlighten me since her wretched soul has caused me to bleed?" Justine whispered as she felt the back of her head, her fingertips returning red.

Gideon took in a slow breath as he weighed the secret he had held on to for so long. It was only one secret among thousands floating through his mind. Loyalty hindered his mouth from opening again. Instead, his eyes closed, and he paused to think before opening them and replying. "Mistress, it is most advisable that you do not ask about such matters again. I am not at liberty to tell. Please understand I do this out of respect for our master."

There was a warmth in Gideon's eyes she had not seen there before. Justine tilted her head to the side and then relinquished the subject for another time. What more could she say? What more could she do? The obvious answer was to call for the doctor to check the bleeding wound on the back of her head. The other answer was to seek out her husband and ask him for clarification, for answers. Neither option appealed to her. But Justine knew she had to take care of herself, if only for the sake of her child.

One for the nightmare and two for the seer, three for the maiden, and four for the fear . . .

December 1971

Annabelle, I love you.

You are better than any woman I have ever known. Our time together will be an eternity. I do not think that will be enough for me. ~~I loved you with everything.~~

I love you with everything.

-M.L.G.

CHAPTER TWENTY

I AM NOT YOUR MOUTHPIECE

WHERE DO YOU SEE US IN FIVE YEARS, Henri?" Percy whispered into the darkness. It was a quiet night because the servants had been dismissed earlier in the day. Five years was nothing compared to the decades between them, yet asking such a question felt intrusive. Percy felt as if she'd overstepped some unknown boundary. No, not unknown. The boundary had been identified the moment he swore to be faithful, to be loyal to the witch . . .

Why was he being so distant? Why was he making her feel as though her presence—her entire existence—was now a burden? It was truly unfair just how quickly, how easily he'd changed.

Percy was pouting into the darkness when there was a sudden onslaught of light as a flame took in the fireplace. It illuminated the entire room within seconds and momentarily blinded her.

Henri continued to kneel by the hearth. His silhouette was dark as her eyes adjusted to the brightness of the fire, but the silence continued. The silence from him was too much. Torturous, this silence was torturous, and he was fully aware. Percy should have felt enraged, perhaps even irritable because of how callous he was toward her feelings, the time she had invested in him. Yet she did not.

"Henri . . . do you know your wife has been meddling? She's asking me questions," Percy said.

"Yes. I am aware, as I am also aware you have had some public tantrums about her in the presence of our society."

"Oh, I have nothing to say in my own defense."

Henri looked over at Percy, but his eyes were shadows, pits of darkness where there should've been a soul, there should've been emotion. This frightened her. Percy felt a shiver form at the base of her spine, and it jerked up her back. Jagged and sharp.

"You are a guest in my home, a guest in my life. You are not entitled to judgment or to speak harshly about my wife. Percy, you will be on dangerous ground if you continue this way," Henri said.

"I *am* your life! You are a piece of me, just as I am a piece of you!" Percy shouted back. Her feelings were hurt, and the wound felt deep, deeper than ever before, and she could not identify why. She could not understand why he was saying this to her. She could not understand why he was so harsh right now. What had she done wrong? She spoke ill about his wife's temper at a tea party with a few key ladies of society.

It should've been Justine who was receiving such a scolding from Henri, not her!

Percy reached out her hand to touch his cheek, but it turned out that she slapped him. The sound of impact resounded in her ears.

"Oh!" She gasped.

"We have an irreplaceable history, which is a vulnerability in my life. My wife is my priority. Second comes Michel and then the staff of my household. You are not my wife, you are not my sister, and you are not my servant. You are my childhood friend, a symbol that needs to be locked and hidden away," Henri said each word clipped and final.

"Oh, Henri! Henri do not say such a thing! I am yours, as you are mine. We have each other, and no one else in this world could possibly understand. Not Michel, not Justine, not Annabelle . . ." As soon as she said the name, Percy understood her mistake.

It was not to be thrown back at her in a verbal confrontation. It was simply not to be acknowledged. This quiet was worse than any argument they might have. The effectiveness of Henri's calm was disheartening to Percy as she tried to calculate what to say next, what to do next. What action could she take to show him how much she adored him? How could she demonstrate how captivated she was with him? This rejection was not possible; it simply made no sense.

They were childhood sweethearts. They shared secrets and shadows no one else could possibly understand. The shadows were far too dark, far too sinister for someone as superficial and frivolous as Justine to comprehend. Their depths were deep, deeper than the ocean.

So lost in the waves of thought in her own mind, Percy did not notice the door to the study open and close. She did not notice there was someone else in the room sitting beside Henri. She did not notice there was another individual sitting on the floor in front of the fireplace. It took her a few minutes to return to reality, and then it took longer for her to understand Henri had allowed Michel and Justine to join them.

The betrayal cut deep into an old scar she had forgotten existed. Oh, it hurt in a way she had not felt in nearly a decade. An ache of true and absolute rejection. What more could she do?

A different conversation was taking place, her own words seeming to have not been said at all. Henri did not seem perturbed in any way. Did he truly have no attachment, no sentiment for her?

"Michel, you need to be married to silence the whispers about your character. It is no longer a passing observation. It is becoming an obsession of society to speculate and to observe you—and through you, our family," Henri said.

"Who will I marry, brother? My prime choice of bride has disappeared, and my other choices seem rather minuscule with people whispering about me. So, I ask again—who will I marry?" Michel replied.

Percy puckered her lips. Why were they discussing Michel getting married? It made no sense. Henri's wife was expecting a child, a potential heir for the Geoffrey legacy. Although Percy knew *she* should have been the one carrying Henri's heir in her belly. She should have been his wife . . .

"You will marry Miss Brough," Henri said.

The silence that fell over the room was heavy, as dark and heavy as a looming storm might be moments before it unleashed its torrential rainfall. Percy must have heard wrong, as she could not believe her former love, her childhood companion, might seek to marry her off to his brother. What was this? They seemed to have forgotten she was in the room, forgotten she had a voice. Her, Percy Brough, to marry Michel?

"Hmm, it seems a reasonable offer, but what does she offer me, brother? She was a ward of our dearly departed father. She was a—she was left an orphan by the civil wars. What does she offer me?" Michel repeated.

Percy was offended. Or was she? It was common knowledge that her father had been "taken in" by the late Lord Geoffrey as the two had a history together, both having served during the civil wars a decade or so before. There had been old rumors circling around the exact circumstances that had landed Mr. Brough in service to the Geoffrey family, but those rumors had fallen on deaf ears.

Percy Brough had been a companion, a playmate for the Geoffrey children. The history was odd, the friendships misjudged, but these were nonissues. The issue had come when Percy took to loving one brother over the other, as could happen when children grew. There was a loneliness, a deep chasm within her chest, she felt even as the playmate of the Geoffrey children. Percy Brough did not belong in the Geoffrey family; this was a thought she had developed on her own many, many years prior to this evening.

So why was she offended when Michel questioned her ability to provide something to whoever she was to wed? This question remained unanswered as she took a hasty step forward, reminding the other three she remained in the room. "If I am to marry, should I not have a word in?" Percy dared to ask. Her voice was rather weak, even to her own ears.

"You remain a ward of the Geoffrey family, of me as the head of this family, until you marry. No, you do not have a say in who or when you marry. You lack a dowry. You lack a family name," Henri answered her, his gaze never leaving Michel.

"You offer me an orphan when I could have had a countess? You mock me," Michel said.

"No, it is you and your behavior that is the mockery. Michel, you are tarnishing our family's name, and that is unforgivable. Redeem yourself, in society and in my eyes, by settling into wedded bliss." A pause as his gaze briefly flickered over to his own wife. "And start your own family. You will have a substantial annual allowance."

"You speak as if I have no other option, brother."

"There is one: your omission from this family."

"Harsh, Henri, to threaten your only brother with negligence," Michel snapped.

"Not negligence. If you do not marry and consummate your marriage to Percy Brough, you are dead to me, dead to this family," Henri replied.

"You . . . you do not mean it. You cannot mean it."

"If you do not wed, you are forbidden from this house and any Geoffrey home. Your name will not be spoken by our lips. I will grieve for you. I will mark your grave in the countryside." Henri spoke in a monotonous voice, his expression blank and his eyes an abyss. Empty and dark.

Michel reeled backward as if he had been dealt a physical blow, his head swiveling around as he tried to see something, anything he could use as a marker, a focal point. There was nothing, as these rooms were not familiar, not anymore since they had been recently renovated. Because they were no longer children, because their father was no longer alive. There was nothing to focus on . . . there was nothing to focus on. Panic surged through his veins as powerful as a tsunami, sudden and overwhelming.

There was nothing left to say, or so Henri felt as he watched the change of expression on his brother's face. The emotions were tumultuous as they weaved through Michel's mind.

Henri stared at his younger sibling, his own thoughts churning in agitation that it had come this far. Why could Michel not understand his behaviors cast shadows across their entire family? Why could Michel not understand Justine was *his* wife, just as Annabelle had been *his*?

"Michel, marriage is a contract. If it assists this family in moving forward to prosper, why not get married to Miss

Brough? She is no stranger to you, and she is no old hag either." Justine spoke in a soft voice, diffusing the tension with a splash of charming logic, a cognition that otherwise would not have been laid out.

"Ah, ah, I see. If I am going to be forced to marry, it may as well be to Percy. There is no harm in marrying Percy because she is a puppet, just as I am a puppet. And the puppeteer maintains control of our strings," Michel said.

Henri felt rage.

Michel felt nothing.

Percy felt betrayed.

Justine felt relief, immense relief.

"I will marry Percy. But do not expect any heirs from our union, for there will be none. I would not curse this world with another of me, another of our bloodline," Michel acquiesced. "The weight of continuing the Geoffrey legacy is upon your shoulders, my brother and his darling wife. You are burdened, whereas I am free."

Justine instinctively spread her fingertips across her rounded belly as she looked across at her husband, then to her brother-in-law. It was curious, the way he had said it . . . It was frightening the way his eyes lit up. The macabre look flickered across his face as they locked gazes.

December 1791

It has been a year since Annabelle died. By my hand? I am still uncertain about the way she died. My hands were holding the glass. Her throat had been slashed. A year. I am married. I am to become a father soon. I am to be a father.

That simple statement is something I am afraid of. I am afraid of failing my child. I am afraid of my child dying. I am afraid of my brother harming my child. I am afraid of harming my child with my own hands.

What kind of monster forgets committing murder?

What father hoards ghouls and skeletons in his closets? My father did. I suppose that makes the phrase true—that the apple does not fall far from the tree.

-H.L.G.

CHAPTER TWENTY-ONE
May the Demons Keep Your Soul

IT WAS NOT MORAL TO ALLOW PERCY TO MARRY Michel without her knowing about his mangled and tarnished mind. This was how Justine felt. Thus, she felt obligated to speak with the other woman in a more intimate manner, and she did not trust Henri be supportive. On the eve of talking with Percy, Justine had planned another confrontation with Michel about seeking holy intervention for his sins. Could his wicked acts be cleansed from his soul, or was he doomed for the fires of hell? Her hand went in the motion of the cross as she whispered a prayer beneath her breath.

One step, two steps, three steps, four. Justine was trying to remember the doorway to her brother-in-law's library, as it was a little alcove of a semi-hidden room. At last, she found the door and knocked on it three times. As her knuckles were about to wrap on the door a fourth time, it quickly swung open, and fingers curled around her wrist. A yank and she was pulled into the dimly lit room. The door closed behind her, and there was a silence, a quiet, a peace that had settled around her.

"What do you want, Justine? Henri forbade me from being alone with you, so why are you seeking me out?" Michel whispered into her ear as he walked around her. Each step was slow, deliberate, predatory, until he was standing in front of her with his gaze narrowed by a frown.

"I need you to treat Miss Brough with respect. She is going to be your wife, and she deserves your loyalty and your name to protect her. You cannot abandon her."

"Who are you to dictate how I behave toward my betrothed?"

"Do not play the fool, Michel. I am aware Henri has made higher demands of you when it comes to this marriage, and the announcement of the betrothal will happen soon," Justine muttered, already exhausted.

"Ah, yes. The betrothal is to be announced before you go into confinement for Henri's child." Michel stared down at the rounded protruding stomach of his sister-in-law and made a *tsk* noise. Dismissive.

Instinctively, her hands curved around her stomach, but Justine did not back down beneath the malicious glare. It no longer chilled her blood as it once had. There was more at stake now, as evidenced by the firm kicks she felt against her palms.

"Do well for your family, Michel. For Henri." It was all she needed to say. Then Justine pivoted around on her heels and left the room. Michel stared at the open doorway with his mouth agape, in disbelief at how his sister-in-law had sharpened her claws.

Why had Justine wasted her energy to speak with Michel when nothing about him had changed? If anything, he seemed more insolent. Her heart felt a familiar ache, an ache of heartbreak over what her husband and his brother were. The toxic environment her child was going to be born into. As if to comfort her, the child gave an aggressive kick that caught her breath and made Justine stumble against the wall. One hand pressed against the wall for support, and the other pressed into her stomach.

Her child was going to have a better life. A strong future. But for her child to have a strong future and a better life, this home required healing. A healing of the relationships between the people who coexisted beneath this roof. How could this happen if Michel held her in utter disdain and Percy accused her of stealing Henri? Justine was determined, and this determination was to be her downfall.

If the truth were to be said aloud, there was no safety within the labyrinth of the Geoffrey household. There were pitfalls and snares, corners marked with the blood of sacrificial lambs. Justine still attempted to understand her husband and his family. She still tried to offer a shroud of peace and of understanding. Her heart, bloodied and bruised as it was, still sought to be a tourniquet. One capable of saving the lifeblood of this family.

Justine did not give a second thought to Michel as she walked down the hallway, turning left and then right. It was difficult to go upstairs these days, but she was hell-bent on making it up two flights to be able to speak with Percy. If this conversation happened in Percy's own rooms, the other woman might feel safe, with the advantage of being in her own quarters. Alas, this plan was not to be followed through, as Justine narrowly missed colliding with Percy rounding the corner of the staircase.

"Why are you on this end of the house?" Percy asked in a hiss.

"I came to seek a truce, Percy."

"Why?"

"You are to become my sister through marriage. We will become family soon, and so I owe you the power of knowledge and foresight into your future husband."

"Oh, you are self-righteous!" Percy exclaimed.

"Percy, humor me."

The two women had not been alone since they'd fought a few weeks prior. Justine had just finally healed a day or so before she had this sudden urgency to warn the other woman. Justine knew Michel had hidden his monstrous shadows and skeletons from the world, from his brother . . . No, maybe not from his brother.

"Very well. Speak," Percy said.

Justine blinked at the abrupt acceptance of the other woman, and it took her a few moments to collect her thoughts. Was this the appropriate place to have such a weighted conversation? She looked down the stairs below her and then to the ones higher above Percy. It was a private part of the property, and servants would not be caught lurking around the Brough woman, as she was not seen as a notable person in the household.

"Michel is a murderer and worse," Justine began after taking in a deep breath. She felt a sharp and sudden pain shoot across her stomach. It settled near her lower back, and there it lingered. "I discovered him with . . . He has an unnatural desire for the dead."

A sound followed, and it was not what Justine had expected. What had she expected? A gasp of horror? An exclamation of gratitude? No, not exactly. But the last thing she had expected was the sound of laughter.

"I have lived with this knowledge my whole life! Both brothers are damned! Their father was worse, far worse," Percy whispered between the pealing laughter. She could not help but to laugh and laugh and laugh. Was this insight from the other woman supposed to frighten her? Was it supposed to save her? Percy found the humor, and she held fast to it. Otherwise, she was lost.

An audible gasp and Justine staggered backward, her legs barely holding her weight as she focused on steadying herself. Her hands reached for the wall, and her fingertips met stone. Why was Percy laughing in her face? Why was she not repulsed? Why was not she not shocked? It took a few seconds for the reality of Percy's words to slither into the darkening clouds of her mind. Michel Geoffrey was a monster, but he was better than his father had been.

Justine felt her thoughts churning over and over as she tried to dig her fingers into the stone wall of the staircase. She still felt unsteady. What had her husband endured? If

Michel was a necrophiliac because of their father . . . what lurked in her husband's mind? What skeletons, what ghosts haunted his memories? Oh! There was a sharp pang in her stomach. It built and built as it wound its way to her lower back. Another gasp as she focused to hold herself steady and catch her breath. There was no relief, be it physical or mental, as waves of pain and nausea overwhelmed her.

"The old Lord Geoffrey used to throw parties, lavish and secretive. He would invite orphans from abroad and host them in the ballroom. None ever left alive. But he did not like them to be alive, not when he shared them with Henri and then with Michel. He hated women. Anything feminine he despised. Elisabeth was a miniature of her mother . . ." Percy had begun to ramble. Then the laughter erupted from her again and again.

Percy kept laughing but softly as her face began to contort with grief and dismay. All the years of trauma, of repressing memories and emotions, began to consume her. It was as if the floodgates had come tumbling, releasing the tears to begin trickling down her cheeks, yet still she continued to laugh. Laugh and laugh and laugh. Oblivious to the earth-shattering waves of pain beginning to overwhelm Justine. The women were mere feet apart on the staircase, and yet there was an ocean between them. An ocean of emotion, of pain, of suffering.

"I was kept alive because of my wardship. It was the only thing that kept me alive despite the Geoffrey brothers wanting me dead. Despite the old Lord Geoffrey tiring of me."

Percy's voice faded off as she stared blankly ahead of her, looking beyond Justine's shoulder.

Everything went quiet.

Justine could no longer feel the harsh stone beneath her fingertips, and she felt only air beneath her feet. Her throat constricted, and she could not scream. She could not breathe. She could only fall.

Down, down, down.

It felt as if a thousand heartbeats trickled by as she only felt air around her and the shushing as it tugged at her clothing, at her hair. Where was the wall? Where were the steps she had just climbed? Panic held her in a shell of silence even as her hands and arms wrapped around her stomach. Her baby!

There was only silence and then the sickening sound of impact as her body at last collided with the stone steps. It was a muffled crunch, the sound of a delicate creature meeting its demise at the claws of a hunter's snare. It was the mortifying moment of truth when she kept falling, down, down, down.

Percy was no longer laughing, and her eyes grew wider and wider as realization dawned. Justine was falling. The pregnant woman, the witch who had stolen her Henri . . . was falling. A gasp caught in her throat and threatened to choke her as her hand reached out for the empty air before her, where only seconds before Justine had been standing.

"Justine!" Percy yelled, her voice hoarse as she stumbled down the stairs after the falling woman, trying her best to not stumble and fall in her pursuit.

Justine fell down the entire flight of stairs, over thirty steps, in a downward spiral of silk, hair, and blood. The picture painted at the bottom of the stairs was horrific. There was blood on Justine's brow, as well as along her skirts.

"Oh, no, no, no! The baby . . . Henri's baby! Help! HELP!" Percy began to scream, louder and louder, as she stood over the still body of her lover's wife. He would never believe she was not to blame if the other woman were to miscarry after such a fall.

Justine heard the muffled screams of Percy, but she felt nothing, only a soft swirling beneath her head. Her eyes remained closed as she drifted in and out of consciousness, until finally the abyss took her away from the screams.

It was to this chaotic scene that Gideon walked in. There was no shock. There was no surprise. There was no judgment. He merely began to assess the situation. He remained stoic as he took Percy by the hand and pushed her through the nearby doorway into the kitchens and forced her to sit down at the table. He rang the bell for a servant but then went back to the crumpled form of his mistress. The red stain on her skirts had grown.

"You poor thing. At least it was not by the hands of your husband or by the hands of Michel. Not this time. Poor, poor dear," Gideon whispered as he knelt beside her, his leather-aged hands cradling the back of her neck as he heard more footsteps and more voices. Another scream, a shriek, and then more voices.

Questions, hundreds of questions all at once, but Gideon did not pay attention to any voice beyond the one of his master. At last, he heard the sound of footsteps that could only belong to Henri. When the scene went into silence again, Gideon knew the master of the house had arrived. There were no words uttered as the old man stood up and lifted the rag doll body of Justine into his arms. He followed his master up the stairs, cradling the poor broken girl.

They walked in complete silence, even into the master's bedroom, where Gideon put Justine down on the bed. Neither man cared about the expensive covering beneath the bleeding woman. Gideon then stepped back and nodded to his master.

"I will call the midwife and the doctor, my lord." It was all Gideon said. Then he clicked the door shut behind him and went off to speak with Percy, questioning and interrogating the shaking woman, no mercy, no sugarcoating. Henri would have been remorseless as an interrogator had he not been wrapped up in the unconscious state of his wife and soon-to-be mother of his unborn child.

The seconds continued to trickle on, turning to minutes, and then a half hour passed. Finally, there was a gentle knocking on the door, and it was opened from the exterior to reveal both doctor and midwife—the doctor, all too familiar with the Geoffrey home and its misfortune with women, and the midwife, doe-eyed and concerned only for the still figure of the pregnant woman. She was alarmed by the blood as it continued to seep into Justine's skirts, into the bedding.

"She fell down the stairs. I think she has been unconscious an hour, perhaps more. The bleeding has not slowed down. Please, do your work and do it well," came the monotonous words as Henri turned black, black eyes on both the doctor and the midwife.

Both nodded, but neither promised to save mother or child, as they knew to make such a promise could mean danger. The doctor had also been called because the head wound was extensive, but the priority was the bleeding continually flowing from between the young woman's thighs.

January 1792

Did you hear the news, Annabelle? Did you? Justine fell down the stairs on the eve of the New Year. She fell! I cannot contain my laughter as I remember the look on my brother's face, as I remember the look on the doctor's face as he left the makeshift birthing room. You might have been devastated on Henri's behalf . . .

I caught Percy earlier. She was blubbering about being the reason that Justine fell. Percy was a mess. Percy continues to be a mess. Grotesquely crying and blubbering on and on and on. Something about telling Justine the truth. Something about that being the reason she fell. It makes no sense. None of it does.

I want her to die.

I want her to die and to never be seen in this house, in our house, again. Annabelle, you should be the only woman in this house. You should be the Lady Annabelle Geoffrey. And I should be the Lord Michel Geoffrey. My brother and his wife should not be here. They should not be in the way.

I don't know what to do.

-M.L.G.

CHAPTER TWENTY-TWO
YOU FOUGHT SO VALIANTLY, ALL IN VAIN

THERE WAS A HEAVINESS, A FOG OF SILENCE blanketed over the Geoffrey house. None of the servants dared to speak; no one dared to even say a prayer aloud for their mistress, as they feared the wrath of the Geoffrey brothers or even the rage of Gideon. There was a sense of hopelessness—an emotion not familiar to those new to the house, but to those seasoned Geoffrey servants, this was only a broken record, a repeat of the history of this family.

A decade before, it had been a young girl, and a little over two decades before, it had been the mother of Michel. Every night since the marriage of Lord Henri and Lady Justine, there had been screams of rage, screams of terror and pain. Screams they had all been ordered to ignore.

Ignore. Silence. What more could they do but obey? They had families to feed and little ones to clothe. They needed to keep their postings; otherwise, they might become destitute, left without a reference and thus without a future. Thus, they ignored and they held their silence. It was this code of conduct within the Geoffrey household that helped keep the Geoffrey secrets hidden, as the servants did not even dare to whisper the truth to each other. There was too much at stake, and they both feared and revered Gideon, the elderly butler who ran the household staff with an iron fist. He was firm but fair.

While the entire Geoffrey staff and halls were eerily quiet, there was one room filled with a raging fire, and it stank of blood, of fear, of sorrow. There was no peace, and there was no quiet in this room as people moved about in a chaotic pattern.

"My lord, I cannot do more for her pain, but her strength is beginning to fail. It is a miracle she woke up at all, but now she feels it all," the midwife was saying into the ear of Henri as his eyes stared at the writhing figure of his wife. He felt every scream. He clenched his jaw and forced himself not to throw an object at the useless midwife.

The doctor was watching Henri and the midwife from the bedside. What more could Henri expect them to do? The baby was not ready to be born, but the mother's body was expelling the child. It was a fight of life. A fight the mother seemed to be losing as her skin grew damp, a contrast to the fever burning her brow. This labor was made more difficult because it had been induced by a wicked fall three days prior.

Three days of labor. Three days on continuous waves of pain, surging and frothing about Justine's body as it tore itself apart. Where was she? Justine could not orient herself through the fog of pain and exhaustion as she heard the muffled drowned-out voices of those around her. It was the same three, maybe four voices she had been hearing the last few hours, or had it been days?

"Oh," she whimpered, twisting her face into the damp pillow to stifle her scream. It was another contraction. They were coming closer and closer together. Stronger and stronger.

There was a soft touch to her cheek as her eyelids remained closed, her entire being beyond exhaustion, beyond fatigue. There was more pain to come. It only seemed to dull in minimal increments at this point. The baby should be born soon. Justine so badly wanted to speak, to ask questions about her baby and if she was going to be able to complete this birth. Yet her voice was lost as her body seemed to both assist and fight against the labor.

It was Henri who spoke for her, who advocated for the midwife to give the laboring mother a stronger tonic to numb the pain further. The doctor spoke in whispers with the midwife, and they both shook their heads, dismayed. But then there was a piercing scream as Justine hoisted herself up on her elbows, tucking her chin into her chest, and she began to push. The midwife was the first to instinctively get into place as she whispered prayers for the safekeeping of both mother and unborn child.

"Focus on your breathing, my lady, focus on your breathing," said the midwife. There was worry written into the furrowed brow, into the hunched shoulders of the older woman's posture.

Minutes continued to tick by, second by second, as the laboring woman screamed and screamed, her body depleting itself of energy as it fought against her efforts to expel the child from her womb. It was too early. It was a traumatic induction caused by the hard fall down the staircase. Minutes transformed into hours. Time did not seem to be in favor of the mother or her unborn child.

Hours were lost as Henri watched his wife fight wave after wave of pain. Her eyes were unfocused, and her brow had gone pale as she collapsed backward into the bed. Why was the doctor not doing anything to help her? Why was the midwife just standing there, worrying her hands in her apron? Something began to break within his mind as he stood rooted to the corner of the room, his fingertips going numb as he began to see red.

Henri was being informed he might have to make the choice between the life of the child or the life of his wife. Justine was no longer able to scream when the pains came. She was far too exhausted. All her energy had been long spent.

"Choose? You are telling me to choose?" Henri was exasperated as his voice broke through the tension of the room. There was nothing he could do. Was there truly nothing he could do?

There was little love in his heart for the body curled up on the bed before him. There was nothing he felt for her, but she was his wife and the mother of his unborn child. Henri heard nothing more of the words whispered by the midwife, nor did he heed the doctor as his hands covered his face. It was the loss of his stepmother all over again . . .

Blood was everywhere. On the floor, on the bedsheets, on the body of Justine. Was it even Justine? The woman reclining there seemed like a broken doll of shattered porcelain. A flash of memory returned him to the darkened room of ash and soot. It reeked of vomit, of sweat, of blood. Death had lingered in the room as a perfume. A curse to never leave his memory . . . Henri shook his head once, twice.

He had returned from the darkness of his own nightmares to stare down at the still body of his wife. He had to choose. It should have been a simple choice—the child. Since there was no love, no affection between Justine and him, it should have been a simple choice . . .

"Give me my child and the life of my wife, or else you are both dead before my wife's corpse is cold," Henri ordered.

An audible gasp as the midwife crossed herself before washing her hands and returning with a new fervor to comfort the unconscious woman before her. The doctor remained calm, as he had heard similar threats before, especially under this very roof. He blinked a few times to take measure of the young man before him.

"Yes, my lord," the doctor said at last.

The doctor and midwife toiled another few hours, each hour crawling by more slowly than the previous. There was too much blood. Her pulse was too erratic and fluttered too slowly. It had been such a terrible fall . . .

A shriek came from Justine as she birthed her child. After her shriek echoed into nothing, there was absolute silence. Utter and complete silence as the newborn did not stir. It did not breathe. It did not cry. There was no life. The doctor turned away from Justine to look at the dead, dead eyes of Henri. He opened his mouth to speak an offering of condolence but was hushed by the midwife as she coaxed Justine to continue to push.

A second shriek escaped the parched and cracked lips of Justine. Then, a second child was born. The silence stretched on as Justine curled into a fetal position and lost consciousness again. The silence was at last broken by the feeble cry of the second newborn. The midwife rushed the little body to a basin of warm water and cleansed it before wrapping it tight in a swaddling cloth.

The doctor was still quiet, as if spellbound. Twins? There had been no indication the woman had been carrying more than one child. The doctor held his peace and exited the room, leaving the mess and the cleanup to the midwife and female servants.

Henri took another few seconds to register the information. He had two children. One was silent, the other crying louder and louder.

"A lusty daughter, my lord," the midwife whispered as she held out the swaddled infant to him.

"And the other . . ." Henri whispered.

"May God have mercy on his little soul," the midwife replied with a shake of her head, her hand making the sign of the cross.

Henri felt the warmth of the little body placed into his hands through the layers of swaddling cloth. The warmth meant life. It meant life. He had two children, but only one had survived. What was he supposed to feel at this moment? His memory tried to recall what his father had done at the birth of Michel . . . and at the birth of Elisabeth. Silence was what enveloped his mind as his eyes lingered on the still form of his other child. Then the words the midwife had said became glaringly obvious. Two children, a son and a daughter. A lusty daughter and a silent son.

Was this a judgment sent down on him by God? There were numerous sins he had not sought forgiveness or reconciliation for. Just as there were countless skeletons hidden within the dark corners of his mind, hidden in the shadows of this home. An answer was beyond his reach, and so he let it drift away. It bothered him but not to the extent that he might pursue it. No, there was too much he had to do.

"Tend to my wife. See that she has every comfort you can give her," Henri ordered as he continued to hold his daughter.

"Yes, my lord," the midwife said as she turned away from him and focused the last of her energies on assisting the exhausted and still form of Justine. The fear of childbed fever or other such complications were savagely tearing through the midwife's mind as she slowly turned Justine left and then right, clearing the soiled sheets from beneath her and then grabbing a basin of room-temperature water to sponge away the drying blood.

The blood- and sweat-drenched sheets were discarded in the corner of the room and were quickly forgotten by the midwife, for she was certain a maid would see to their cleaning. Her focus was to see this young woman survive to see and hold her daughter. After such a labor and the loss of one child . . .

The blood loss had been too much. The fall . . . Would this woman survive to see the morning? It was a question unspoken by those in the room, lurking in the shadows and creeping along the floorboards. Again, the hours came and went with the ticking of the clock. *Ticktock, tick, tick, tock.*

Everything about her recovery was utterly unknown.

January 3, 1792

My daughter is born.

My son has died.

My wife continues to . . . be abed.

My daughter. I have a daughter. She is a little thing. She is a fragile thing.

Will she survive? I pray that she does. Do I believe in prayer? Do I believe that God will hear me? Do I believe in God? Not at all. But I do pray that my daughter survives the night. Why? I am a father, and she is mine to protect.

—H.L.G.

CHAPTER TWENTY-THREE
At What Cost?

WHAT MORE DO YOU WANT FROM ME?" Justine screamed into the frigid air, no one there to hear her. She screamed and screamed and screamed with the truth: her questions did not matter; her grief did not matter; none of it truly mattered. There was no sanctuary. There was no escape. And there was no absolution.

This house was her prison. This house was her casket. There was no one to hear her as she yelled and cried. The sorrow was too deep; it felt too powerful. It swelled higher and higher and came crashing down over her head, again and again. It was drowning her. There was no one, yet everyone was there. The eyes were open; the mouths were shut. And they heard nothing. They saw only what they were meant to see. They heard only what was meant to be heard.

Justine's anger did not bother them. Her sorrow did not bother them. Justine felt . . . she felt nothing. It had all slid away into the wintry air, drifting away as she collapsed against the windowpane. Someone had closed and locked it.

"Justine, come rest. Lay your head down. They will say prayers and bury the body. Lay your head down," came a murmur into her ear, a soft touch to her shoulder as she went limp.

"What is the cost, Henri? What further price must I pay?" Justine whimpered, exhausted.

Henri froze, his arms wrapped around her waist as her cheek nestled against his chest. There were no words he could surmise to speak aloud to her, as his own grief was constricting his throat, burning in his chest. A chasm had split his heart, the anguish pouring out and filling his entire being. Too much, too much, it had all become too much. There was no turning back. There was no turning around and seeing it all as a dream, as a nightmare. This was the truth. This was the absolute truth.

Is this grief what had driven his father into true madness? There had been whispers inside of Henri's own head as he grew from childhood and into the early days of his youth. The old Lord Geoffrey had made questionable choices, had taken actions bound to be set before God on Judgment Day. There was no reckoning in this life, but there had to have been justice in death.

"Lay your head down, my sweet. You need to rest or else I fear I may lose you too," Henri pleaded with her as he walked over to the canopied bed.

The servants had freshly changed the sheets, but the smell of blood still lingered. The stench of sweat clung to his wife. It did not bother him; it only served as a reminder.

"I want to hold him, Henri. I want to hold him." At last, she spoke in a strong voice. Although her body was still weak and she felt sick, Justine fought to keep her eyes open as she stared up at her husband. She saw her own grief reflected in his eyes. Tenderly, she reached up and curled her hand around his cheek.

"Let us hold him together, Henri. Then . . . we might say goodbye," she said, a little more softly this time as she turned her head toward the maid who held the silent bundle. Silence. After hours of anguish, of screaming, of burning pains . . . there had been silence when the baby was born.

Henri nodded toward the maid as he settled his wife down on the bed, as he curled around her diminished form and held out his arms for the covered baby. He felt his mouth work as he fought against his grief, as he felt the cool skin. So soft, so cold. The loss was too profound, too fresh. All at once, his sadness transformed into rage, and he sneered at those who stood watch.

"Get out. All of you. Let us mourn in privacy. We have no further need of you!" It came out as a thunderous growl, all his anger, all his dejection swelling the words into a rage. At once, those statuesque bodies rushed toward the doors and slid out. The room then truly became silent, tranquil.

What was tranquility when there should have been the wails of a newborn son? Henri could not look down to the child his wife held so fondly, so delicately. Yet he watched her fingertips trace along the little nose, the puckered lips, the closed eyelids. There were no words to speak. There was no action to take except to hold her. Thus, Henri wrapped his arms around his wife's shoulders and buried his face in her hair. Tears warmed his cheeks as he tried to breathe, as he tried to focus on her breathing. In and out, in and out, in and out . . . The silence followed. Minutes ticked by as they ever so quietly held each other and their dead son.

How could this have happened? Henri tried to imagine the scene Gideon had come across. The elderly servant had spoken in a quiet concerned voice when retelling the discovery to his master mere hours before. Or had it been days? Time seemed to have been lost in the chaos and the worry for both his unborn child and his fallen wife. Why had she fallen down the stairs? Justine had started to take great care of where she went within the house and in the gardens. She had been aware of her balance being hindered by her expanding belly.

So, why? Henri had allowed his mind to become lost in seeking out the answers. They swirled and danced beyond his reach. No clear reason became apparent as he sifted through grief and sorrow, confusion and pain.

"Is the girl alive?"

The question was sudden, spoken in a choked jagged voice. Henri hardly recognized it as coming from Justine. It startled him from his reverie. It was Justine who'd spoken, for there was no one else in the room. How much time had passed? Had he fallen asleep? The room had grown cool as the embers in the fireplace flickered and crackled, struggling to keep aflame.

"Yes, our daughter is doing well. She is with the wet nurse now. I chose only the best. She came highly recommended from the prince's mistress."

"Oh," Justine responded while staring down at the silent lifeless body of her son. He had been born first, mere minutes before his sister, but his birth was marked with silence, whereas his sister had wailed from the moment she entered this world.

"I was going to . . . to name him . . ." Her voice broke, and no more words could be spoken. Justine was once more submerged beneath the waves of guilt, of shame, of rage. Oh, why had he been born dead? *Stillborn* was what the doctor had whispered, a curse. A damned curse that she could not have given birth to two children, two live children. Why had he been born dead? He was of similar size to the girl. Tears stung her eyes as she held on to the bundle with one last embrace. Then she set it down beside her.

"I have killed your heir, my lord, in my distraction . . ." She was mumbling now, her fingers twining through her hair and pulling hard. A keening noise, a wounded animal sound, poured from her lips as she began to thrash about. Justine began clawing at her own face, her nails digging into her cheeks. What had she done? What had she done?

A resounding slap sent Justine reeling as she stared down at the lifeless baby and then looked up and stared at her husband. Her cheek burning. Her emotions wiped away.

"You did not murder our son. You did nothing wrong."

"You're wrong. You've always been wrong. You were wrong to protect Michel for so long. You were wrong to keep Percy." The accusations were said, strung along as if pearls on a fine necklace slowly wrapping around her husband's throat. Constricting, tightening. Hastening the pressure of his own guilt, of his own grief.

Henri fought against it with all he could while feeling himself begin to fall beneath the surface, where it was harder to breathe, more difficult to focus. His chest felt heavy. It throbbed as a drum, boom, boom, booming in his ears, and the tension began to tighten his shoulders.

"Justine, you know that I have not forsaken our wedding vows." It was all he could respond with.

"Do you know what she has said? Do you know who she has said these things to? Do you know what she has said to me?"

Henri did know, and he did not care. He really did not care as there was so much more he needed to be concerned with. Michel had gone missing. Gideon had suffered some medical catastrophe, which had left him absent from his familiar duties. Henri did not care what Percy did. He did not care what Percy thought, and he would curse her feelings to hell. Percy could not have been further from his thoughts. Instead, they whirled with grief, with rage, with disappointment, with tenderness, with betrayal.

"It does not matter what words she speaks, for she does not matter. Her behavior, her feelings, her existence are the least of my concerns. You are my wife. Michel is my brother.

And now our children . . . our daughter," Henri replied, curbing his own wave of grief. It was still too fresh. Justine had given birth and nearly died in the process. But she had survived the birth, and now she had to focus on healing, on healing and not dying of childbed fever.

"Percy matters because she thinks she matters. In her mind, in her insanity, she believes herself in love with you, and this makes her dangerous."

"I concede the truth in your observation, Justine, but your focus must not be on Percy or her tantrums. Instead, focus on yourself and healing." *Please, please become better and do not perish in childbed.* The words were left unsaid.

Justine was not blind to her husband's own struggles; she was just too exhausted. She was just too empty. Her heart felt as a void at this time. There was nothing more she could have desired but for her children—both of her children—to be alive and well. Crying and protesting at belonging in this cold, cold world.

Where had they taken the girl? Henri said a nursemaid had been brought for her. Only the best for a daughter. What would have been enough for their son, the heir? Justine convinced herself she was the reason her son had died. She had sinned greatly indeed for her son to be dead without even being able to take a breath.

Maybe he breathed in angel's dust and slept on their wings . . . No, that was not possible, for no prayers had been said for the lost little soul. She was so tired. She was so, so tired. Her eyelids fluttered and suddenly felt heavy, as if stones were weighing them down, down, down. It was only exhaustion; it was only fatigue. It had all been too much, too much.

"Henri, I will sleep now. Tell the parish to say a hundred prayers for our heir, as he was born into our sins and our sins were too much. We must atone for his soul to remain out of the depths of hell. Those horrible flames, eternal flames. Promise me . . ."

"A hundred prayers for our son and a year of masses to ensure he is not locked in purgatory. I so vow," Henri replied, resting his chin on top of his wife's head. His hand stroked her shoulders as he began to hum the lullabies his own mother had sung to him. He felt his wife's shoulders stiffen and then gradually relaxed. Her body curled into his warmth and his embrace, accepting the comfort, accepting the bond grief had afforded them.

What else could they say? What else could they do? The loss was too heavy a burden for only one of them to carry, yet they understood little of each other. And so, they could not offer one another comfort beyond the simplicity of a gentle touch, a softly spoken word. Was it to be enough? They had a healthy daughter, a little girl in the room next door who was cradled in the arms of a nursemaid.

Justine could not imagine holding the little girl, the surviving child. The unwanted child. Is this what her mother had thought of her when she was born? A longed-for son and heir yet only a girl had been born. Only a daughter had survived infancy, survived childhood. Only a daughter to inherit a portion of a dowry, and then the family name and her father's legacy was to be absorbed by another. By her husband and any son born of their wedlock. Any son born of her body was to inherit her father's land, her father's title, and her father's wealth.

Only a daughter . . .

January 5, 1792

Did you know his name?

-Justine Geoffrey

CHAPTER TWENTY-FOUR
What Is It We Have? Nothing . . .

WHAT MORE WAS NEEDED? WHAT MORE was necessary? The lists seemed never-ending, ever-changing, and multiplying. A higher and higher demand as the sun continued to rise in the east and gradually descended in the west. All the clocks within the household continued to tick, tick, tick as the seconds continued on. Justine did not want to be sleepless, to be restless, to be hurting. She did not want to exist. Not in a world where she had lost a child . . .

Her memories of the hours prior to the birth were clouded, remaining just beyond her reach as she did her best to remember where she had been or who she had been speaking with. An argument. A feeling of air surrounding her entire body. Justine sat up in her bed and stared over at the fireplace as the fog lifted from her memory for just a moment, but it was all she needed. Percy. Stairs.

The truth. The disgustingly dark truth. Oh! It would have been better for her mind to have forgotten what Percy said. Michel was just a copycat of his father. Henri was just the guardian of the family's darkness. Henri was the gatekeeper. Percy was a victim but also a villain. All three of them were victims, but they had allowed themselves to become monsters. Oh, Henri . . .

Justine closed her eyes, the images of the truth flooding through her imagination as she put it all together. The old Lord Geoffrey had been a monster who created monsters out of his sons. The daughter? She had not lived long enough to make a debut into society, so her name had been easily lost and buried in the ashes of this home. What about Henri's mother? What about Michel's mother? They had been two separate women, Justine knew. Lady Rockwell had tried to keep her secluded and shielded from the gossip of society, but Justine had been too curious, too earnest in her pressuring of the servants in her old guardian's home and had learned that much.

The baby girl had yet to be named as both parents were torn by such intense conflicting emotions, marveling at her growth and her beauty while also mourning the loss of her brother, the weight of the unknown. This little child was sleeping so soundly in her cradle beside her mother. Justine kept putting in effort to bond with the child, but she felt her own lacking.

"You are not the heir this family needed. You are not a son. Why are you alive and your brother died?" Justine was whispering to the little girl, her fingertips outlining the child's face but not touching her.

The wet nurse was attentive to the child, but she remained quietly in the corner, keeping a sharp eye on the Lady Geoffrey. She had heard stories of noble women going mad in the weeks after birth, mad enough to smother their infants, mad enough to cause harm. So she was vigilant as a guardian for the little girl. A little girl who was not cherished by her mother. A little girl who was doted on by her father from a distance.

Justine was aware of the other woman in the room. She was always nearby wherever the little girl was. Why did she forget the wet nurse's name? Fog and smoke continued obstructing her attempts to recover her memory.

It is the fog of childbirth . . . It is the exhaustion . . .

So many explanations were whispered to her, failed attempts to soothe and soften the anxiety beginning to build within her mind. Why was this so difficult? Justine had daydreamed about holding her child in her arms, crooning and adoring the little face and smelling the newborn scent. Why could she not hold her daughter? Even the thought of touching the little girl sent shock waves through her body, caused nausea and bile to rise in her throat. Why?

There was an argument between her and Percy. There was another argument with Michel. Yet another with Henri. A continual series of arguments and disagreements. Bickering had begun to erode at her mental state prior to the birth. Her anxious and distressed state of mind came from far more than the fog of childbirth or the exhaustion of labor.

It was the dancing corpse. It was the pale, pale eyes that never closed. It was the shadows twisting and contorting with the sickly sweet stench. It was the memories haunting her every time she tried to close her eyes. Why was she being punished? Justine could not pinpoint why.

She was not guilty. She had not committed the atrocious sin. She was not guilty. Or was she? Justine knew she was guilty of complacency, of not purging the sinful act from the house. She was guilty of fear, of shame. She was guilty of cowardice. Perhaps her cowardice was what had caused the death of her son. The awareness began as a warmth in her mind, slowly spreading its reach down her spine and into her chest. It had been her cowardice.

Unaware of the passing of time, Justine appeared to be in yet another comatose episode, according to the milk nurse. The little girl had started to cry, and the mother did not stir. She was not bothered to even blink. Quietly, so quietly, the milk nurse went over to pick up the little girl with a gentle shushing noise. Instead, the woman let out a loud yelp as a strong hand suddenly wrapped around her wrist, preventing her from touching and soothing the little girl.

The milk nurse looked up into the cold exhausted eyes of the Lady Geoffrey, and her free hand immediately started to make the sign of the cross. The lady was not herself!

"My lady, may I feed your little one?" the milk nurse murmured, turning her gaze down to the now screaming infant.

"You will not take her away from me. Do you hear me?" Justine said.

"No, no, my lady. I am only going to feed her, if it pleases you." Oh, where was the father? It was unlike the Lady Geoffrey to be near the little girl for this long.

"Do you hear me?"

"My lady, please, let me feed her . . ." she began to plead.

"Do. You. Hear. Me?"

A silence followed as the milk nurse began to shake. This was not the assignment she had been promised! The promise had been a position in a prestigious household, with ample pay and leisurely days. The promise had been to nourish and care for the Lord and Lady Geoffrey's firstborn child. Not to be so poorly mistreated. She felt tears stinging beneath her eyelids. How was she to reply? The lady did not listen to her. There seemed to be no reasoning with—

"You may take the baby, Madame Katharine. Please, console her," a gentle voice said from behind both women, breaking the frigidity encasing them. The little girl was still screaming in the cradle, but she was quickly scooped up into the warm embrace of the milk nurse. A hasty curtsy and then Katharine fled from the chamber with an ache in her chest.

"Treat Katharine well, Lady Geoffrey. She came from the prince's own mistress. You should not be frightening her with your behavior." The figure sat down in the chair opposite Justine.

There was worry on the face of the older woman, who now gazed openly and unabashedly at Justine Geoffrey, formerly Justine Ayling. Worry transformed into a blend of fear and anger for how her former ward was presenting herself. Was there no recognition? A frown rested along her pale eyebrows as she reached out and gently, ever so gently, rested her hand along the younger woman's forearm.

"Are . . ." Lady Marie Rockwell closed her mouth before speaking more, as she soon recognized the signs of childbed trauma. The vacant stare. The lack of bonding with the child. The odd posture. "Oh, my sweet . . ." she murmured as she slowly knelt before Justine and rested her cheek on the other woman's knees. "Justine, my sweet, sweet girl, what has happened to you?"

Silence.

"Justine, I should have visited you far sooner than now. Your lady mother would chastise me for not being with you," Lady Rockwell whispered.

The words were laced with regret and self-loathing. It would be a difficult task to get the young woman out of the dark embrace of childbed trauma. Lady Rockwell was haunted by the look in her niece's eyes, as it was a ghostly reflection of the eyes of her sister mere days before her sister had perished. This could not be allowed to be a repeat of loss, of shock.

Lady Rockwell had poured her entire being into raising her niece to be the very best of her sister; because if the little girl was able to live and to thrive, it meant her sister still lived as well. Pieces of her.

Those pieces were now shattered into a thousand fragments of who Justine had been. The cold, cold gaze looking back at her could have startled anyone who had not witnessed it once before. Lady Rockwell did not dare speak aloud again until she witnessed life return to her niece. If the screams of the infant did not even faze this new mother . . . Was she too far gone? The fear was soon overcome with anger at the mistreatment and neglect of Justine. Why had Lord Geoffrey done nothing for his wife? Clearly, he cared only for drinking and womanizing, just as society had murmured about both Geoffrey brothers.

In a tender gesture of absolute love, Lady Rockwell began to guide Justine from the chair. How long had it been since they'd bothered to feed Justine? To bathe her? It was alarming, the waif who stood before her, swaying back and forth as if the effort to stand was too much. Oh, she was so weak!

"You will recover from this, my heart. I am so grateful the prince's mistress allowed Madame Katharine to come into your house. I am so grateful your husband was honored by the gesture and allowed her to be of service here. It is thanks to Madame Katharine that I became aware of your suffering . . ." Her voice faded out as she turned away from her niece. She rang for food and hot water.

The servants were flustered at the strange woman who was suddenly ordering them about, but they did not dare disobey. The older woman's voice carried strength and authority they were unused to hearing from a woman, especially a woman in the Geoffrey house.

It was not going to be long before word spread that someone new was tending to the lady of the house. Lady Rockwell was fully aware of this and knew she was to see Henri or Michel before the evening meal was prepared for the household. Oh, but she was to be disappointed, as there were three people who entered the room when the meal was announced. She had been mentally prepared to face Henri or Michel, as they were the men of this house, and they could order her to leave. But Lady Rockwell was unprepared to see the Geoffrey brothers enter the room, followed by the shadow of a woman. Once more, she felt anger on behalf of her niece. This anger strengthened her backbone, allowing her to look upon the three faces with her own expression set in stone.

"Who is to blame for this?" Marie asked directly, her voice cold.

January 16, 1792

Do you know his name?
I cannot remember. I have not named them. My babies.
Do you know his name?
My aunt came to visit. Why did she bother to make such a trip? I have failed to be a wife. I have failed to be a mother. Just as I failed to be a daughter. Just as I failed to be a niece. I have failed.
Do you know his name?
I want my son.

-Justine Geoffrey

CHAPTER TWENTY-FIVE
Welcome to Our World, Be Wary

YOU ARE WELCOME TO STAY WITH US FOR AS long as you desire, Lady Rockwell," Henri said. Wariness was written in the older woman's body language, in the way her gaze was focused and stony.

"Yes, yes, welcome to our world . . ." Michel whispered over his brother's shoulder, a chilling smile on his lips as he then looked over to his right and stared at Percy. A silent communication took place between Percy and Michel, silent but visible to the wary eyes of Lady Rockwell.

Lady Rockwell gave each a nod of acknowledgement, even as her body slowly shifted closer to the sleeping Justine. What had this home done to her niece? The young woman in the bed was feverish and weak, appearing as if she had barely been tended to since the birth. Twins . . . *Oh, my dear, dear niece.* The undercurrent in the room had shifted when the three of them had entered.

"I am grateful for your welcome, Lord Henri. I came to pay a visit to your wife. I had not heard from her in some time," she said with a smile, though it did not extend beyond her mouth.

Percy hovered behind the two men as guilt and shame burned her cheeks and seared her already fragile mind. She fought against the waves of guilt and constant demand for confession, for atonement, for forgiveness. Percy knew the older woman was a familial relation to Justine, and this knowledge intensified her shame. No words could undo what she had done, but if only the other woman had died, then Henri might have finally been her own!

Henri was unaware of the internal conflict Percy was struggling with, and he was equally unaware of the morbid fantasies his brother was entertaining. *Will there ever be a calm day where there is no conflict, no drama, no guest?* Henri was worn down by the grief of his child and the strain of worrying over his wife. Why had he even been so obscenely worried about her?

An answer was flitting between the boulders in his mind, but it slipped beyond his grasp as he continued to stand in silence and observe the older woman. Lady Rockwell had entered his home unannounced and uninvited. Those two factors alone were splinters. Small fissures in the etiquette so delicately sewn together by the society they all lived in. Was he to allow these infractions by ignoring them? Or was he going to cause a scene to prove a point? Henri was too drained.

"On behalf of my wife and I, you have our deepest apologies for not notifying you in the last weeks of her well-being. Justine experienced . . . a traumatic birth, to put it politely. I was too worried over her and our daughter to properly notify you—or anyone else—with information," Henri finally responded, his voice husky and burdened with emotion.

"Naturally, it must have been overwhelming for all of you. Lady Justine was not due for another month . . ." Lady Rockwell replied, letting the end of her sentence hang with something unsaid. An accusation was clearly seen in her eyes, but no words were uttered.

"What are you insinuating?" Percy spat. She took steps forward in an aggressive manner as her temper flared. Who was this woman to imply anything negative about her Henri? It did not bother her that it was also implied toward her and Michel, but Henri should have been left out of this.

A sharp intake of breath gave Lady Rockwell's surprise away. Who was this impudent girl? No introduction had been made. Despite the other woman's pallor and her earlier silence, she had dared to interrupt—and so rudely.

Henri reached out his hand and pulled Percy back and away from Lady Rockwell. He leaned down and hissed something into the woman's ear, and she blanched, withdrawing into herself. Lady Rockwell took a mental note of the odd behavior and dynamic she witnessed.

A troubled silence followed as Lady Rockwell refused to degrade herself by answering the younger woman. She also refused to be the first to speak after such a display of distemper. Instead, she took slow and deliberate steps to be closer to the bed where Justine was resting and sat down at the edge. It made no sense to keep standing in the presence of the two men and young woman, especially with their blatant disrespect.

Henri took note of this but made no open remark to contradict of the actions of the older woman. There was no point in doing so when the power struggle had already been knocked out of balance with the older woman's sudden unannounced visit to his home. A frown settled on his face as he finally observed that his younger brother had remained in the room. Michel had stayed quiet and unnoticed—as he enjoyed it when observing those around him. Only, Michel's eyes had focused on Justine and had not moved from her. Why?

Henri followed his brother's gaze, and the frown lifted as relief bolted through his chest and through his body. Her eyes were open, and Justine was slowly looking between the four of them. Her eyes were open! A jolt of joy ricocheted through his body. The Grim Reaper had not taken her soul; for if her eyes opened, it meant she had survived another slumber.

Lady Rockwell was also hit with a wave of relief as she noticed the focus in her niece's gaze. Oh, this meant she was coherent and no longer a wandering soul within her own mind! It took all her self-composure and self-control to not lean over and embrace her niece, largely because of the other three people in the room.

"Thank you for your concern, all of you. Michel and Percy, you are dismissed. I must discuss a personal matter with my husband and my aunt." Justine's voice was hoarse but firm as she pushed herself into a seated position on the bed. She waved her hand to dismiss her aunt's fussing over pillows and the blankets. She gave no mind to her own disheveled appearance when meeting her brother-in-law's stare.

"You are dismissed," Justine repeated.

"What do you mean, I am dismissed?" Michel finally said, disdain in his voice.

"Brother, go. Take your fiancée to the gardens. Take a walk," Henri commanded.

Michel made a dismissive *tsk*, but he obeyed, executing a quick bow toward his brother and then again toward Justine and Lady Rockwell. He put his arm around Percy's shoulders and escorted her out with him, not giving Percy another moment to have a fit.

The uneasy silence returned to the room once the doors to the bedchamber had closed. It was not a priority for Justine to play the role of hostess, as she was still healing, sore, and aching. The burden was then transferred to Henri, and he shouldered the weight with grace. Quietly, he began to move two chairs from before the fireplace and set them down on the side of the bed where his wife was. Only then did he make the motion for Lady Rockwell to choose one of the chairs and to take a seat before he did. As was only proper.

"What is the topic you wish to discuss, my dear niece?" Lady Rockwell began after she had taken the chair closest to the bed.

Henri sat down just as quietly as he could and simply looked between the two women. He had not noticed it earlier, but they had a similar facial structure. There was nothing else he felt the need to say or do other than simply exist with them. Justine shifted her weight back and forth until she felt more comfortable.

"Our daughter. She will be named as my direct heir, as I am the heiress of the Ayling family. I needed two witnesses to hear me say this. Then it is legally binding as a will and testament for the lawyers," Justine said simply.

"Your daughter?" Lady Rockwell affirmed.

"Yes, my daughter. Henri, I have decided to name her Elisabeth. Yes, Henri, Elisabeth. You cannot and will not change my mind. Elisabeth Rose Geoffrey will be named as heir apparent to the Ayling family," Justine said with finality.

Henri instantly felt every muscle in his body tense, and the chaotic pounding began in his head. His vision blurred, and he could barely contain his rage. Elisabeth? Why had she chosen this name? His jaw clenched and unclenched, the muscles working as he leaned forward in his seat and placed both his hands on the edge of the bed. His knuckles went white as they curled into fists.

"We had assumed you were too unwell to make such complex decisions," Henri said at last, his voice cold and each word clipped with rage.

"Justine, my dear, God bless her with a long life, but not many infants make it beyond their first three or four years of life. You put a target on her back by naming her as your heir when she is still so young," Lady Rockwell said, her hand reaching out to touch her niece's cheek.

"Elisabeth is and will be my heir, the heir apparent to the Ayling family. There is nothing further to discuss on this matter. This way, she does not rely on the name or the wealth of her father's house." Justine stared directly at Henri as she said this. Each word was said with such intensity, it stole Henri's breath away. Justine turned her cheek away from her aunt's touch.

"Yes, madam," Henri answered as he nodded his head and relinquished the fight. It was a loss, but it was worth it—not fighting his wife over the inheritance of their daughter. Even if only for the time being to allow his wife to feel at ease with the future of their daughter. Even if her name was a curse rippling through his mind.

Elisabeth. It stirred the skeletons and the shadows into swirling clouds of chaos and disdain. Why had Justine chosen to name their daughter Elisabeth? It was going to be asked another time when Lady Rockwell was no longer present in his home.

Lady Rockwell looked between husband and wife, seeing the power struggle and then the power shift between the two. It was a different power struggle than she had observed between Henri and the other woman, Percy—a name she registered into her memory and made a mental note to ask around about. The moment to pester her niece to change her mind or to parry a reply against the decision was to pass.

"Let it be so, Justine." Lady Rockwell nodded as well, surrendering.

"Elisabeth Rose Ayling is my heir, then." The strength written in Justine's expression and the iron within her voice had startled both her husband and her aunt.

Startled them but also succeeded in having both agree to her statement. It could have been a difficult argument and an uphill battle if both had gone against her; rather, they had folded easily, and Justine began to doubt how easily it had happened. Justine distrusted her husband's agreement and feared for an argument once they were alone. The lawyers must be called first thing in the morning.

Justine stared long and hard at her husband before she turned to her aunt and smiled. It was a sad smile, sad and tired. "Aunt, I name Elisabeth as the heir to my parents' wealth because Percy Brough made an attempt to murder me the day I went into labor."

An explosion seemed to go off as a chair flew across the room and the water jug was flung and smashed against the wall. A roaring of rage, of grief, of disbelief resonated throughout the chamber. Both women were frozen in place in trepidation by the temper being displayed by Henri, Lord Geoffrey. His entire body was tense as he swung his fists into the wall and hurled any movable object within his reach. The roaring continued into a yell, then faded down to a growl. The growl was the most savage, most raw sound either woman had ever heard.

Lady Rockwell sat rooted in her chair to avoid being targeted by the blind rage Henri was experiencing. The older woman could not blame the man for his rage nor the display of it. Her own mind was streaked with red as she digested the words Justine had said so simply and matter-of-factly. It was the woman who had just been in this room. The sheer audacity!

The room was suddenly silent. Lady Rockwell kept her gaze averted to her clenched fists in her lap to avoid having her own flared anger seen. It was Justine who stared at her husband, and she had continued to do so throughout his outburst.

"I command you to inaction, my lord. In the name of our daughter, do nothing. Let Miss Brough wallow in her own guilt and let it feed her anxiety until she chooses to confess to you," Justine said calmly, her gaze locked with her husbands as his chest heaved with the violent waves of emotion.

"How dare she put a finger on you? How dare she?" Henri shouted.

"Henri, do not touch her. Do not speak of it to her. I only said it so that you and my aunt are aware of *why* I have named Elisabeth as my heir. In case I do not survive her childhood . . ." Justine steadily said each word, even though her shoulders were shaking and her body suddenly felt heavy with fatigue.

"As you wish, wife," Henri acceded for the second time in one day.

January 30, 1792

Did you know? Did you know, Annabelle? Annabelle, did you know that my brother was going to force my marriage to Percy? He pushed it earlier. Damn him and his wife and his daughter! Damn them all!

Percy was meant to be sent away. Her confessions to me would be enough to send her away to a nunnery, to an asylum. Anything but to send us more quickly down the aisle! Marriage? Hah!

Annabelle, you are my one and only. You are mine. No one will take you away from me.

-M.L.G.

CHAPTER TWENTY-SIX
MY GUILT AND SHAME, WILL YOU LOVE ME?

PERCY WAS TO BECOME A GEOFFREY THROUGH marriage but not to the brother she had loved since childhood. It was Michel whom she was going to wed. It was Michel whom she was going to fall asleep next to and would wake up to see in the mornings. The last few days had felt like an eternity, from sunrise to sunset, with her skin crawling and her mind fighting with itself. She was not happy in the knowledge that soon she was to be settled with Michel, but it was better than nothing. It was better than where she had been before—a burden, a ward, a leech on the Geoffrey family.

She was to be one of the ladies married into the Geoffrey name, a prestigious but notorious name. There was a sense of pride she felt as she sat up a little straighter in front of the mirror. It was a pale face staring back at her, with dark circles beneath the tired eyes and a pouting mouth. Pride did not ensure happiness. There was going to be a social event this evening where society was to be introduced to Michel's fiancée.

Slender fingers reached up to graze along her cheeks as she continued to stare at herself, ignoring the servants standing quietly behind her. They were lined along the outer wall with various objects in their hands: gowns, gloves, powders, hairpins. Henri had ordered both Geoffrey women to be glamorous tonight.

"I am not ready to be dressed yet. Draw me a bath first," Percy declared, focusing her gaze on her own reflection. She did not glance between the servants' faces to see their reaction.

Percy knew they judged her and belittled her within their own minds. They always had. It made no sense for them to despise her as they did because she had always tried to be kind, to be gentle. Except for when she screamed, except for when she threw objects . . . There was a shuffling of footsteps, and the staff left the room with a gentle click as the door closed behind them.

That was simple! Oh, she was going to enjoy this new level of luxury her life had been raised to—the beauty of having servants at her beck and call, something she had not experienced before. It was all perfectly acceptable but for the glaringly obvious fact that she was to be married to the wrong man. Percy slammed her fist down onto the chair and immediately whimpered to herself as pain jolted up her arm.

"I should be the lady of this house! I should be married to Henri. I should have been the one to give him a son. A living son. The witch did nothing for my Henri but cause him grief and misery over the death of his heir. His heir must have died because that witch was its mother," she mumbled to herself as she grabbed the hairbrush from the vanity's surface and slowly brushed out her long hair.

There were further mutterings and cursing as she tried not to become enraged by her own triggering thoughts, but her emotions began to boil, leading to more anger and frustration. Anger because she was not the one married to Henri and frustration that she was so poorly treated within the Geoffrey home. The servants had not even answered her request with a simple acknowledgement before they left. The cowards!

What more could she ask for? When she was the second lady within the Geoffrey house, she would no longer be a lowly creature slipping through the shadows, intended to be forgotten. She had been cast aside by Henri, and he had sent her down as a rag doll before his brother.

"I am more than they know. I have more potential than they have ever given me credit for," Percy whispered to her own reflection.

The time began to go faster than she'd prepared for, and she was soon wrapped in the heavy and lustrous volumes of fabric that glittered and swirled around her. There was a moment when she felt beautiful; she felt treasured; she felt as if she were a princess in a fairy tale. Oh, but this was not the case.

Percy was soon standing with her gaze settled on her would-be love as he was ordering the servants to settle some final details prior to the party starting. It was an unsettled feeling that began to stir within her chest and caused her breathing to hike, her pulse to quicken.

Was this anger? Was this love? Was this passion? The swirling emotions were difficult for her to pinpoint as she stared at him.

Only a few seconds passed before Henri turned and saw Percy staring at him. He arched an eyebrow at her and waved his hand for her to come to him.

As a well-trained well-behaved creature, Percy leapt at the attention he paid to her. It meant the world that he wanted to speak with her! There had been so many cold moments since the dinner announcement of her engagement to Michel, as Henri had not given her a second to breathe or to react or to express her outrage. Henri did not want to be berated by both women in his life; he had enough troubles to handle without adding drama and hazardous emotions into the whirlwind of his household. Thus, Henri had heavily avoided both women, but colder and more deliberate was his manner when it came to Percy. This acknowledgement of her presence felt as refreshing as a cool sip of water on a hot summer day.

"What did you need, Miss de Brough?" Henri said as she paused to stand in front of him.

"Why are you not saying my first name, Henri? Are we no longer friends?"

"You are my brother's fiancée. I am merely being respectful of your new status within this house. It is a fragile balance we have. What is it you need?"

Percy recoiled as if his words had scalded her, as indeed they had, for it was a sharp contrast to the relief she had felt moments before when he had looked at her and beckoned her forward. Why was he so cold?

"Percy, you need to accept our paths were not destined to be the same. You were meant for Michel, as you come with no dowry, and he is a second son. You are lucky to be marrying him. You are lucky you will not remain a spinster," Henri said nonchalantly.

"Why are you acting as if we never had anything between us? Why are you treating me as a stranger, something to just be casually tossed aside? You said you loved me. You promised to love me and to take care of me. You said you would never make me cry, not like your father . . ." Percy was beginning to shake, her throat constricting and her words becoming heavy with emotion. Why was he doing this?

Why were women such emotional fickle beings? There was no need for such a display of passion, of emotion to be coming from the woman before him. Henri felt the tension in his shoulders grow as he gritted his teeth to keep from lashing out at her. Why was he doing this? Why was he acting as if they were suddenly strangers? There was no clear answer he could give her. There was no clear answer he could even give himself. Though the answer did surface in his mind, but he chose to ignore it.

Instead, he remained quiet and only stared at Percy as she struggled to collect herself. There were tears, and she was visibly shaking. Such a nuisance. Henri, at last, exhaled to calm his own temper as he turned his body in the direction of the door. He chose to ignore her questions and to ignore the answers floating through his own mind.

"There is a party to attend. Be sure you are in the ballroom in half an hour," he said before stepping out of the chamber.

Henri had no intention of speaking to Percy again until he was walking her down the aisle to be married to his younger brother. There was too much between them for him to keep walking. It took every ounce of willpower to keep himself from throwing her to the ground and beating her bloody. Especially since the traumatic birth of their babies, caused by this woman. It was another broken part of his heart. There was too much. Thus, he did not bother to look over his shoulder to see the shock and the dismay on Percy's face.

Percy was left in the chaos and turmoil of emotion, of heartache, of rage, of confusion. *Why, Henri, why?* She crumpled to the floor with a heaving chest and a headache throbbing in her temples. Time continued to pass her by as she stayed on the ground, her hands balled into fists on the floor as she stared blankly at the wall. Why was he being so . . . distant, so cold?

There was a deep and dark history between them. It could not be escaped, and it could not remain hidden for long.

PERCY CAME BACK TO HER OWN MIND, TO HER OWN body when she felt warm fingers curling around her wrist, and then she was staring up into the dead eyes of her betrothed. Michel was frowning down at her in such a way that caused chills to plummet down her spine and into her stomach, creating knots and twists. Percy swallowed and did a faint curtsy to him in acknowledgement of his presence. He did nothing.

"Michel, my lord, are you displeased?" Percy whispered.

Michel did nothing and continued to do nothing. He just stared down at her. This caused her to be uncomfortable and feel nauseous as she looked up at him, not fulling knowing what to say or what to do. Was there anything she could do? How could both Geoffrey brothers be mad at her? Their displeasure was too much. Percy could not handle Henri's and Michel's annoyance of her.

Tears began to stream down her cheeks as her gaze slowly lowered to the ground, her shoulders trembling as she struggled to breathe. Once more, she had lost control of her emotions, and Percy was angry at herself for breaking down in front of Michel. He was heartless, and he was the true son of the monster once known as old Lord Geoffrey.

No words of comfort came from her fiancé as he continued to stare down at her with his cold eyes. People moved around them as the party began to fill with society's finest, all come to congratulate and gather intel on the newly engaged couple.

Such a spectacle they had already begun to witness! It was to be a few minutes of too many eyes staring and too many mouths whispering before a third body stood between Percy and Michel. A warm hand rested on Percy's shoulder and turned her away from Michel; it was Henri, who'd come to her rescue again. It was Henri who saved her from the cold, cold eyes. It was Henri who guided her to the dance floor, and it was Henri who danced with her. The first dance should have been with her fiancé . . .

"Henri, I did something terrible. It is leaving me restless, unable to eat or to sleep for fear you will hear of it from someone else. I need your forgiveness. I need you to keep loving me. I cannot lose you," Percy half whispered, half sobbed as Henri led her in the graceful movements of a beautiful dance. When had the music begun to play? When had she begun to feel the warmth of tears on her cheeks?

The murmuring crowd around them seemed to disappear and merely become the sound of a babbling creek, a soothing sound echoing through her fears. Percy felt invincible when Henri was beside her.

"What is this terrible deed, Percy?" Henri asked as his fingers curled into the skirts around her waist. "What have you done this time?"

His voice was salt to her wounds, stinging as it healed her. The tears had not stopped streaming down her cheeks even as she was smiling up at him. A confession was building in her mind, and she could not hold it back, but she also could not figure out how to word it the best way. She could not articulate it to where Percy was the victim and Justine the villain, the witch. No, instead Percy confessed her spite, her hatred, her jealousy, and her involvement in the staircase.

"The witch was arguing with me over your brother, and she was saying the most heinous of things about him. That vile woman was going to bring ruin to your house with what she was saying. She deserved to fall. She deserved to be hurt far worse than she was. That witch took you away from me. She was not supposed to be the mother of your children." Percy had become unhinged, her voice laced with venom and anger. "I was supposed to give you a son. I could have given you a son. Instead, the witch—"

There was a resounding slap, a clapping of thunder within the ballroom, as his hand met her cheek. Stunned silence echoed throughout the gathered crowd as Percy inhaled sharply.

"Lady Geoffrey is your superior in every way. Are you telling me you dared to harm her? Are you telling me you are the reason my son died? You are the reason my daughter almost died? *You* are the reason my wife almost died?" His voice grew louder and louder as he raged in her face, no longer aware of the world around them as everything blurred red, bloody, and bruised.

Percy whimpered and clasped her hands to her stinging cheek. "The witch was sending us all to hell with her rumors and slander!"

Henri heard the roaring build, build, building within his ears as he stared down at the woman before him. He knew she was capable of terrible deeds, as he had covered up many of her unfortunate dealings and mistakes. But this was too far. This had harmed his protégé, his wife . . . Justine had spoken true.

Percy continued about the insanity of corpses, of rumors, of witchcraft, of madness. It was clear she had allowed her mind to become fragmented. Weak!

"You are lucky to be alive. Go to your room and stay there until you are summoned for the wedding," Henri bellowed.

Percy fled in a rustling of tears, skirts, and murmurings. It took Henri time to calm himself down as he stared where Percy had run to. There was hardly anything left of his dignity as his gaze slowly moved and landed on his brother. Michel had not moved an inch in defense of his betrothed or to comfort her. He was as a statue, cold and lifeless. What was going through his brother's mind? Henri said nothing further as he waved his hand for the orchestra to continue playing its music.

The silence of the guests was deafening each time the music faded. Henri and Michel now stood side by side, both saying nothing. The evening had been whispered about with excited anticipation. Now it was riddled with unspoken rumors, unanswered questions, and too many eyes had witnessed the disarray that was within the Geoffrey home. Where was the Lady Geoffrey? Society had assumed her presence was inevitable, as she had given birth more than a month prior.

Soon, the silence wore thin, and the guests began to murmur to one another—behind their hands. Questions. Accusations. Splintering the truth into half lies, half stories that were to be repeated and fractured again and again.

"Maybe this is why they do not house guests regularly?"

"What brutes they are!"

"Now that you mention it, they do not entertain in their residence much at all. The last gathering they hosted was when Lord Henri announced his engagement to the Lady Stanley..."

"You mean they do not host other nobles?"

"No! Not even well-known artists or musicians. Everyone gets turned away!"

There was an individual who'd paid particular attention to the scene as it unfolded before the crowd. Justine hovered on the outskirts of the gathered guests, trying to stay hidden, staying quiet. Henri had ordered her to attend this engagement party, but he had not ordered her to make her presence known. There was a moment of hesitation when Justine thought to speak, to reach out her hands to embrace her aunt.

The moment passed. With its passing, a sadness settled in her chest. Heavy and dark. Justine had not thought to see her aunt again. Why? She could not say. The quiet of the room, the shock and the dismay of the guests caused Justine to retreat. She had no desire to speak with anyone, not even her aunt. She had no desire to be seen.

It had been a few weeks since Justine was surprised by her aunt's sudden and unannounced visit. Weeks since Henri had promised to take better care of his household. She shook her head, seeing the feeble excuses Henri spewed.

February 1, 1792

Did you forget that I belonged here? Did you forget that I am the master of this house? Michel does not seem to remember that this is my home, this is my lordship, and that everything he has is because of me. I am Henri, Lord Geoffrey. I am the firstborn son. Michel is my half brother. Michel is the second son. The spare.

I have ignored his pleadings for answers, for a change in his life. He does not want to marry Percy, even though he agreed. He wants her to be sent to a nunnery. He even suggested that the woman be sent to an asylum.

In the same conversation, Michel said Justine should also be sent away.

What am I supposed to do? He is my brother. But he is a parasite to this family. He is . . . a burden. I suppose I can send him and Percy off to the countryside after their wedding. That would clear the house of their filth. That would make my daughter safe. Right?

Percy will never touch my daughter. Michel will never touch my daughter.

—H.L.G.

CHAPTER TWENTY-SEVEN
Listen to the Sounds the Darkness Makes

F YOU WANTED TO BE CHERISHED ON YOUR WEDDING night, this was not the way. If you wanted to be loved on your wedding day, this was not the way. If you wanted to be happy, this was not the way. Percy could hear the words echoing through her mind as she stared at her own reflection in the mirror. The woman she saw was familiar and yet seemed to be a stranger to her as the beautiful charm of the pale wedding dress shone in the candlelight. This was her special day. This was the day she became a Geoffrey. It just . . . It was just . . .

"I am marrying the wrong brother," she said aloud. There was no one else in the corridor with her, as all the servants were tending to the guests, to the pastries, to the orchestra.

"If you wanted to be a corpse, this was the way."

Percy inhaled sharply and spun to look around the hall, her eyes gone wide and fearful. The voice had been so hauntingly close. The voice had belonged to the late Lord Geoffrey, a favorite saying, a familiar phrase once again triggering panic at the forefront of her instincts. No, no. It could not have been the old lord. He had long since died. She'd seen his dead body for herself. She had punched and kicked his corpse in a frenzy of tears and tantrums. In freedom.

No longer! No longer was she the old lord's marionette. No longer was she controlled, no longer was she used against the one she adored—Henri. Ah, the shadows were curling and whispering in her memories as her thoughts drifted back to her childhood. Why had her father died? Why had her mother died? They had abandoned her in the hands of a monster. They had delivered her into the life of her destiny, her love with Henri. It had been a blessing and a curse.

Is this what she was always to be? A blessing and a curse?

"Mistress, they are starting to play the music. You are needed," came a gentle voice through a now cracked doorway, and indeed, the orchestra had started up again. A lovely song. Percy focused on the lilting notes of the violin.

The doors slowly opened more and more until they stretched out as if to embrace her into the warmth of the grand hall. Hundreds of eyes turned to stare at her as she walked slowly through the entry. The faces all blurred together as her panic rose and her feet carried her forward. There was no bouquet, as it was not the season. The household was still in mourning for the loss of Henri's son. There was no one to walk her down the aisle, as her father had died long ago and Henri had scorned her request to escort her.

There was only the sound of the violin and the clouded face of her fiancé. Michel was there physically, but Percy understood the vacant look in his eyes. Fine. If only she could also escape to another world to better endure the reality of this day. She was being married to the wrong brother! Her cheek gave a phantom sting where Henri had struck her mere days before.

Ah, the daydream came as she disconnected from the reality where she was marrying Michel and not Henri. Instead, her daydream had her smiling and laughing up into the loving warm eyes of Henri as they said their vows. Vows of devotion, of eternal love, of forgiveness. It was perfect! Henri was lightly touching her hand as they turned to face the priest. Henri slid the wedding band over her finger, the symbol that they were forever man and wife. It was Henri's lips she kissed.

Percy continued to daydream her way through the remainder of the wedding ceremony, through the congratulations, and into the reception. The hundreds of eyes never seemed to leave her. What were they looking for?

PERCY RETURNED FROM HER REVERIE WITH AN UN-settled heaviness in her chest. She was in her wedding dress. She was beside Michel—her husband—with her hand on his forearm. Michel was whispering into her ear, his breath warm and foul against the side of her neck. They were having their first dance together as husband and wife.

"I will not love you. I will not protect you. Do you hear me, Percy? You are a burden my brother has laid at my feet, nothing more."

"Yes, I heard you perfectly fine. You are not the man I wished to marry," Percy snapped.

"Excellent. May you forever pine for my brother." Michel leered, his face turned away from his bride.

Percy hissed in reply as she looked at her husband and saw the Cheshire cat grin on his lips. Oh, not a safe sign. Where had her daydream gone? Where had Henri gone? He was just there caressing her cheek and toasting the room, loudly declaring his love and his passion for her.

"If you wanted to be a corpse, this is the way." The old Lord Geoffrey's voice sounded through her mind again, shattering her. The panic returned in full force as she came crash-landing into the reality: She was married to her lover's brother. She was married to a man who loathed her. She was married.

It was meant to be a memorable affair. An event forever marked in one's mind as a new beginning, a turning of a page, and the fresh stroke of a pen. It was meant to be beautiful, to be emotional. A wedding was supposed to be a blissful day for a blushing bride as she was teased about the wedding night to come. It was not meant to be a nightmare. It was not meant to be troubled. Percy could no longer hold the smile on her lips, and her expression began to melt as her mind fractured.

As the minutes passed, Percy was unaware of when her husband left her side. She was unaware of the subtle change within herself. It was impossible. Her mind spiraled with how impossible it all felt—this new reality.

Henri appeared, having noted the shift in Percy's posture from across the room. It was Henri who took ahold of her cold, cold fingers and took her to the dance floor. It was Henri who held her waist in his warm hands. It was Henri she was suddenly staring up at. It was always supposed to be Henri. Henri. His name went through her bloodstream. It became the drum for which her heart thudded for.

"Keep smiling, Percy. We've made enough gossip to entertain society for the next fortnight, if not through the winter. Keep smiling, even as your heart is breaking," Henri whispered into her ear.

One for the nightmare and two for the seer, three for the maiden, and four for the fear . . .

Oh! He knew her so well. Tears began to fall down her cheeks, and she was smiling up at him, so radiantly. Yet her sorrow and her fears were written clearly in her eyes. Percy was so utterly and completely devoted to him. She smiled and smiled until her cheeks burned.

"I will always smile when you are near me," Percy cooed as her fingers curled into the fabric of his overcoat.

The dance between them was meant to last an eternity. It was what Percy wanted. What she most desired was to dance with and to be held by Henri for the rest of time. Alas, the dream was never to be, and she had to accept it as a simple truth. All too soon, the dance ended, and Henri walked away from Percy without giving her a second glance. Her heart ached.

The minutes turned to hours, and as the evening continued, the guests seemed to drink and to laugh more openly as they became intoxicated. The bride and groom remained sober.

This day marked a permanent change in the function of the Geoffrey home; both bride and groom were aware of this change. Percy was no longer a mere ward of the estate, a cast-off from the old Lord Geoffrey. Despite this, there was still an emptiness in the Geoffrey family that even a mindless guest could see. It was the absence of Lady Geoffrey, Justine.

It had been weeks since she had given birth, and the public was anticipating her return debut into society. Many had bet Lady Justine Geoffrey was to return to society during the engagement party or at the least during the wedding and reception.

Lady Marie Rockwell was amongst those more vocal guests questioning Lady Justine's continued absence. The older woman was not quiet. She spoke against the harsh treatment Henri had displayed at the engagement party. The milk nurse had not sent her another message about the health and goings-on within the Geoffrey household—this fact the woman kept to herself, wisely so.

"I heard the lady is deceased. Gone with childbed fever not two days after she gave birth."

"I heard she gave birth to a monster and fled to the countryside in shame."

"My servant heard, from a reliable source, that the Lady Geoffrey is alive but living closeted away in shame because she did indeed give birth to a monster. A two-headed thing also tucked away into the shadows."

"Quiet now, ladies, before the hosts overhear us. I know Lady Justine Geoffrey is healing, as she is entitled to do." Lady Rockwell spoke up and hushed the gossip. But why?

The prestigious lady had been observed as a harsh critic of the Geoffrey brothers, more so at odds with the elder brother.

It was not her concern whether people were watching her or gossiping about her shift of attitude toward the Geoffrey brothers. Lady Rockwell had become increasingly worried over the silence and continued absence of her niece, who had been wed to Henri Geoffrey for a year. It was a year during which Justine had made fewer and fewer public appearances. Lady Rockwell did not care that this was another wedding for the Geoffrey family. She did not care if the bride was happy or sad today. Her only focus was obtaining more information about her niece.

Lady Rockwell approached Percy, now the second lady of the Geoffrey family, with a false smile and a kind expression. She reached out her hands to clasp the cold, cold fingers of the younger woman. The bride was as cold as winter's air!

"Congratulations, Lady Percy Geoffrey, on your wedding day. May you be blessed with an abundance of happy years in your marriage. You are blessed to have gained a brother and a sister this day." The last statement was said more hushed as Lady Rockwell leaned into place a quick kiss on Percy's cool cheek.

"Oh! Yes. I have gained a niece as well. She is such a beautiful little girl. Her father is so very proud of her." Percy began to ramble on and on about Henri and his adoration of the little girl.

It became clear to Lady Rockwell that Percy was enamored with Henri Geoffrey. Marie already knew the young bride despised her niece and had tried to murder Justine.

The bride said not one word about the child's mother. The rumors surrounding this young woman and the Geoffrey brothers were . . . obscene.

"You need to be careful, dear girl. God sees and hears everything," Marie hissed against Percy's cheek before she turned and walked away.

Was there another way Justine might be contacted during the night? The staff in attendance were not going to be of help. The other guests were going to be more of a hinderance than helpful. Unless she might be able to create a chaotic scene everyone's eyes were focused on. Then she might step out of the grand ballroom unnoticed and be able to explore the Geoffrey home. No, it was not going to be possible tonight. As much as it pained her heart to acknowledge it, Lady Rockwell abandoned her ideas of being able to sit down with her niece tonight.

The night continued as the celebrations went on and on, guests getting more and more ill-mannered as the hours went on. A few more toasts were said to salute the bride and groom; a few more dances were enjoyed. Then the hour came when the servants began to escort people out politely and effectively through the front doors. The noisy and boisterous crowd wandered to carriages and stumbled down to the main street of town, singing and laughing.

There was no sound inside the Geoffrey home once all guests were closed out. The staff were silent as they went about the task of cleaning and taking down the decorations of the event. It was a momentous task, but they were diligent. Inside the walls of the Geoffrey home, the silence endured for the remainder of the evening, as each member of the family took to their own sacred space. There was no ceremonial consummation of the marriage by the newlyweds. There was no informal familial cheers and toasts. There was only the silence.

February 10, 1792

I will not bed her.

I will not be defiled by the whore of my brother.

I know that Percy gave herself to my brother. She gave herself, over, and over again to Henri. The little whore. Annabelle, you have my dedication. You are an angel.

Percy is a whore.

I have said the vows, and I have placed a band of gold around her finger. I have pecked a kiss to her lips, and that is the only physical contact Percy will get from me. I need to stay pure for you, only for you, Annabelle, my love, my angel, my beautiful.

Percy does not know about you. Justine has kept that to herself. I think.

Percy would be fool enough to speak to me about you, the jealous pathetic whore that she is.

Percy will never be enough. She is not meant to be Lady Geoffrey. She is not meant to be anything more than my brother's whore. A page in history that died when my father died.

I will not bed her.

I swear it.

—M.L.G.

CHAPTER TWENTY-EIGHT
WE ARE NOTHING BUT ASHES, ASHES

D

O YOU THINK . . . DO YOU REALLY THINK I relish maintaining this façade? I smile at you in front of Henri only out of courtesy. If you think there is anything of friendship or kinship be- tween us, then you are sorely mistaken. You are abhorrent to me," Justine spat out at her brother-in-law.

It was the morning after his wedding to Percy, and Michel seemed to think himself atoned in her eyes. Justine seldom had patience or energy to play pretend with him. Her focus had shifted from disentangling the twisted and tangled relationships within the Geoffrey household to her daughter's upbringing.

"Stay away from my daughter. You will not look at her. You will not touch her. And you will not speak to her. You have only seen her a handful of times in her short life. Let's keep it that way," Justine finished.

It was challenging to feel any sort of attachment for her daughter. Her emotional struggles were known only to herself and her husband, as Justine tried to keep such struggles hidden away. A daughter was still a child, an offhanded heir if no other children should follow. A daughter was hers until the girl was to be wed. A daughter was . . . a daughter.

Michel had kept to himself since the confrontation with his brother and sister-in-law at the dinner a few weeks prior, more so than was typical for him. The servants knew better than to murmur about the changes, as Gideon kept them in line with subtle threats or gigantic rewards. Loyalty was the best possession a servant could have—such was Gideon's motto, and he tried to ingrain it in those below him.

Michel blinked once, twice. Then he simply stared at Justine with blank eyes, his expression crestfallen. Why did she have to be like this? It was so disappointing, as he had thought their bond had made improvements when she first witnessed Annabelle and him. How much had Justine observed? *Oh. Oh yes.* She had not been too happy about the whole scene. Michel remembered the drama that had unfolded. What had his brother said to him? Henri had not been too happy with the whole scene either. Months had passed!

It was tedious, trying to fathom the emotions of Henri and Justine. What more did he need to do? Or rather, what more did he need to not do? Henri had been adamant. Henri had been ferocious. It had both intrigued Michel and frightened him. It was a warning, oh! Henri did not want Michel to touch Justine because Justine was his wife. What did she mean to his brother? Again, trying to figure out what he could and what he could not do to Justine was entirely tiresome.

"You plainly do not understand what it is that I create. It is a tourniquet that halts the demons from entering this world, a bridge that assists those who need to enter heaven. I am . . ." Michel said, his words slurring off as his attention shifted from Justine's face to the window just beyond her shoulder. What was it like to feel the sunshine at this hour? The world appeared in a golden halo, swathed in pristine resplendent light. An illumination drifted over Justine, covering her.

"Do not worry, my lady. Nothing will come to harm your precious baby. I keep my deeds hidden from the world and its judgment, its scorn. You were not supposed to be wandering the halls. Henri had said you would be kept occupied and not to be concerned about your whereabouts," Michel at last mumbled, focusing back on his sister-in-law in a steady manner.

"You are a monster, Michel. Why are you acting as if your acts are not sinful? Are not an abomination?"

"*You* are mistaken. *You* are the fiend. *You* are the enemy," Michel snapped, his head whipping from side to side as he spat out the words. His finger pointing in her direction. His eyes flashed with a feverish brightness as he stood still, frozen. His shoulders heaved as he took in gulping breaths of air, as if surfacing from being beneath the water's surface for too long.

It was not enough! How could his trust in her not be enough? He had not sought to harm her after she discovered his tryst with Annabelle. He had not thought—no, the truth was not so simple. He *had* thought to harm her, to seek her out and harm her to make her silence guaranteed, but Henri had forbidden it.

Henri said he could not do any harm. Was Henri always right? Yes, yes, yes, he was. Henri was the god in his universe, the sun of his earth. Oh, he knew his trust in his older brother was absolute. For was it not Henri who had rescued them both from their own demon, their father?

Justine went still and could not breathe, afraid of his verbal retaliation but more terrified by his sudden stillness. He was so still but obviously not calm. This was not . . . this was not safe. Why had Michel entered the library mere moments after she had? Why was there only one door leading in and out of this library?

"Michel, you do not know me, as I do not know you. Yet we share a bond with Henri, with your brother," Justine said softly, melodically, trying to pacify his temper even as she took slow, painfully slow steps backward in the direction of the closed double doors.

Burdensome! This was all so terribly burdensome. Michel was already thinking far beyond the simple conversation he was having with Justine. He was far beyond even seeing Justine in his mind's eye.

"We are nothing but ashes, ashes and bone dust, did you know?" Michel replied, ignoring the words she'd said.

"Why?" she asked despite all the words swarming in her mind. All the questions, all the doubts, and all the hatred. Yes, Justine could grasp the truth: She hated Michel and the liability he posed to her life. If his secrets were discovered by anyone outside of this home, outside of this family, they would all be implicated in his obscenities.

"We are nothing but bone dust and ashes. We are nothing. Nothing. Nothing. None of what we do truly matters. None of what we feel is permanent. It will all simply become ashes and bone dust." Again, Michel ignored her as he looked up and down, side to side. "This is why we are gods. If we can grasp this understanding, then we can become as gods."

"Even the gods—Even the gods have a sense of cruelty, of awareness for what is just. Even the gods do not minimize the dangers of toying with mankind, with the taking of life or the creation of life. Michel, even gods need to be accountable."

"Even gods need to be accountable. But you see—or perhaps you do not see—the gods cannot be held accountable, for there is no one superior to them. Gods cannot be held accountable as they are—supreme," Michel replied, his gaze settling over her features with a darkness in his eyes. A darkness that seeped into his voice. It crept along the floorboards from where he stood and began to march toward Justine. Little shadows hissing and churning, prowling for a weakness, seeking, seeking a vulnerability.

Justine was not intimidated by her brother-in-law, not anymore, as she had lived in the same house as him, ate at the same table as him, as well as seen the horror of him and the corpse. He was a demon in the room on that damned night, a true beast of evil. Again, came the constricting in her chest and the pounding of her heart. Boom, boom, booming. Harder, harder, and harder.

It hurt. It hurt to breathe. It hurt to think. It all began to hurt so bad. What was this? There was no physical pain. There was only emotional—no, not even emotion. It was as if there was power in his gaze, power chaining her down, holding her down.

"Gods are supreme, complete. And within my own realm, I am a god. I become all supreme, the only one to pray to for mercy or for death. When you control life and death, when you control yourself to maintain a balance . . . it is being a god," came the words, punctuated and controlled, and with each word spoken, he had come a step closer. Until with the last utterance, Michel was standing right before her, and in his eyes was a feverish glow.

Oh, no, no, no. Justine felt her head begin to throb, the same pounding as in her chest. A vicious rhythm clawing its way through her entire body. It hurt so bad. It hurt so bad, and she could not move. She could not turn. She could not do anything of her own volition.

Why? There were no physical restraints on her wrists. Her neck was bare, and her ankles were free. But she felt weighed down. She felt burdened and heavy, as if there were chains all around her. And then it all came crashing in, a roaring in her ears.

"Am I your god, Justine?" he whispered, his lips brushing along her ear as his fingers sought to wrap around her throat. Michel saw her pulse. Her heart was racing, and it was alluring to him, teasing him. Ah, he could not touch her, as his brother had commanded. Michel meant to obey. This created quite the dilemma while Michel hovered ever so close to her. The power, the control, the tilting of her world was so, so tantalizingly close. Self-control. It was a trait he did possess, but it was difficult to withdraw. It was rather cruel to pull away.

"Yes, the answer is yes—I am your god," he said.

Michel then began to take steps back and away from her. His gaze was vacant, his expression frozen as a mask—a mask he had so carefully, so meticulously sculpted throughout his life. It became what he made it with his facial expressions and his body language. He knew how to become what the world wanted or needed to see. He knew how to control the perception, the image—

His thoughts were cut off by Justine's voice.

"You are nothing. You are a ghastly excuse of a man. You are nothing. You are not my god. You are nothing to me."

Oh, those words were so cleanly said he felt them slice through to his core. He was nothing? Not acceptable. How disappointing.

"That is what you may believe now, Justine. Be cautious, for your faith may change. Your world may crumble, and I will be your only salvation. Then you will see I am your god," Michel taunted as he turned away from her, turned and walked away.

Michel left behind a tense Justine and a chaotic atmosphere. There was nothing more to be said. There was nothing more to be done. Not then. It was not the right time. Not yet.

Michel licked his lips and slowed down his pace as he turned down one hall, then another, not truly paying attention to his surroundings until he came face-to-face with the dark oak doors to his study. The sight made his heart skip a beat. It stirred something feral within him.

Survival launched itself to the forefront of his thoughts, of his mind, and everything else blurred into red. Survive. Survive. Why was the door slightly ajar? It had been closed and sealed tight when he left the room not an hour before. Who could have trespassed into his library? Justine would not have dared. Henri knew about this place but lacked the time to search it. Leaving only . . . Percy.

The doors swung open with a bang. Michel still only saw red as he entered the room in a whirlwind, fueled by rage and retribution. Then time both froze and quickened, leaving him in a pool of red. Red. Everywhere was red.

Michel felt . . . nothing. Nothing but rage. There was no sorrow. There was no pain. Just as there was not guilt. There was no shame. Nothing was as it should have been, not with his brother, not with his father, and certainly not with his love . . . Nothing. There was nothing left. There was simply this existence, where he felt as if he were suffocating by the cold skeletal grasp of the Reaper.

Michel did not feel vulnerable, but he did not sense he was dauntless. Rather, there was a heaviness about his mind. A fog had darkened and intensified the nothingness within.

It never bothered him, this emptiness. It was what he had always known.

Yet he was obsessing over Justine because of the changes within his brother, Henri. Henri was more concerned with his daughter than he was about Michel. It was petty, but Michel needed to be acknowledged by his elder brother. Yet there was nothing. There was nothing left. Nothing of their childhood, nothing of their survival together as he looked down on the fresh body sprawled on the floor before him.

There is nothing left.

Late February 1792

I will kill him.

-H.L.G.

CHAPTER TWENTY-NINE
In Our Final Hours

November 1780

I was in love with ~~Alice (my stepmother)~~ her. I had to destroy my sister. This meant I would be the only focus of my stepmother. If ~~Elizabeth~~ she was gone, then I would be the only one to comfort my stepmother.

She was so beautiful. Her blue eyes always wide in fear, doe-like. Her fingers always trembled as they played the pianoforte. I was in love with her. Do I remember what it tasted like? Do I remember the salty bitter taste of victory?

~~My stepmother hated me and feared me after Elizabeth died.~~

~~The bitch knew.~~

~~I swear that I hate her.~~

I swear that I love her.

My stepmother disappeared a week ago. Two? My father does not seem to care. He says, "Be quiet! She was a whore anyway. Speak no more of her."

~~But i loved her.~~

I turned thirteen today. My father does not seem to care.

-M.L.G.

PERCY, WHY DID YOU HAVE TO SCREAM, TO rage? I was going to be a decent husband to you. I was going to ensure you were provided for. You were . . . well, not . . ." Michel began mumbling his thoughts aloud as the silence was stifling.

The blood was curling around shards of glass, shards of porcelain, shards of bone. Why was his head roaring? Why were the waves crashing higher and higher, suffocating him further and further into the depths? He had seen red. Michel had heard nothing after he'd seen Percy sifting through his desk, his papers strewn before her, and the look of guilt she had given him as the dark oak doors swung open. The blood was still warm. Her cheeks were still flushed, and there was still a burning glow to her eyes. They stared at him, accusing him and taunting him.

"You should never have looked through this room. This room was never accessible to you, to any of us as children. So why did you have to come here, today of all days? I swore to Henri I was going to marry you. To marry you, not to bury you. Bones and ashes, Percy! You were meant to be my wife, not this!" he shouted, over and over. "Not this! Not this!"

"Do you think I wanted to die, Michel?" her voice whispered through his mind, condemning.

"None of them wanted to die, Percy. Annabelle was not an exception; she was not amenable. My father did not want to die. My mother did . . . She . . . My little sister . . ." His shouting had begun to dwindle as his voice lost its strength. Michel began to reel with the brutality ripping through his thoughts and exploding in his mind as flashes of screams, of blood, of more screaming.

"Do you think it my fault? I did nothing wrong, Michel. I did nothing wrong . . ." Percy continued to whisper through the explosions, through the storm surging through his mind.

"I did nothing wrong! I did nothing! You . . . YOU!" Michel was screaming, his cheeks wet and his hand gripping his stomach. Fingernails digging into his skin as he knelt, his knees dipping into the red, red floors. The blood soaking into his pants. There was no echo. There was nothing coming back. There was nothing. He was nothing. He was . . . he was nothing. Not a god, not a man, not a brother, not a son . . . Michel slammed his forehead down into the shards of bone, shards of glass, and shards of porcelain.

Michel slammed his head against the ground. Again, and again and again. In his attempt to silence the whispering voices in his head, Michel ignored the building pain in his abdomen and head. It was not just Percy accusing him, not just Percy whispering his deeds. It was his brother. It was Annabelle. It was his sister. It was his mother.

"You were not my lover, Michel. You were merely a plaything. A revenge."

"Michel, my sweet child, why have you destroyed my sacrifice? I died so you might live, my sweet Michel. You were named for the angel, not for the demon. My sweet, sweet child . . ."

"You are nothing to this family. You are nothing to our name. You are a hazard. You are doomed."

"Michel, I do not know why you did these things, but please, please, Michel, let me speak with Henri. Let me speak with him! Does he know about your confessions, your journals? Michel . . . No, no . . . Don't throw it! Michel!" Percy screamed in his head.

The scene began to replay in his mind's eye, and he was shaking, shaking. The glass of wine crashing off the table as he threw it all down. The porcelain vase shattering as he took hold of it and swung it down over her head. The crunching of her skull on impact. The hissing silence after she thudded to the ground.

Michel began to tremble. Why had she read through the pages of shadows, of webs, of lies? His heart began to pound against his chest. *Boom, boom, boom.* His ears were filled with a ringing, a chiming of chaos as his body keeled forward. Michel pressed his palms to his ears, his breathing labored as he fought the urge to vomit.

"You did this! You did this, Percy!" Michel was sobbing, his shoulders shaking as his body heaved forward and backward. There was no longer any control, there was no longer any . . . emptiness. The nothingness had lifted, and he felt it all. The lashings, the trauma, the nightmares, the fears. The weight of the secrets pinned him down. The heaviness of his wrongs forced the air from his lungs. His ears were ringing, roaring.

There was nothing left. The boundaries had been broken. The walls of his fortress had evaporated within a moment's breath. All the memories, all the moments flashed through his mind and slammed into one another. A battlefield of emotions he had not felt since . . . since childhood. Fear. Anger. Sorrow. Oh, what was this? Why had Percy read the journals?

Why was his stomach heaving? Acid burned the back of his throat as he vomited the contents of his stomach across the floor.

Michel slammed his head down a final time, and then he became still. His eyes were wide open, staring over at the body of Percy, and he felt warmth oozing from his forehead, from his ears. He no longer saw red, but he could no longer ignore the storm within. The monster had been overcome.

What more was there to be done? Michel staggered to his feet and then fell back down to his knees, his eyes locked on Percy's body. Oh, Henri was going to be furious. Would his brother forgive this mistake? It was another mistake too soon in the wake of the other. Annabelle had been gone a year and a half. Her notoriety had faded, and fewer mouths whispered her name as the months continued on. But Percy . . . After the announcement of their engagement in the papers, after their wedding a week ago . . . Percy would not fade.

What could fix this? Michel's mind began to race, faster and faster, as his hands reached out to touch the side of Percy's face. She was already cold. His breathing was labored, and he was not sure what to do next. There was nowhere to go. They were supposed to be dressed and going downstairs for the family dinner—a grand display of the Geoffrey's' family unity and celebration of this new marriage. Close friends and figureheads of other prestigious families were gathering.

Henri was supposed to discuss something with him prior to them all entering the grand hall. What more could be done? How could he fix this problem? Michel felt his forehead and saw red on his fingers.

"Michel, you are not going to survive this one. Your brother will never forgive you. Percy meant something to Henri. You are a monster," came Annabelle's whisper through his mind.

"Be quiet! You temptress!" he shouted.

There was little else he could say aloud as Annabelle's words danced through his mind. They tangled into his thoughts and began to tighten their hold, constricting his mind to darkness and suffocation. There was nothing else to be done.

Michel stared down at Percy's body. It was not to be. His head had become foggy, heavy. His tongue felt heavy, thick, and sluggish in his mouth. His fingers were curling around a shard of broken glass in an absentminded gesture. Was someone else holding his hand, pressing his fingers into the broken glass? Michel did not want to die.

There was nothing else to be done.

Michel could not remember when the glass had left his grasp. He could not feel his fingers. He could not feel his hands. The slice felt like a quick burn. It stung for only a moment. The laceration was deep.

His body fell beside his wife, his blood seeping from his veins and emptying itself around her. Michel stared straight ahead. There was nothing left to be done. Was a servant going to sound the alarm? It was fine . . . Michel knew he was going to be gone soon. Only a man. Only a man. He had only ever been a man.

Goodbye, Henri. Michel was too weak to truly speak aloud, so the words crawled through his mind as his eyelids closed, and this time, they did not open again.

What misdeeds were to be forever silenced by his death? Michel had not confessed to his brother the truth of Annabelle, the truth of Elisabeth, nor the truth of his own cruelties. The shadows seemed to grow and strengthen as if to celebrate the passing of Michel.

As the light of the setting sun glistened and glowed off the droplets of blood still drip, drip, dripping, the shadows began to twist and dance, the silhouettes of three figures appearing along the floors. One was masculine, kneeling and in a weakened position. Two were feminine, both standing over the kneeling silhouette with their arms outstretched. There was a shifting and changing of the figures, as if they were in a struggle.

One might assume that Michel was being pulled down into submission by the ghosts of Annabelle and Percy, as a smaller, more petite shadow lingered in the corner. There was a heinous history being erased as the blood dripped down, down, down.

March 10, 1792

CHAPTER THIRTY

Did You Forget How We Cried?

I CANNOT DO THIS AGAIN. THIS IS MISERABLE. How can you expect anyone to live like this? Walking around in a glass prison with delicate walls and cracking floors. I cannot do this again and again. I need more than this. I need stability." Justine was choking, sobbing the words out as she clutched the bloodied blanket to her chest. Her throat hurt. Her chest felt constricted, tight.

"Justine. He is gone. There is nothing more we can do. He was never meant to be with us. Justine . . ." Henri whispered, reaching out his hands to touch her. He felt her trembling beneath his fingertips. Why had he not seen the depth of her wounds, the true depth of her hurt? Because he had felt it himself, because he blamed himself for their loss.

"I felt him kicking me! I felt him—" More sobbing, tears dripping down, down, down.

"Forgive me, Justine, forgive me for the part I played," Henri said.

He was answered with a laugh, a sound of hurt and betrayal. A laughter meant to be a scream that could have been a sob. The sound of her laughter tore his heart from his chest. Justine swung around to face him with her hand balled into a fist, fingernails digging into her palms.

"You think I would forgive you? *You?*" Justine screamed. Her voice broke.

There was to be no forgiveness. There was to be no forgetting. There was to be no turning of the other cheek. No, not for this. Not for the terror she had felt when Henri's hands curled around her throat and he had shouted profanities in her face. The terror had sent shards of glass through her body, shots of pain into her belly.

Her babies . . . her son. Her tears could not be stemmed, except for when Justine embraced the anger, the rage. When she felt the anger warming her blood, it lessened the grief, and the sorrow was banished into the hole in her chest. It became easier to breathe; it became easier to focus. Anger was cleansing; grief was degenerating.

"Justine, our daughter is growing every day. The milk nurses say she can hardly be satisfied with how much she drinks. She is beautiful." Henri spoke in a calm voice, recognizing the change in his wife as he took a step away from her.

The bloodied blanket she cradled so tightly against her chest was the last evidence of the traumatic birth of their children. It was a corner of the coverlet Justine had found and hidden away before the servants cleaned the room. No one had been aware of her being awake in those hours following the birth. Henri took a few more steps backward and away from his wife.

"You will never be forgiven, Henri. There is so much blood on your hands. I cannot envision a future where you are around our daughter. God forbid your actions, or lack of, harm her as well," Justine said quietly.

Henri felt the jagged wounds in his heart break open, slowing ripping with each word she said aloud. To not be allowed to see his daughter, to hold her or to share in her laughter . . . He stopped moving and stared over at Justine. An icy abyss separated them, and it seemed to span a thousand miles as her words died into silence, as his heart bled. Internalized. He kept it all internalized.

"You do not have such power, dear wife, to say these threats and be able to carry them through. Our daughter is more mine than yours. You forget yourself," Henri replied coldly. He turned his back to her.

"No. *You* forget yourself. We are supposed to bury your brother tomorrow. We already buried Percy."

"Be quiet!" Henri raged. "Shut up!"

Justine closed her mouth but continued to stare at him, no fear in her steady gaze. There was so much loss, so much pain, too much trauma between them. They were suffocating.

"Michel is dead, Henri. While you drifted through the halls in denial, I saw to the details of his burial. Death by suicide. It took a hefty donation to the church for them to allow him to be buried in Percy's family's tomb." Justine spoke quietly again, her voice monotone.

Henri was in denial of the truth in her words.

It was not true.

It was not true.

It was not . . .

It was . . .

It . . .

It was . . .

It was true . . .

Again, Henri felt the decades-old scars peeling backward, and those ancient wounds began to weep. Michel was gone. Percy was gone. His son was gone. Elisabeth was gone. His mother was gone. His father had caused all this loss. All this pain was his father's legacy. Henri remained silent as the seconds trickled by, transforming to minutes as they stood and stared at one another.

At last, Justine sighed, heavy tears streaming freely down her cheeks. The droplets splattering down, down, down to the touch the crimson-stained blanket. What more could be said between them? They'd had to bury their firstborn son. They'd had to bury his childhood and lifelong friend. They would have to bury his brother. Justine had not thought all this hurt, all this pain would break her own heart.

It was difficult to remember where she had been over a year ago. A newlywed young woman—no, a girl in truth—with glittering eyes and a hopeful heart. The world had been hers, with all the opportunity, all the magic of the unknown. Where had her hope gone? The hope was buried beneath the scars of violence between them, the screaming, the hitting, the crying. All the damned crying. Too many tears.

The magic of the unknown had been snuffed out when she discovered Michel's morbid secret and thus discovered the first of the Geoffrey skeletons. Oh, but that was only the surface of the skeletons and the shadows lining the halls, lining the closed doorways. There was so much more.

"Elisabeth will not be at the burial. The weather is turning foul, and I do not want her to get sick," Henri said aloud.

It was such a mundane thing to say, so simple. Their infant daughter could get sick so easily, and so she was seldom allowed outside unless it was sunny and warm. There was a tickle of laughter that passed through the air. The laughter grew and grew until they were both smiling.

"Our daughter will stay behind with her nurse," Justine agreed.

It was one of the first agreements they had reached in their relationship, excluding her agreement to his marriage proposal. This moment could have been ignored and hidden away beneath the folds of grief, the creases of anger. Instead, the two continued to smile as they looked at each other with the shared love and devotion for their daughter. Was the infant their hope?

Henri blinked once, twice and then let out a slow sigh. He was exhausted. Always exhausted.

"You will not be able to take our daughter away from me, Justine. That is not how our society functions. What are the details of Michel's funeral service?" he asked.

"As I said, it took a hefty donation to the church for the priest to agree for Michel to be buried in the Brough family tombs. He will still be buried on holy ground, albeit not in your family's tomb." *I'm sorry . . .* The words left unsaid clung to the back of her throat.

"Will a prayer be said over the coffin?" He was afraid to know the answer.

"Yes, there will be a short prayer said for his soul. We can pay more tithes for masses to be said." Justine fought the urge to reach out and touch her husband's shoulder.

"Elisabeth will not be there. You will be my only family in attendance. Will you walk with me?" Henri turned his face away from her, ashamed of his own vulnerability.

"Yes. I will remain by your side throughout the funeral service. We will be united as we bury your brother," she said so quietly the words were barely spoken aloud.

The room was so quiet around them that Henri did not have to strain to hear her whisper, even as her words were spoken more and more softly. There was nothing the servants feared more than silence, as silence meant death. Justine glanced around the room and felt her fingers loosen their tight grip on the bloodied blanket.

"How have the servants been faring?" Henri suddenly asked, as though their minds were somehow linked even as they remained strangers and even enemies, but for their daughter.

"We lost three maids. One manservant chose to leave as well. The four who left were only hired within the last year. All the others remain loyal to the Geoffrey house. They honor you, my lord, in their quiet servitude."

All the secrets, all the shadows, and all the demons had crept back beneath the floorboards when the little maid had screamed out upon discovery of Michel's and Percy's bodies. The poor thing had had the early morning duty of emptying the chamber pots and relighting the fires in each room if they had died in the night.

The little servant's screams had awoken Gideon. Then more servants had begun to stir. It was Gideon who was the second to enter the disastrous scene of the study. Silence had followed once the young servant fainted from shock. Gideon did not catch her as his old eyes took in the chaotic morbid scene before him.

It was as if a flash of history had been brought from his memory and laid out before him. What kind of macabre joke was this? Denial was the first emotion the old man felt as he took a few steps forward and placed his fingers on Michel's shoulder to scold the young man—until he felt the shoulder was stiff and the cold of the corpse seeped into the old man's fingertips.

It was not a sick jest. It was a reality Gideon once more experienced—a grizzly death scene within the walls of the Geoffrey home. It had been over two decades since the last bloodied room had been discovered.

How was he to tell his lord? How was he to approach his already mourning master about the death of his only brother? Gideon had stumbled backward and sunken down to the floor. At a loss for words, at a loss for action. It had been the other loyal servants who chose to awaken their mistress before the master of the household. It was Justine they whispered to as they brought her to Michel's study and held her fast in the doorway, whispering words of warning and of misery.

It had been Justine who stepped through the doorway and took in the silence, the stillness of the four bodies in the room. Her pupils had dilated, and her fingertips had reached out to touch Gideon's shoulder, stirring the old man from his own shock. It had been Justine who held a frozen finger to her lips to quiet the old man from speaking.

Justine had scooped the young servant into her arms and carried her to the other servants, who'd started to gather just beyond the gory background. No words were spoken, merely an exchange of stares and one nod. Gideon had remained in the room. Justine returned to his side and knelt beside him. She did not reach out to touch him again. Instead, she bowed her head and folded her hands together in her lap. Justine then began to pray. With the aftershocks of the loss of her stillborn son, still healing from the traumatic birth, prayer was all she could seek.

Henri had not been informed of the double loss, not so close to the death of his son and heir. Michel had been the presumed heir since their son had been stillborn. This meant the house was weakened, the bloodline put into a precarious position with no heirs.

It had been another near fatal blow to Henri as the exchange of information was said without emotion, without attachment as Justine succumbed to her own darkness. Michel and Percy had been wed not even a fortnight ago. The death of their son had been two months before. They went from grieving to putting aside their mourning to celebrate the wedding, and now . . . Justine was never going to forget the anguish on her husband's face when she had uttered the words.

Henri existed in a comatose state. Justine continued to barely function as she ran the household, giving directions for the local priest to be contacted, and she began to arrange for a double funeral months after she had buried their son.

Why? It was the question reverberating throughout her entire body as she went through the daily motions of living, of breathing, of planning. Justine could not fathom why Michel had murdered Percy. They hadn't been fighting. They had both been reluctant but agreeable to be married, to obey and please Henri. They all had tried to satisfy Henri, albeit in their own forms. Henri was the center of their lives.

The question remained: why?

An answer lingered just beyond her grasp as she thought over the days leading up to the murder-suicide. The only thing out of place was where their bodies had been found—in Michel's private study. Perhaps Percy had brushed off the rule and entered the study despite the looming threat of punishment. Justine closed her eyes and sighed. It did seem logical for Percy's intrusion to be the reason.

Justine kept up the appearance of maintaining the household, replying to letters of condolence, sending out letters for funeral arrangements and expenses. In the days following their deaths, Justine lost pieces of herself and truly doubted she would regain the fallen bits. There was no time to visit her daughter, no time to console her husband, no time . . . Shock weighed so very heavy within her chest, even though she had despised her brother-in-law, even though Percy had tried to kill her.

324

March 15, 1792

I killed him. I killed him. I killed him.

What would Henri do if he knew the truth?

—Justine Geoffrey

CHAPTER THIRTY-ONE
WHERE DO WE GO FROM HERE?

*O*NE FOR THE NIGHTMARE AND TWO FOR THE *seer, three for the maiden, and four for the fear . . .*

The blood was caked on her hands, burrowed beneath her fingernails, and it was drenched in her hair. She felt it on her scalp. The metallic taste coated the back of her throat. It was difficult to breathe. It was difficult to focus on anything but the red, all the red. She was drowning in the red.

Justine woke up sweating and panting, tangled in her sheets as she clamped her mouth shut. A scream had been building in her throat, pulsing and burning as it fought to be released.

There was no release.

It was just another sleepless night.

Her feet remained bare as she tiptoed through the hallways toward her daughter's nursery. Minutes passed while Justine lingered just outside of her daughter's door, her fingertips dancing along the doorknob. The knots of guilt, the cobwebs of grief weighed her down, causing her to be suspended in inaction.

Her fingers were slender and clean, no trace of blood on them. It was only a nightmare. This was her reality. She turned the doorknob and slipped into the quiet dimly lit room. The nurse was asleep in the antechamber.

Justine padded over the cool floor and peered over the edges of the cradle, staring down at the little girl cocooned within. Even in the dim lighting, the child was undoubtedly lovely, with curls of strawberry blond hair as a crown atop her head and eyelashes thick over plump cheeks. Why was there no tenderness warming her heart when she looked at her sleeping child? Why was there no emotion within her as she watched her daughter? Justine reached into the cradle and picked up her little Elisabeth, gently shushing her as she held the child against her chest.

The infant stirred but readily settled into the warmth of Justine's arms with soft coos. There was still no deep connection linking the mother to her daughter. Justine was keenly aware of the emptiness in her heart and in her mind. This little girl was not enough. Her daughter was not enough to quiet the storm of grief draining her soul. The trauma was still too fresh, the pain still too acute.

"Do you see your brother in your dreams, Elisabeth? Tell him Mommy loves him. Tell him Mommy is so sorry she could not—" Justine's voice broke as tears began to streak down her cheeks. A few droplets fell onto her daughter's face, which startled the infant. Elisabeth awoke with a high-pitched wail of discontent.

It seemed as though no comfort was to be given to calm and quiet the wailing little one. Justine felt panic, as well as a whiplash of anger. Nurse Katharine came into the nursery with a worried look, her expression changing as she dipped into a curtsey with a murmured "Milady." With trembling hands, Justine passed her daughter over to Katharine and pivoted away as quick as she could, her eyes burning and her temper blazing white and hot beneath her skin.

"Please quiet her down. Elisabeth was crying when I came into the room. You need to be more attentive; do you understand?" Justine's tone was sharp.

"Yes, milady. I am sorry, milady." The milk nurse stumbled out the apology as she swayed back and forth, deftly unbuttoning her blouse and allowing the little girl to root and then begin to nurse.

The little nursery was silent except for the hungry gulping of Elisabeth. Justine did not bother to dismiss the nurse to depart, nor did she remember to grant the other woman permission to sit. Preoccupied, her entire mind was preoccupied with everything else she was required to maintain and see to. Her daughter was moved lower and lower on her list of priorities, a fact that did not hurt Justine. Not as it should have.

The silence continued until Elisabeth unlatched, cooing in contentment as Katharine patted her back until a tiny burp came out. It was not long until the girl was asleep once more and the nurse had gently swaddled her back into her cocoon prior to laying her back into the safety of her cradle.

"You may go. I will sit here with her for a little while. Thank you, Katharine," Justine said at last, her voice hoarse and unsteady.

The nurse dipped into a quick curtsy. Then her hands nervously wrung in her apron as she ducked out of the nursery and went to fetch Gideon. The young woman remained leery of Lady Geoffrey being left alone with the little girl, as she sensed the lack of warmth and connection between the mother and child. It had been two months since the baby was born. A detachment this severe should not have lasted this long.

Bone-tired and unable to stand once the other woman had left the room, Justine sank into the nearby rocking chair. She felt the cool wood behind her neck as she leaned all the way back with a ragged sigh. Her entire body trembled.

Why?

The single-worded question kept racing through her thoughts, overwhelming any design she might have set for herself, as nothing was able to prove a suitable distraction. A whirlwind of questions and doubts leaked through the barricades she had attempted to place in her mind, the foundations weak, the walls already crumbling.

"Would . . . would you have murdered me, Michel? I trespassed into your private study, and you threatened violence. If your brother had not interceded . . ." Justine murmured to herself, cautious to keep her voice low even as her throat burned with another suppressed scream. She swallowed hard against the tightness in her throat, her hands curling into her hair as she leaned forward.

The scream continued to build within the back of her throat, and eventually, Justine released the pressure with a low and quiet keen. Her teeth sank into the flesh of her lower lip to keep herself hushed, intent on not disturbing the sleeping child a few feet from her.

It was a nightmare. This life had been a nightmare from the first night, from the moment she had said her vows at the altar. The nightmare had grown more and more garish as the days wore on. Her husband had proved to be abusive, manipulative, and cruel. Her brother-in-law had proved to be a vain psychopath. There was no one within the Geoffrey household she could wholly trust. Gideon was loyal to Henri. Even the milk nurse who cared for her daughter . . . her loyalties were questionable.

Wave after wave of paranoia began to amass as her thoughts continued into the downward spiral of a slippery slope. Was Elisabeth even safe within this family? Or would the little girl be better off dead? It had been God's judgment to take her son away before he took his first breath. Perhaps it was also God's judgment for her daughter to return to heaven.

Justine sat up straight, her fingers clenched into the fabric of her nightgown as she dry-heaved onto the floorboards before her. Nothing came out as her body tried to release itself of the growing stress. Her stomach knotted to a painful extent. Why was she being punished?

As the shadows descended around her heart and her mind, Justine became detached from the world around her. Thus, she was unaware when the nursery door clicked open and then closed again. Her eyes were staring over at the cradle, but they were unseeing as the figure moved from the doorway over toward her, kneeling at the side of the rocking chair.

Muffled words came from the figure's mouth, but Justine did not coherently register someone had spoken to her. She was internally drowning. Piece by piece, she fractured within herself, the edges jagged and smoldering.

Henri noticed his wife had not heard the first words he'd said to her; he recognized the glazed-over eyes and the too-pale skin. He had been ensnared in his own hell, in his own internal battles for the last few days. Or had it been weeks? Time had been utterly lost to him until 9:20 that morning, when Gideon had slapped him across the face, hard.

"I am sorry I failed to shield you, Justine. You deserved better than for your husband to withdraw into himself. I have failed you again," Henri murmured against his wife's cheek. His hand settled across her knee in a hesitant touch. Gone was the possessive energy. The dominance had dissipated. Loss after loss had taken a brutal toll on his own mental strength, utterly depleting it. "What do you need from me? No. I will not ask you. I am here, Justine. I am here." His words strained with emotion.

"Leave me alone," Justine whispered. "I need you to leave me alone."

"That is not possible, not when you are near our daughter. Elisabeth is healthy. She is growing. This would change if someone were to harm her. If you were to harm her."

An audible gasp left Justine's mouth, and she abruptly stood up from the rocking chair. The sudden movement almost knocked them both off-balance. Henri held steady, his hand catching his wife's elbow to keep her upright as well.

"You do not know me at all if you think I could harm my own child!" Justine spat out.

"On the contrary, wife, I do know you. I know you wish it were our son sleeping in the cradle and our daughter were in the grave."

The truth sent a lightning strike of shame and guilt down her spine. Justine had been harboring those dark thoughts to herself for weeks now, desperately combating them with futile efforts of identifying her daughter's beauty and her sweet disposition. An innocent child—yet Justine blamed the little girl for taking the life meant for her brother. How did Henri know this? Henri had been detached from their private life after the news of his brother's death. So how did Henri know?

"You trust servants' gossip over your own wife?"

"I trust Gideon. You are burdened more than you should be, so freshly postpartum . . ." Henri huffed out a sigh as his fingers curled more tightly around her elbow.

"I am not a threat to our daughter!" Justine lashed out, her nails digging into her husband's hand as she clawed at him.

"You promised to be at my side at Michel's funeral. I need you to regain your strength, Justine. I need you to not be a threat to our daughter, my only heir . . . your heir." Henri allowed her to temper to flare, for her to inflict the deep gouges along his forearms if it meant keeping her in reality, far from the ambiguous shadows still lurking along the corners of his own mind.

"Elisabeth will not be harmed, not by my hands. I swear." Justine breathed out, calming herself as best she could.

Her words brought a wave of relief through his body, yet Henri remained vigilant as he took a step and then two steps away from his wife. He felt the trickle of blood dripping down, down, down his arms and did not bother to glance down at the damage she had done. Henri did not want to frighten his wife, nor did he desire to lay blame at her feet.

"Henri, I am exhausted. I do not know how much longer I can keep everything balanced. I needed you, and you were lost within yourself," Justine confessed, her hands curled into fists at her sides. What else could she say to him? She wanted to promise she loved their daughter. She wanted to say she was fine. Those would have been lies. Henri hated when she lied to him.

"I am here now, Justine. I am here. What may I do to help you?"

"You need to start writing response letters to our friends and the peerage." Justine glanced down at her fingertips and blanched at the blood on them. This whole excursion had started as an attempt to run away from the blood in her nightmares, the blood that had been coated all throughout her hair and on her hands. Blood was now sticky and warm on her fingers. Nausea assaulted her senses, and she swayed backward.

"Justine!" Henri exclaimed as his hands shot out and wrapped around her waist, unintentionally pulling her against his chest, causing both of them to tremble at the sudden physical contact.

They had not embraced one another in a year, not since Justine had confirmed her pregnancy with the doctor. Her proximity caused a fire to explode in his chest, searing him and taking his breath away. Over and over. Henri had forgotten what it was like to hold her, to feel her near him. It was excruciating.

"You and I allowed this to happen to our family, Henri. You hid your brother's sins, and I helped you. Both of our souls are damned," Justine whimpered as her shoulders began to quake, her body surrendering to the sobs. Tears rolled down her cheeks unabashed as she pressed her forehead against Henri's chest.

Henri kept his arms tight around his wife's waist as she sobbed and sobbed. He was able to understand the tremendous amount of strain she had been under while he'd allowed himself to drown in grief and self-pity. It was no excuse that he knew grief had a way of destroying. Henri loathed himself for succumbing to the weakness. There was no grace allowed as he berated himself internally.

March 17, 1792

Do you know his name? My son. My only son. My little boy.
Mommy loves you.
Mommy misses you.
Mommy did this atrocity to protect you.

-Justine Geoffrey

CHAPTER THIRTY-TWO
There Is Only One Hope, She Is Fragile

THE WORLD WAS A FAITHLESS THING AS LIFE marched on in a steady march after the burial of Percy Geoffrey. The sun continued to rise in the east and set in the west. As each day came and went, it felt erroneous. It felt as a betrayal to the memory of his brother. Henri had become a shadow of himself. Barely eating. Barely sleeping. A phantom who wandered the halls of his home with dead eyes and a pale complexion. The servants began to whisper about his madness. Henri was weighed down by the burden of grief: for his son, for his brother, for Percy. There was even a whisper of loss for Annabelle, although she had been dead for over a year. He dug his fingers into his scalp and bent his head over the desk, his eyes closed tight as he fought against his own memories.

Henri heard all of them laughing, and he saw them twirling around in the small space of his study. Henri saw them all as clearly as though they were alive, as if they were once more flesh and blood rather than bones and ashes. The strain of emotion encased his face in a grimace as he looked on to the celebration happening before him: Elisabeth was dancing around in a white frock trimmed in lace with soft pink slippers on her feet. Annabelle was twirling in the arms of William, the late Lord Geoffrey, dressed in a beautiful lavender gown with ruffles along the neckline. Percy was laughing and clapping her hands, swaying back and forth in her wedding gown of lace and layered skirts. Michel was looking away from Henri, laughing and smiling as Elisabeth pulled him in to dance with her.

Three other ghoulish silhouettes were floating along the background, hidden behind a curtain of smoke and treachery. The reflections were distorted and fractured. The three ghouls were feminine, each with a different shade of hair. Each with a hideous contorted smile on their face.

Henri began to lose the contents of his stomach as he heard their laughter, their clapping, and their music echoing through his mind. Why were they so happy? They did not seek to dance with him. They did not seek to acknowledge him. It left him feeling despondent, abandoned once more to be the only survivor. The last one who was truly breathing, the last one to truly be flesh and blood, not bones and ashes.

The noises echoed louder and louder until Henri had to press his palms against his ears to drown out the noise. He began to rock back and forth, keening in agony as he watched those he had once loved dance in merriment about their own graves.

"I am nothing without you all! I am nothing without you, Father, and your wisdom to guide me . . . Michel, your steady presence beside me . . . Elisabeth, your little hand to steady me . . . Percy, your love to cleanse me . . . Annabelle . . ." Henri was sobbing, breaking further and further into the void opened wide at his feet. It had engulfed him. Darkness and streaks of light, flashes of their faces, and the white noise of their laughter, their voices.

What could he do?

What else could he do?

Awareness dawned in his mind. Henri slowly moved, his body uncurling itself as he stood. The tears had dried on his cheeks as he stared at the corpses before him. Henri had awoken, returned to the reality of his life: he was alone. What else could he do? An answer screamed loud and clear in his mind as he walked over to his bookshelf. His fingers reached to the third shelf and went deftly behind a few of the older tombs. At the withdrawal of his hand, there followed a low creaking noise, and the bookshelf swung open.

Henri took quick and deliberate steps, leaving behind his study and entering a dimmer, dry room that seemed more like a cavern, except the floor was made of smooth cool white marble. The walls were lined with glass display boxes, each with an oil lantern hanging before it. The flickering unsteady light of the oil lamps revealed the grotesque contents held within.

Henri paused before the third glass box and pressed both of his hands, palms flat, against the cool glass. His gaze met the marble eyes of his father, the late Lord Geoffrey, and the nausea and overwhelming wave of emotions of sorrow began to drain. It was a continually odd experience to walk into this cavern, into this quiet room where time was eclipsed by the pause of death, of loss, of grief. This was where Henri sought the comfort of his father's advice, and the two of them could stare at one another, one seeking solace and the other merely there, merely a corpse.

"Why did you not train Michel in the ways of being a lord's son? He was the second son, the spare, but he should have been held to a higher standard. You failed all of us by lowering your expectations of him," Henri whispered, his forehead pressed against the glass and his eyes tightly closed. It was still difficult to speak against his father, to speak in criticism for the formerly great and domineering shadow who had consumed his childhood and his youth.

"Why are you not responding? Why are you not spewing some venomous statement about my own failures, my own shortcomings and how they were the cause of Michel's lack of success?" Henri began to yell, his voice echoing in the confined space.

Silence, perpetual silence surrounded him, and it felt as though it were draining him. The silence dug its nails along the back of his mind. What was the purpose of coming here if all he heard was the sound of his own ragged breathing? In coming here, Henri always expected an answer, guidance that never came. Another emotion stirred beneath the fragile surface of his mind, grasping at the edges of his thoughts as he turned and looked to his right.

"Mama . . . do not weep. You are a grandmother. Mama, why do you request the unthinkable of me? My wife . . . she will not understand why you are in here. She will not allow your granddaughter here. This remains my great secret. I am sorry, Lady Mother." Henri spoke in a hoarse whisper. Tears streaked down his cheeks as he stared at the once beautiful face of his mother. She appeared to be sleeping, with her eyes sewn shut with golden thread, her mouth downturned in a frown in an expression of discomfort.

Henri let out a keen as he crumpled to the floor before his mother's still form. What more was he supposed to do? Justine had all but forbade for little Elisabeth to be told of the family's tragic history. Justine had discovered enough fragmented truths. She had been able to piece together a picture of his father's depravity, Michel's childhood trauma, and the trauma of his own childhood . . . the numerous murders, the vanishings . . . Henri held both sides of his head in a viselike grip, his fingers clenching and pulling at his hair.

"Mama, little Elisabeth is not old enough to meet you. She will not understand. Neither would her mother. I will try to bring your granddaughter to visit you soon. I will tell her stories about you, about your beauty and your wisdom. Through these stories, she might learn to love you as I love you—" His words stumbled, and his voice broke with another keen. Another wave of loss struck him through the chest faster than a lightning bolt and harder than a ship colliding with the rocks of a hidden shore.

The back of his throat began to burn and to ache. The wail that came from his mouth was dying down as he felt the rawness of his throat. When was the last time he had drank something? Anything? It had been a week since his brother's funeral service. Henri knew he had dined once or twice with Justine between then and now . . . It had been no more than two, perhaps three days since he had consumed anything.

Nothing mattered anymore. Justine hated him and barely spoke to him. Michel was dead. Percy was dead. His son was dead. His father was gone. His mother too. Nothing seemed to matter beyond the simple fact of his daughter, his sweet Elisabeth—who was cursed to never meet her namesake.

"One day, Elisabeth will come to visit you. She will come to visit all of you," Henri said aloud to the corpses lined around him, their unseeing eyes looking beyond his soul. He knew they heard him even though they gave no answer. They always heard him. They always listened to him whenever he came to visit.

March 20, 1792

I buried Percy. I was barely able to remember the sound of her voice, the touch of her skin . . . I was not unfaithful to my wife. But I do miss her. Even though she almost killed both of my children. Even though she did kill my son. Even though she . . .
I buried Percy.
I cannot bury Michel. I need my brother.
I hate my brother.
But I need my brother.

-H.L.G.

CHAPTER THIRTY-THREE

Are You Burning in Hell?

THIS PARISH WAS ON THE OUTSKIRTS OF THE city in a district that was impoverished, and thus, when the parish required a hefty donation to be made on behalf of the lost soul, Justine did not blink at the sum.

It was a miracle that this parish had accepted her plea for a burial service, as the church condemned suicide as a mortal sin. Justine was wholly and fully aware of the monster her brother-in-law had been. Despite this knowledge, she was frustrated by the church and their rules of burial. Her efforts were not futile, as she had eventually been granted permission to bury Michel in the Percy family tomb—as the tomb itself was located on the external perimeter of the holy burial grounds.

An unsteady breath in allowed for Justine's mind to clear itself of fog and mist. She steadied herself in the front pew of the church. The heavy black skirts of her mourning gown swished gently along the ground as she swayed side to side. Her teeth worried the flesh of her lower lip as she kept a wary eye on her husband, not daring to touch him, but also not daring to step away from him. Henri had been so . . . fragile since the news of Michel's suicide. Fragile and shattered, his confidence utterly vanished and his purpose seemingly destroyed.

"Selfish bastard, you owed your brother more than this," Justine murmured beneath her breath as she glanced over at the closed casket. The deep mahogany wood was smoothed and polished. It held the corpse of the would-be god, the selfish fool who had thought himself above the laws of God and man. "Are you burning in hell, Michel?"

Any form of an answer would have been better than the white noise that surrounded her: the shuffling of feet, the whispers of dozens of people, the chanting of the choir. The white noise wrapped around her, smothering her senses, and caused Justine to turn to face the closed casket. Michel was dead. She had seen his corpse, seen his blood pooled on the floor of his study. Yet she could not shake an eerie feeling that he was not gone.

The church itself was cramped; the half dozen pews were barely enough to contain the guests that had begun to arrive. It was mostly noblemen who came on behalf of their great families, leaving behind wives and family members. The funeral service itself was under scrutiny and a topic of heated debate within the salons of high society—thus, the fewer eyes and ears to witness the service, the better for the Geoffrey house.

A slim man stepped forward to the podium at the front of the nave. He cleared his throat and adjusted the folds of his priest's robes. The white noise of the gathered nobles grew quiet until there remained only the shuffling of feet and the soft sound of fabric rubbing against the pews. The priest began to pray:

"In your hands, O Lord, we humbly entrust our brother. In this life, you embraced him with your tender love; deliver him now from every evil and bid him eternal rest. The old order has passed away: welcome him into paradise, where there will be no sorrow, no weeping or pain, but fullness of peace and joy with your Son and the Holy Spirit forever and ever. Amen. We are gathered here to say farewell to a cherished . . ."

Justine could no longer focus on the words as the priest drawled on and on. Another noise caught her attention. A lullaby she had heard Henri whispering to their daughter.

"Swing my hands; swing my hands, ever near and ever far, from the flames of hell, from the flames of hell. Swing my hands, swing my hands, oh-ever love, oh-ever love, to the gates of heaven, to the gates of heaven . . ." Henri sang the childhood lullaby beneath his breath as he stared straight ahead, unseeing and uncaring. He began the melancholic tune again and again, a broken repetition as he sought to soothe himself. Why was his brother dead? What had caused Michel to make a sacrifice of himself? Why had Percy been another casualty? Why were they all dead?

As the questions circled through his mind as ravenous and predatory as vultures, Henri paid no heed to the priest standing before him. Henri ignored the mahogany casket and the vibrant bouquets of flowers. He remained isolated as the funeral service ended. The twenty-odd guests that had dared to appear were lingering, whispering to one another.

Henri let them think he was not overhearing every rumor, every slanderous whisper they shared. His own thoughts were not the vultures, it was the faces surrounding him with glistening eyes and lying lips. Despite the searing pain of the false words, the accusations and the rumors swirled around and round. Henri stood and walked down the center aisle of the pews, only to pause as he heard peculiar details, no one outside of the Geoffrey home should have known.

"A murder-suicide?"

"Do you ever wonder about Lady Stanley's disappearance?"

"I heard that Michel left a confession letter."

"Michel killed his wife in cold blood! He was tired of being cuckolded by his own brother. Then the damned fool committed suicide out of his own guilt. Can you imagine?"

"No, no . . . I heard that it was the wife who murdered Michel Geoffrey. Then the maid killed the wife. A love triangle gone wrong!"

"Oh, be quiet! All of you!" Justine spat out, her tolerance had been nonexistent hours and hours before the funeral service had even started. How could she ignore the remarks? The audacity these noblemen had was baffling to her. She glowered at them; the harshness of her expression blurred behind the spiderweb-fine black lace that covered her face.

"No offense was intended, Lady Geoffrey," one of the

gentlemen simpered, lowering his gaze and bowing his head in a gesture of respect. It was far too late. The words had already been said aloud, and they acted as a stimulant for the grief engulfing Henri's mind, causing the man to spiral into the abyss.

Justine cast a quick look at her husband's face, where she saw the deterioration occurring beneath the frail façade of his calmness. His mask was going to fall. A cruel thought pulsed through her mind as she fought against the impulse to let her husband crumble into a thousand pieces before his peers. It would be a fit punishment for the violence he had committed against her; however, it would cause harm to their daughter's future if society saw the weaknesses in Lord Geoffrey. Grief was acceptable, but a public breakdown was intolerable.

"Let us mourn our loss without your insipid murmurings. My lord and I thank you for your generosity, and we appreciate your comforting presence. Now please seek refreshments elsewhere." Her words were clipped, edged with impatience. Something sharper threatened to break through her composure.

All the emotions threatened to overwhelm her. There was anger; there was confusion; there was grief. All of them in conflict within her own mind as she stepped closer to her husband and gently laid her hand across his forearm, curling her body into his chest in a display of weakness—her own weakness, so any slight or offense could be blamed on her feminine qualities.

Thankfully, the priest understood the cue from Lady

Geoffrey, and he made his way toward the double doors of the church. It was a clear indication to the guests it was time to leave. The guests lingered a few more seconds before they began to shuffle out, clearing out row by row. An unnatural quiet shrouded the small crowd as they looked between Henri Geoffrey and his wife, questions and opinions flitting beneath the surface. Gossip and details were to be shared over and over again, twisting and turning into fantastic stories of death, of grief, of jealousy, of madness.

In the brief time it took for the church to be emptied, the last of Justine's resolve collapsed, and she fell backward into the nearest pew. Her head ached, throbbing as she closed her eyes and fought the unexpected wave of nausea. It was all too much. All the deaths in quick succession devoured her from the inside.

The despair had engorged itself on the sadness, on the grieving, on the broken-heartedness that never diminished. As wave after wave of nausea coursed through her body, Justine pressed her cold palms against her closed eyes until she saw lights sparking in the back of her eyelids. There was no length of time she could be allowed to truly mourn, to curl up and sob for hours, if not for days. It had been barely two months since her stillborn son was born with eyes closed and no breath in his lungs...since she named her daughter as her heir should anything worse befall her.

It was an unfamiliar emotion beginning to surface, rearing its hideous head through the fractures of her mind. Justine regained control of her body, and its physical symptoms of stress melted away as she turned her head to stare over at her husband. At the man who was the center of her world, who was supposed to be the provider and the shield of the family. Disgust is what crawled out of the depths of her soul by clawing its way through flesh and bone, blood and ashes. This disgust flooded through her mind and clouded her judgment.

"Henri, be a man!" Justine spat out. Each word trembled with unshed tears and contempt. There was no one left in the church to hear her, no one except for the priest and the unhearing ears of her brother-in-law. Justine wanted to scream. Instead, she stalked over to her husband's still form and slapped him. The sound of her hand smacking his cheek reverberated throughout her entire body. There was no regret as the disgust began to evolve within the pit of her stomach. It began to burn, to mutilate her internally.

Neither of them heard the footsteps of the priest as he fled the scene. This left them completely and utterly alone in the church.

Henri heard her. He had been fully aware of the whispers of his peers and had heard the hypocrisy of the entire funeral service. The prayers could not possibly salvage the damnation of his brother's soul, the words of healing and of forgiveness never to be fruitful. Henri had been aware of everything around him despite how he had remained frozen in place. He had allowed his wife and the others around him to believe his grief was so overpowering that he was not aware of them. His cheek prickled with the sensation of pins and needles where her hand had made contact.

"You have an abundance of daring to touch me. Do you truly not fathom the extent to which this has damaged our family? Our foothold in society has been weakened. My bloodline has been shortened. My brother is dead, Justine. And you expect me to be a man? What do you want me to do? What should I do when my own brother is *dead*?" Henri's voice rose higher and higher with each word until he was bellowing into his wife's face.

"I expect you to be a man! I want you to be the pillar for our family, for our daughter! I want you to grieve for your brother and his wife. I want you to grieve and then look ahead for the plans that we need to make!" Justine screamed back, her spine hardening along with her resolve.

"There is no time to grieve! You are a fool. A pathetic rancid fool. All the planning in the world could not salvage the damage that my brother has done to this family. Michel was a scoundrel who existed only for his self-centered desires, his only focus his morbid impulses. Society needs to forget about our family. They need a new scandal to focus on," Henri shouted back, the veins bulging from his throat as he raised his hands and pushed against her shoulders. Forgotten were the unwritten rules of charity, of kindness when in the Church of God. He wanted to hurt her. Henri wanted to smash his fist into the pretty face of his wife, to knock the sneer from her.

"Henri, if I am a fool, then you are worse. You are a simpleton. You never dared to—" Justine choked on her own words as her cheek began burning after her husband slapped her. It was not surprising, nor was she startled.

"Be quiet, you ungrateful despicable woman! You do not know what my brother suffered through. You do not know anything! Keep your wretched mouth closed if you wish to speak about Michel in a damning light. Only God may lay judgement on my brother's soul, because only God knows what we suffered and survived." Henri once more was shouting each word into her face, his hand raised again as if he desired to strike her again and again.

Quiet. Quiet and curling into herself, her body shrinking away from the wrath of her husband's voice and his face. Justine had seen him angry. She had felt the pain he could inflict if he wished to be cruel, but even in those times, she had not felt fear. However, fear was what began to wrap its cold, cold fingers around her spine, and she felt it clawing at the back of her neck. A tangled disaster.

"YOU KNOW NOTHING!" Henri bellowed.

Justine bit her tongue to keep from shouting back at her husband about the knowledge she possessed, about the truths and half-truths she was aware of. Deep down, she was aware saying such things in this moment would prove futile. There was no reasoning, there was no logic when she knew the color Henri saw—red. An angry blistering red.

All was quiet as Justine continued to make herself appear small. There was no one else in the nave. Each of the pews was empty, and the air around them grew eerily still. Justine could have sworn she heard laughter echo from within the coffin. It appeared Henri heard it too, because he slowly turned away from Justine. Then even more slowly, he took calculated steps toward the mahogany coffin.

Justine held her breath as she watched her husband come to a standstill beside the coffin. Her brow was furrowed with intensity—an intensity that was focused on every minute movement of her husband's body, because they had both heard the echo of laughter muffled by wood.

Henri pressed his forehead down on top of the coffin, his eyes closed and both of his hands pushing down against the smooth surface. It was a dream to have any fraction of hope Michel was still alive, alive and openly laughing at the bickering between man and wife. It would be like Michel to waltz into an argument and disperse the tension with some mocking statement that taunted both Henri and Justine.

There was only silence.

EPILOGUE

EATH HAD MARRED THE GEOFFREY HOUSE-
hold in such a profound way; it was not a surprise
to society when the lord and lady continued to
decline social invites. The invites slowed down
to a mere trickle as time ticked from days to weeks and
weeks to months. In this postmortem existence, the London
townhome became uncommonly quiet with a singular exception—the noises of young Elisabeth Geoffrey. Her rages
and her joys could be heard throughout the empty halls. Her
cries reverberated through the house. In a way of treating
the grief and the heartache, Lord and Lady Geoffrey seldom
scolded their daughter. Elisabeth had become their beacon,
their lighthouse.

Justine had been utterly depleted by the procession of
funerals, of parties, and of condolence letters. Each smile she
had to politely give, each murmur of gratitude stole pieces of
her soul as the same faces said the same things once, twice,
three times. The insincerity had become glaringly obvious to

Justine as she first buried her son, then buried her sister-in-law, and finally buried her brother-in-law, all within a span of a few months. A few horrible months when her heart continued to break and be beaten.

Her sorrow and grief over the loss of her stillborn son had never left her. It never became eclipsed by the loss of Percy or by the loss of Michel. No, the murder-suicide within the family had only created a heavier thicker shroud around her sorrow.

Justine had not been allowed to properly mourn, and she was bitter about this. Deep within her heart, the bitterness had taken root. She despised her husband for his role in the tragedy, although it had played out nearly a decade ago. It felt as if only days had passed, when in truth, Justine had been in and out of a comatose state. A vast majority of her days were consumed by a heavy weight, her mind shrouded and her body somnolent.

"Elisabeth, you are meant to put the needle through the fabric, not your finger! Tsk," Justine admonished with a frown marring her lovely face.

The girl sitting across from her started, not realizing her mother was present in the room. Elisabeth did not question the way her mother was there but not always present. It was difficult to explain to her dolls and teddy bears at teatime. Golden ringlets bounced as she ducked her head down in shame.

"Yes, Mama. I-I was daydreaming . . ." Elisabeth murmured the answer, glancing up at her lady mother through thick lashes. Her blue eyes flashed defiance even as she appeared to be subdued in her chastisement.

"Again? You were permitted to play outside in the gardens all this morning, tending to the flowers and then the herbs. Was it not satisfactory for you?" Justine's expression was stern, but her voice softened with each word until a smile transformed her entire face. Soon, she was glowing while looking over at her beautiful girl, her only child to have survived infancy, to have survived birth. There were too many little crosses near the property's tree line, little crosses Justine did not care to think about.

There was a lapse of quiet as mother and daughter watched each other, one with sad and ancient eyes, while the other possessed fresh and spirited eyes. Elisabeth adored her mother, more so than her father—her mother felt safe, whereas her father felt dangerous. Again, it was something the little girl struggled to name as she sat with her dolls fanned around her on the nursery floor. Even in the weeks her mother had vacant glassy eyes, she still felt warmth in her presence. Whereas with her father, Elisabeth felt on edge and unhappy.

What could be a better description? Elisabeth worried the flesh of her lower lip between her teeth as she started to work on her needlework, her hands moving slowly as she thought about how to draw a picture of her father, a picture others might understand. Why did this matter? Elisabeth wanted her dolls to be careful around her father, as careful as she tried to be. Her father was quiet, but there was a dark in him, a dark similar to the anger of the chained bear at the Tower. She could sense it, but it was never fully visible.

"Mama?" she chirped as she put her needlework carefully in her lap. Her head was tilted to the side as she waited for her mother's attention.

"What is it, my angel?" Justine whispered back, setting aside her own embroidery and looking to her daughter with exhausted eyes.

"Why are you not allowed to meet Nana?"

"Nana?" The single word was clipped, the voice heavy with dread.

"Yes. Nana. Why are you not allowed to meet her? My lord father says I will get to meet Nana soon, but you cannot. He does not tell me why." Elisabeth was going to say more but for the look of pure terror that paled her mother's face. "Mama?"

"I do not know, my angel. Have you told your brother I love him today? Have you told him about the chamomile we have been able to plant this year?" Justine's voice was unstable.

"Mama?" Elisabeth knew her mother was deteriorating again. Her mother was going to slip back into the pitch-darkness of her mind. Tears burned her eyes as she reached out her small hand to grab ahold of her mother's knee, but it was too late. Her mother's eyes were glazed over. The warmth of tears tickled Elisabeth's cheeks as she sat back on her stool.

"I will tell my brother about the chamomile before we fall asleep tonight. And I will tell him just how much you love and miss him. I promise," Elisabeth whispered as she picked up her needlework again and focused all her attention on it, doing her absolute best to not prick her fingertip again. Soon, time was lost to her as she continued to thread the needle in and out of the fabric.

The young girl began to hum a lullaby her father tended to favor, as she'd heard it thousands of times. Elisabeth glanced up to look at her mother now and again to see if the vacant look in her beautiful eyes might have left. Each glance proved a disappointment, and the tears continued to slip down her cheeks, quiet and unwanted.

Why was her mother not able to hear about Nana? This was only the second time she had mentioned Nana to her mother, and again, her mother quickly faded into herself. Elisabeth bit down harder and harder on her lower lip until she tasted the familiar coppery tang of blood. With a huff and a sniffle, she tossed down her needlework and curled up into a ball, precariously balancing on the narrow stool.

Why was Nana not here every day? Why was her mother here and then gone again? Why was her father so secretive? Why were the servants so quiet? A hundred and a thousand questions swirled around her head as she squeezed her eyes shut and the tears finally abated. Why was there so much silence in the house? Elisabeth peered over her bent knees and stared at her mother, her lips forming a pout. It did not make sense. Her mother and her father did not argue or treat each other meanly. Rather, they seemed to ignore each other and lived in different worlds altogether. Her father was often away on business trips or hunting on this gentleman's estate or another.

Elisabeth was not able to remember all the names her nanny, Mistress Katharine, attempted to teach her every night before teatime. Names Mistress Katharine wanted Elisabeth to repeat to herself and to her dolls to learn them as best as she could.

No, there was something more to the shadows and to the quiet, the silence that dominated her childhood. It had been two or so years ago, but Elisabeth remembered hearing a whispered conversation between two of the maids. They were making a complaint about the acrid stench of frankincense in her father's study, oblivious to the eavesdropping ears. Their master had apparently been heard shouting at himself for hours. Why would her father yell and argue with himself?

A huff escaped from Elisabeth as she continued to watch her mother. Her mother's face was serene but stricken. Worry lines plagued her beauty. Again, Elisabeth bit down on her lower lip and yelped at the sharp pain. She had forgotten that she had already drawn blood from biting down so hard earlier. It was time to investigate her father's study—the only room in the whole house Elisabeth had been forbidden from entering. Both curiosity and defiance fueled her impulsive decision.

Elisabeth's stockinged feet were quiet when they touched the floor below her, and the soft skirts of her dress brushed around her knees. As she always held tightly to hope, she glanced over to her mother to see if there was life in her eyes once more. But it was not to be. Perhaps her mother would be absent the remainder of the day. This made Elisabeth more determined to be successful at discovering something during this adventure of hers.

"I promise to not break anything, Mama. I will be back before teatime, so Mistress Katharine does not worry." Elisabeth pecked a quick kiss on her mother's cool cheek before she quietly went out of the parlor. It was one of her mother's favorite rooms.

Some time passed as Elisabeth merely stood in the hallway to gather her confidence for the exploration she was about to partake in. *One for the dreamer, two for the seer . . .* At last, Elisabeth felt her chest expand and surge with the warmth of courage. She had good intentions for breaking her father's rule. The potential for answers to her thousands of questions was much too tempting to keep away. Thus, her white-stockinged feet pitter-pattered through the empty hallways of her home, and she went straight to the double doors of her father's study.

The wood was dark. The archway appeared to be leaning forward to cast its shadow over any who dared to enter. The hairs on the back of her neck bristled just as Elisabeth shushed her own fears as nonsense.

"I can do this. I can do this. Right, Charles?" Elisabeth whispered over her shoulder at her own ghost, her twin brother. Mama had refused to name her deceased sibling, no matter how many times Elisabeth had cried and cried. Mama simply could not bring a name to something that had been lost to her, as with all the other little ones Mama had lost . . . "Keep an eye out, okay, Charles? Warn me if you see our lord father . . . or worse, Sir Gideon."

A shiver splintered down her spine. Elisabeth gave a defiant flip of her golden ringlets, her blue eyes flashing bright as she grabbed on to the doorknob and turned it. The ancient doors—as ancient as they appeared to her ten-year-old eyes—opened without a noise.

"Wish me luck, Charles," Elisabeth murmured. Her imagination had begun to go haywire as she pictured shadows and ghouls, werewolves and Frankenstein. But there was nothing visible in the dark and quiet room. Nothing alive.

Elisabeth had barely taken four steps into the room before the doors swung shut behind her, the latch clicking. It was the loudest sound she had ever heard. Her heart began racing, and she spun around to open the doors again. They did not budge. They were locked. How? Frantic, Elisabeth pivoted back around to face the interior of the room. There were shadows of a desk, of chairs, of a sofa, and an expansive bookshelf across three of the walls.

She became engrossed in searching the titles of the books. Many were dusty and must have been untouched for a hundred years! Elisabeth was ready to pick one off the shelf when a darkness began to weigh against her shoulders. A dark that was heavy, that was all too familiar. A violent jolt shot through her body when she heard her father's hollow voice behind her.

"Elisabeth, have you come to meet your grandfather?" Henri said.